The Carrion King, A Novel of the Dark Forest
Michael Panush

Bestiary of Characters

Noble and Wealthy Beasts:

Esther Essen, daughter of the Court Rat of the Grand Sable Empire.

Eleazar and Yelena Essen, her parents.

Titus Tarr, a merchant, a squirrel.

Sir Alexi, a boyar of the Winterborn Empire, a lynx.

Mercenaries and Soldiers:

Sweeney, bodyguard of the Essens, a wildcat.

Sir Volkbert, bodyguard of Titus Tarr, a wolverine.

Smiling Spike, jester and leader of the Laughing Company of mercenaries, a porcupine.

Reynardine, a hired blade of the Laughing Company, a fox.

Jacopo Draco, mercenary brute of the Laughing Company, a monitor lizard.

Contessa Vivaldi, poisoner of the Laughing Company, a

dart frog.

Niko Nikaros, once a soldier of the Fortunate Few, now fighting with the Hoppite rebels, a pine marten.

Sir Thomas Mulberry, another former soldier of the Fortunate Few, now an actor, a bullfrog.

Artemesia De Leon, a swordsmonkey, once the Fortunate Few and now a criminal enforcer, a Golden Lion Tamarind.

Troubadours, Outlaws, Alchemists, and Spies:

Rinaldo the Wrinkled, a musical toad of the Mendicant Merrymakers.

Rosa Fumes, a knife-throwing skunk of the Mendicant Merrymakers.

Zipporah Schall, a master thief, a mouse.

Zoya Schall, her adopted daughter and apprentice, a rat.

The Great Flammarion, a renowned inventor and engineer, a possum.

Septimius Von Stahl, Imperial Intelligencer to the Grand Sable Empire, a ferret.

Monks, Peasants and Commoners:

Brother Ambrose, a monk and master gardener of the Abbey di Ecco, a salamander.

Moll Mullen, an innkeeper in the village of Woolery, a mole.

Maggie Mullen, her daughter.

And the Hero:

Nathan of Nestovich, known as the Rat on the Road, Bold Sir Squeaky, the Orphan Prince of Tock, a rat.

CHAPTER 1. ON ST. CUTHBERT'S EVE

In his dreams, Nathan's home burned all over again.

He stood outside his house in Nestovich, whiskers quivering as slaughter and carnage spread crimson through the surrounding streets and the town square. Swords rose and fell. Goat hooves pounded against the earth. Torches arced through the smoky air like obscene shooting stars, hurled by the paws of the attacking Winterborn hares into the homes of Nathan's friends and neighbors.

Slain, because they were rats.

But it was own house, the rooftop already smoldering, that gave the nightmare its venom. It had been different—the real sacking of Nestovich. His father, fur singed, and eyes panicked, grabbed Nathan and shoved him into his mother's arms before a saber cut him down. She hugged Nathan close, using her body to shield him from the rain of arrows that riddled her back.

In the dream, though, it was different.

Nathan just stood there. Hungry flames licked the roof of his house. Goat hooves galloped past. Rats squeaked in terror and begged the Supreme Rodent for help that never came. His parents' voices as well.

They called to him.

He couldn't move. He just stood there—feet rooted to the earth as the flame danced and the blood spilled.

Unable to do anything but watch.

His eyes flashed open. His breath burst ragged from his throat. No fire—no Nestovich. It was gone—burned away almost two years ago. His parents with it. He was in an expansive cottage, well, a sprawling manor that was *called* a cottage. It was the country estate of Eleazar Essen—Court Rat of the Grand Sable Empire. Far from his home in the Dark Forest.

As safe and comfortable as a rat kit could be.

"It's all right. Just a dream." Who was he talking to? Himself? He didn't need comforting.

He wasn't a little kit anymore.

Nathan slid from his bed in the guest room. Outside, spring sunlight filtered through windows of real glass. Breakfast—and Nathan was ready for it. He gave his face a quick wash and dressed, then headed out—whiskers still soggy. He wore fine clothes that Yelena Essen, the lady of the house, had purchased for him: a comfortable doublet, in stripey blue and yellow. Probably the nicest suit of clothing he'd ever owned.

Such luxury was everywhere in the world of Eleazar Essen.

And the best part of that world waited for him at the breakfast table, slathering boar butter over a loaf of golden bread and grinning at him—her red eyes shining.

Eleazar's daughter, Esther.

His own age, and the reason he was here in the first place.

"Hello there, Nathan!" Esther waved to the table. "We've got butter. We've got honey. We've got fruit and sausage and stuffed eggs—and three varieties of cheese." She wore red, a crimson gown that matched her eyes, and contrasted with fur the color of fresh-fallen snow.

Esther seemed delighted at the breakfast, and just as happy that Nathan was there to share it with her.

She was quite the rat.

"Oh—amazing. Looks scrumptious." Nathan sat across from

her on the wide, richly-laden table. He reached for his glass, but Valencia—the old mole nursemaid who had practically raised Esther—filled it first with clear well water. Nathan smiled weakly at her. He'd been here for months and still hadn't gotten used to having servants. "Ah, thank you."

"Such a polite young fellow." Valencia beamed at him and filled his plate.

"That he is, Valencia." Yelena Essen crossed into the room, a letter gripped in one paw. Her white fur matched that of her daughter. A tall rat, willow-thin, and clad in simple, formal black. She looked at Nathan over the letter, eyes flickering with concern. "Did you sleep all right, young sir? We heard some, ah, some noises from the guest bedchamber?"

Oh—they'd heard. A little kit, disturbed by nightmares. Fires burned in his cheeks. He couldn't look at Esther. "Perhaps I'm, ah, not used to such comfortable sheets and fine pillows."

"Perhaps." Yelena patted his shoulder. "If there's anything you need, my dear, you have only to ask."

What did she mean? "You and Master Eleazar—you've been so nice to me—"

"Please, Nathan. We merely did what's right—what any rat would do for a rodent in need." The kindness slipped away—she was all-business again. "Received a letter from your father today, Esther. All the way from Erminium." The capital of the Grand Sable Empire—Nathan had never been, but it was the center of a power that spanned half the world, so it must be an amazing place. "He's busy at court, you know. But not so busy that he can't take an interest in his daughter's studies."

Esther popped a square of Misty Islands cheddar into her mouth. "He will find them proceeding at an excellent rate." She put on a satisfied smile as she looked back.

Yelena rolled her eyes. "I'm delighted that you think so. Now, your tutor has provided me with some reading and work for you to accomplish while I oversee the spring planting—I utter a prayer to the Supreme Rodent that both will be done and done well by the time your father returns from the Feast of St. Cuthbert."

"The Feast of St. Cuthbert?" Nathan asked. There seemed to be so many saints—the Blessed Beasts. Rats did not worship them, and he'd but rarely heard their names before leaving Nestovich. "What's that one about?"

"I don't know. Maybe the illustrious St. Cuthbert, whoever he is?" Esther shrugged. "It sounds boring. A chance for noble-ferrets and weasels and the like to talk endlessly about the dreary affairs of state. My father would have me greet them and listen to them drone on and I'd have to be polite—trust me, Nathan, it's a good thing that we're missing it."

Fair enough. Though it might be fine to see Erminium. He'd visited the Free City of Katzenberg, the clockwork town of Tock, and many other wondrous places in the Dark Forest—but his wanderings had ended here, in this comfortable, vast cottage with its servants and warm hearth.

But he was safe here. He was happy here—wasn't he?

Esther sprang from her chair. "Very good. Nathan and I will begin our studies—we'll dedicate ourselves to them with laudable industriousness." Falsehood in her smile. She'd do this sort of thing often to her mother, making a mockery of what a good and obedient Court Rat's daughter should be. "We'll amaze you with our acumen, mother, and the birds who donated the feathers for our quills will be happy that they sacrificed parts of their bodies to give such scholars as we a chance to—"

"Just finish your work," Yelena muttered. She glanced at Nathan—a sympathetic look. An 'I'm sorry for what you must deal with' look—but why would she think that? Esther was amazing. "I'll be close by, overseeing the garden if you need me."

"Can we study outside, by the field facing the trees?" A ruby twinkle shone in Esther's eye.

Oh—of course. The forest—where all their goodies were stashed.

"Well…" Yelena said. "I'm not sure if the greenery is a suitable place for study."

Valencia was already starting to clean the table, stacking plates ably with her huge paws. "Pardon me, your ladyship—but it's far too nice of a day for young kits to be inside. The sun's shining bright and the grass is growing green. Not too hot, and not too cold either. Why not let them enjoy it?" A wink with one of her bright, little eyes.

Oh yes. She knew.

A sigh. "Very well, Valencia. You've convinced me. Your wisdom is matchless, as ever."

"Thank you kindly, madam." Valencia made her way to Nathan's plate. "Would you be liking anything more, Master Nathan?"

"No thank you—and breakfast was wonderful." And it was—far better than anything his father could cobble together back in Nestovich. Having a beast dedicated to cooking for you, and to clean up after you, and care for you—the noble and the rich of the world certainly had discovered the best way to live. He slid from the table, stuffed a final piece of cheese in his mouth, and scooped up another for the road. "I'll go and get the books and quills, then."

"A true gentle-beast, young sir." Yelena gave Esther a quick nuzzle, a squeaking of contentment leaving her mouth as her daughter made another in fond annoyance. She paused and patted Nathan's shoulder. "We are so very pleased to have you here."

And Nathan was just as happy to be with them.

Far away from the flames of the nightmare.

+++

A set of carved wooden tables, sturdy for the elements, waited outside the cottage—facing the forest. The garden stretched on the other side of the house. Yelena wasn't merely growing flowers. She'd planted rows of vegetables, intending to send them to the Dark Forest to help rats in need. With all the wars there, and those running to escape it, there were plenty who fit that category. Around the tables, flowers shone red, yellow, and blue in the sunlight, and a little creek trickled pleasantly in the distance. A nice enough place to collect stones or to let a boar graze.

But the expansive grove of trees, opposite the Essen House, was the real reason Esther had wanted to be here.

Nathan had to work on his writing. His letters always had too many loops and looked somewhat wilted. A dip of his quill into the inkwell seated on the table and he began. Ah—Supreme Rodent—that looked miserable. Maybe, if he added a curve around it, it would look like a mighty sword.

But he shouldn't do that. Shouldn't doodle. He dipped the quill again—went to the next letter.

Wielding a blade, thievery, intrigue, riding a boar, alchemy—he'd studied them all. He could make his letters neat.

Esther was staring at him, looking at him over the open pages of her book—a treatise of comportment that, according to her, was as monotonous as beating dust from a rug. "How're those letters coming along, Nathan?" She pulled a leaf from the grass and set it against the pages to mark her place. "A shame, I think—beasts have written about you and your adventures. You shouldn't have to practice writing."

He showed her the page. "I'll get it, I suppose—how's the, ah, book you're reading?"

"I think I'd rather be smacked about the head with it than read another page. Who knew there were so many ways to curtsy?" She sputtered. "You want to take a break?"

They shouldn't. He needed to be a good student—to do what Yelena asked of him. "Yes. Absolutely."

"Excellent." Esther's smile made breaking the rules worth it. She set the book on the table and sprang onto the grass. "Come along, then, Sir Nathan—Rat on the Road, Orphan Prince of Tock —and see what the she-demon bandit queen Esther Essen has in store."

Rat on the Road. The Orphan Prince of Tock. Those were the names in some of the stories about him. Published tales that he hadn't read, sold through the Dark Forest and as filled with falsehoods as certain pastries were with berries.

How should he feel about that? How should anyone? And the same with his sudden fame.

They neared the trees and the cool shade. "Master Nathan? Mistress Esther?" A kindly voice from behind. Both kits stopped. Valencia stood outside, bearing a basket of washing. She grinned at them. "Neglecting your studies?"

Nathan looked at his feet. Esther folded her paws—for once, at a loss for words.

Valencia chuckled. "Oh, that's all right. It's a child's right to avoid drudgery. But you don't take too long, yes? A few moments, and then return. We wouldn't want your dear mother growing upset."

Esther beamed at her.

They went on, weaving through the trees—going to the center of the grove. A giant hollow stump waited there, at the edge of a large clearing speckled with vibrant wildflowers. Nathan had found that stump soon after arriving. He'd kept his old satchel, his shadow-black cloak from his days as a pickpocket, an old stuffed dragon and—most important of all to keep secret—a Winterborn dagger. He'd worked a whetstone over his blade, keeping it sharp—though what was there to slice now, besides cheese and sausage? A letter from his mother too, and a necklace with a rat's tooth at the end.

All he had left of his parents.

But Esther didn't go for the stump—respecting his privacy. Instead, she went to a fallen log, the moss emerald bright against the sun-whitened wood. Behind that, a case of good leather. Esther tugged at the straps and drew out what waited inside.

A crossbow.

Solid dark components. A stiff metal band and a taut string, with a clockwork crank. Next to it, a little bag of lethal metal bolts.

Esther drew one and tapped her paw against the needle tip. "Shall we begin the day's practice?"

"I suppose so." Nathan settled on the log. "We'll just have to be careful." Did that make him sound like he was trying to ruin her fun? He didn't want that—but he didn't want Esther injuring herself either.

Or him.

"Thank you, Nathan." Esther worked the crank, gritting her teeth a little—but she managed. "I always appreciate your caution." She carefully placed the bolt and brought the crossbow to her shoulder. "But you don't need to worry. I'm the she-demon bandit queen." She leapt to the top of the log, balancing on one leg, and spun around. "Apple, there at the top of the tree."

The crossbow twanged. Her bolt shot out—an iron blur. Nathan didn't even have time to exhale before a meaty thump and a gentle plop hit the air. An apple tumbled from the tree at the edge of the clearing, the bolt wedged deep inside—nearly splitting the fruit in two.

Her practice was paying off.

Nathan picked it up by the bolt and gave it a shake, dislodging the apple—then cleaned the bolt carefully on his jerkin.

"Well done!" He passed her the arrow. "A good shot."

"I'm getting better." Her usual confidence faltered. "The apples of the world had better look out. I've shot my share of them, and stumps and tree trunks. But you, Nathan—you've been out in the world. You've become the Rat of the Road. A legend." There was no artifice or joke in her words.

The sunny warmth of the clearing was nothing compared to the shine in Nathan's heart.

Esther cranked the clockwork mechanism again to draw back the cord. "All right—your turn."

"You'd like me to try?"

"Come now—it's not fair that you just watch me shoot targets. I bet you're a deadeye." Esther tossed him the crossbow. Supreme Rodent—more danger! He caught it, careful not to press the trigger and send the bolt flying back into the Essen House. "There we go!" Esther didn't even seem to notice his nervousness. She hopped next to him—thankfully, away from the point of the crossbow. "All right—what do you want to shoot?"

"Um..." Oh, he was sounding like a true fool. "Well, what do you think? What's a good target?"

Esther laughed. "I don't know—you're the noble knight. You pick something. Oh—how about the knothole over there, on that stump?"

A good swirl of dark wood. Not too far away either. He could strike that—and not look like some blind idiot rat in front of Esther. He brought the crossbow up.

"Hold on, Nathan—your position's almost perfect, but not quite." She drew closer to him, a paw settling lightly on his arm. "I've been studying some martial manuals—Sweeney's been nice enough to share them." Eleazar Essen's wildcat bodyguard—a Gallowglass. Nathan was too scared of Sweeney to even ask him to pass the salt during dinner. "You want to bring it up, to your cheek."

She pushed an arm up—her paws, warm from the sunlight, settled against his fur.

His heart was pounding so fast. Maybe she could hear it?

Then Esther stepped back. "All right, Bold Sir Squeaky—show that knothole what for."

He pressed the trigger. A sudden click, a hum of the string clicking home. The crossbow shook, the impact rippling through his arms and down to his belly. He lowered it and looked for the bolt.

Nowhere to be found.

Nathan passed Esther the crossbow. He grinned weakly. "The sun—or maybe it was the crossbow—or—"

Esther gave him a sympathetic smile. "Just some bad luck, Nathan. But you'll get it next time. And it's only practice."

"Only practice," he repeated. But impressing Esther was truly important—and he certainly hadn't done that. "I'll find the bolt later—I won't lose them. Your turn, as promised."

"As promised. What should I shoot this time?"

A scream came from Essen House.

Yelena's voice.

Clear, unmistakable, bold—and terrified.

For a second, Nathan and Esther stood there. Yelena couldn't make that noise—it just wasn't possible. She was too dignified, too confident—but then her scream came again, and there was no doubt that Yelena had the kind of terror you only felt when a nightmare had burst from the land of sleep and become real.

Esther looked at him, panicked, clutching the crossbow. "Nathan?"

Asking him for help.

And he needed to be there for her. He couldn't freeze up—if there was danger here, he needed to be ready. He needed to protect them.

He couldn't let what happened to Nestovich happen here.

"Esther, come on." He took her paw, leading her to the hollow stump—staring through the trees and back at the estate. His heart drummed differently now as fear brightened Esther's crimson eyes. "Go inside the log and grab my satchel, please." She crawled inside the log, grass clinging to her fine gown, as Nathan started back toward the cottage.

And the screams.

Through the branches, he caught a decent view of the Essen House. A trio of wagons had ridden to the front and rested on the dirt road by the garden fence. Bizarre wagons, pulled by gray goats. Checkered flags of red and green. Pennants showing a leering jester's face. They looked like they would deliver a band of mummers to a village, bringing a whole carnival with them. One wagon, however, had a cage of solid iron set in the back. What carnival would have a thing like that?

Armed beasts, at least two score of them, boiled from the wagons, trampled the garden, and surrounded the Essen cottage. Halberds and battle swords flashed in the spring sunlight.

Oh, Supreme Rodent. They'd killed one of the gardeners—a nut-brown weasel from the nearby village of Glückenhoff, who had been helping Yelena with the planting.

He lay amongst the seedbed, the red pooling around his head visible even from where Nathan stood.

It had been a long time since Nathan had seen death. The callousness of it, the coldness of that grim sight on a warm spring day—it was terribly wrong. His ears flattened and his tail writhed like a dying worm.

No—don't be scared. Think straight. The Essens needed him.

Where was—there. Yelena. The armed beasts had grabbed her and dragged her to the wagons as she fought and squeaked. No hesitation in their movements. No pause before hurting another beast. They were well-used to violence.

Mercenaries, maybe. Soldiers of fortune. Nathan knew the type.

Valencia came running from the house and neared the table where they'd done their studying. She looked through the trees, her dark eyes filled with terror as she stopped at the creek that marked the edge of the grove. She switched to a harsh whisper. "There you are!" She'd come to warn them. "Is Mistress Esther—"

"Back in the woods."

Her pointed nose twitched back and forth. "Good. Now stay there, young sir—stay there—stay hidden! I'll send them away."

He should run down. Help—fight. But instead, he did as he was told, ducking back behind a tree—following an older beast's instructions, like a good kit. He peered out from his hiding place. Watching what was happening.

Valencia spun around, pretending that he wasn't there.

Two more beasts crossed the grass. Valencia tried to run, to lead them away—but she was an old mole. They caught her before she left the bank of the creek.

Supreme Rodent—no! His claws dug into the bark.

A hulking monitor lizard, his diamond-shaped head wedged between broad shoulders, set a huge, clawed hand on Valencia's shoulder—holding her in place. A breastplate covered the puke-green scales of his belly and a falchion that looked big enough to chop a boar in half rested on his belt.

His forked tongue flicked in and out. "Who were you talking to, old one?"

She shook her head. "No one, sir. I—I mean you no harm."

Next to him stood a fox. A lean and artfully dressed fox,

with sunset red fur and a fine suit of dark brocade and a lacey collar. He swept a rapier from his hip—fast enough to make the air hum. "Jacopo Draco, my friend, you waste your time." An insolent voice with an Argent accent. "Why would the two squeaklings be in the forest? Why would they not keep to the comforts of their fine house?"

"We'll find them either way, Reynardine. No one's coming to help them."

Squeaklings. A cruel term for rats and mice.

That meant they were looking for him and Esther.

"I can take you to the house, sirs." Valencia lowered her muzzle—servile and terrified. Yet still trying to lead them away from Nathan and Esther.

He had to help. No more being a well-behaved kit.

Nathan slid from his hiding place. "Wait!" he called down, voice shrill. "I'm right here. Please—let her go—you don't need to —"

Reynardine stared at him, his tongue lolling.

He stabbed Valenica.

Nathan gasped and covered his mouth. The fox had driven the sword deep into Valencia's belly, enough so that the reddened end burst from her back. Valenica let out a gentle murmur as the swords-fox slid his blade out with sickening ease. Her body collapsed into the stream.

Nathan stood rooted to the ground, frozen.

His parents. Valencia. Dying because they tried to help him.

Yelena too, maybe.

And Esther.

Jacopo stared at Reynardine and sighed—like an old friend had told the same bad joke for the hundredth time. He started across the stream. "Come along, little rat. We've got a long journey ahead of us." The fox followed.

"Valencia!" Esther's voice. She'd left the log and now stood behind a fallen tree alive with moss, looking down at the creek.

She'd seen everything.

Fox and lizard ran for them. Nathan spun. Come on—run to Esther. Get her out of here.

But he'd started too slow. The monitor lizard reached him first and smacked him. The blow made the trees dance, a sudden flash of pain as the sky turned and danced and burned.

He dropped on the grass.

"So much for the Rat on the Road." Draco loomed above him, tongue flicking in and out.

Reynardine sprang up past them, the crimson rapier in one paw. "I'll get the other one!" He flourished with the blade, going into a dramatic bow before Esther. "If you would be so kind as to come with us? We are to bring you to your mother and father, my dear, so that the entire Essen Family will be together." A flash of white teeth. "Nathan of Nestovich shall accompany us. I guarantee that you will not be harmed. Please, my little darling, I mean only—"

Esther hoisted up the crossbow from behind the log and pressed the trigger.

The familiar mechanical click and hum. The bolt streaked out, flashing toward Reynardine's face. She didn't aim properly —that was the only thing that saved him.

Instead, the bolt ripped into the side of his face, tearing away an eye, and leaving a redder track on his orange fur.

Reynardine wailed, his cry going to a piercing shriek. He sank to his knees and tumbled onto his back.

"Hellfire!" Draco's tongue danced--amused. "Look at that, Reynardine—she took an eye out of you, if I'm not mistaken." He looked down at Nathan. "Stay put, Lord Squeakling."

He left Nathan on the grass, still sucking in air.

Then he surged ahead, heavy tail flicking on the grass, and reached the fallen log. Esther flailed with the crossbow, bashing it against Jacopo's belly. It clanged against his breastplate—doing nothing more than making noise.

Jacopo Draco lunged out, grabbing Esther's arm.

He wrenched the crossbow away and threw her against the fallen log. "There now, Mistress Essen. You just stay put for a moment."

Reynardine yipped from where he lay. "Carve out her squeakling eyes—bring her to me and I'll show her what pain means!"

"And upset Smiling Spike? I don't think so."

Smiling Spike? Somewhere in the fear, the grief, the chaos —that name struck a terrible chord. He knew Smiling Spike. A porcupine blade for hire. A child killer—or rather, one who had so little regard for life that slaying a child meant nothing to him.

A veritable clown in the circus of death.

But Spike wanted Esther alive. The same with Yelena—and Nathan was to be captured as well.

He could think of what it meant later. He had to get Esther out of there.

"Up we go, little darling." Draco grabbed Esther's tail and dragged her—away from the crossbow. "Time to go and join mommy in the cage."

He looked up from where he lay. What could he do? Bite? Claw? Jacopo Draco would cut him in half. Reynardine, even with one eye, would do the same—and laugh at him for trying.

Wait. Something glittered at the base of the tree, jutting partially into the dirt and revealing just enough of the metal point to shine in the sunlight.

The crossbow bolt. The same he'd sent hurtling away earlier.

Their eyes weren't on him. He held his breath. Inched closer.

He grabbed the bolt.

Then he stood and charged, holding the bolt below his cloak. He weaved away from Reynardine, who was still writhing on the grass, and ran for Draco.

The lizard turned and watched him, tail batting back and forth as he held Esther's tail—amused. "Oh—you. I can see why they sing so many songs about you, Bold Sir Squeaky. Spirited— a spirited rat boy—"

He plunged the crossbow bolt into Draco's foot—driving it as hard as he could through flesh and into the grassy earth below. Draco wailing as the bolt bit down, pinning him to the earth. Scarlet welled up between his claws.

Then he darted back, ran to Esther, who had grabbed the fallen crossbow and slung it over her shoulder on its leather strap. "Come on!"

They ran. Draco wrenched the bolt out and followed. Limping, clicking his teeth, hissing—but still up.

Esther's paw clasped Nathan's. She dipped down, passing him his satchel from where it lay on the forest floor. Nathan dug inside. The pommel of his Winterborn dagger. He never had gotten around to giving it a suitable name. But it could still slice —oh yes, it could do that. He drew the blade and spun, just as Jacopo Draco reached for them.

The blade hummed out and gave Draco's arm a slice. Clumsy, with Esther leaning on him, but the tip still carved a red line through the scales. Draco hissed, tongue flashing and stumbled, landing on his belly in a reddening heap.

"The kits! The kits are here!" He bellowed as he did so—giving everything away, then started pulling himself back to his clawed feet.

Nathan and Esther ran down to the creek, now flowing red with Valencia's blood.

Esther gasped.

"You don't need to look. You don't need to look." Nathan spoke softly. Kept hold of her paw. They crossed the shallow water. Made it back to their tables where their books still rested, waiting in the sun.

A lifetime ago. Before bloodshed and chaos had invaded their lives and a nightmare had become real.

Sudden heat in the spring air. The mercenaries—Smiling Spike's beasts—had set fire to the country manor.

Not enough for them to abduct Yelena—and nearly get Nathan and Esther. They had to kill servants, to add some butchery to their work, and to burn down the home that had sheltered Nathan these past years. What had happened to Nestovich was happening here, the slaughter leaving his memories and nightmares and coming to the peaceful world of the Essens and—no—he couldn't despair. Not next to Esther.

Not until they were safe.

"A little closer to the stables. That's all we need. Then I'll get us out of here." Nathan led Esther back toward the garden as the fires started to spread through the house. Inky smoke drifted up. But they didn't have long. The Beasts-at-Arms on burning duty glanced up, staring at them as Jacopo Draco cried—already reaching for the assorted blades on their hips.

Then Smiling Spike himself came around the side of the country house in a wild run that was half jig and blocked their path. "Uh-uh!" He waved a finger at the soldiers. "These two are mine."

He'd rather face Draco and Reynardine. He'd rather face almost anyone—but Smiling Spike.

"Nathan!" False pleasantness in Spike's words—like he was

being reunited with an old friend. "My, my. It has been too long!" The porcupine still had red and green checkered garments and a jester's cap outfitted with dancing bells. His quills jutted out, an array of dark spines that rattled and clicked as he moved, and his tail batted the ground. His eyes—ink dark and somehow shining—settled on Nathan with a virulent joy. "I've been looking forward to our reunion since that day in Katzenberg. I prayed to the Blessed Beasts, and do you know what? They heeded my prayers."

Was he paid to do this? Or was he just spreading chaos and death because it was what he liked to do?

The stables waited, past the well and the garden. Could Nathan's voice reach them? It was either that or pit his dagger against Smiling Spike, who carried a brutal flanged mace in his paw—and was far bigger and stronger than him. Esther had retrieved her crossbow, but she hadn't had a chance to load another bolt.

Besides, she was terrified, saddened—she'd never been anywhere close to a situation like this.

Nathan had.

He whistled as loud as he could.

"What are you doing, Nathan?" Spike asked. "Calling for help, like you did last time? I'm sorry to say that no help is coming." He played with his mace, spinning it like a musician's baton. It had bells on it, which rang merrily with each twist. "But you go on and beg. Every joke needs a punchline, after all." His mouth opened, showing even teeth. "And the Laughing Company loves nothing as much as a good joke."

Was that rustling coming from the stables? A stall door creaking open? Hooves on the straw-strewn floor?

Had to keep Smiling Spike talking—which wasn't hard. He loved to talk.

"The Laughing Company?" Nathan made his voice clear. Did

he sound brave? He hoped so. "These clowns following you around?" He looked back at the forest. "Esther shot a crossbow bolt through your fox's eye. I nailed the monitor lizard's foot to the forest floor. I think you need to find some new clowns, Spike."

The porcupine hopped closer, brandishing the club. Nathan hoisted the dagger. "You'll be singing a different tune, little Nathan. I'm supposed to bring you in alive. Same with the squeakling maiden there. But maybe I'll break both your legs— just to hear the music you make."

"I wouldn't try it, Spike." Movement in the stables— definitely. But Nathan didn't look. Kept his eyes on the mad face of the porcupine. "Remember what happened last time."

"Ah." Spike drew closer now, bringing the mace back. The little bells rang. "But things are different now."

The stable door flew open. Hooves pounded on the green grass of the meadow.

"Yes," Nathan agreed. "They are."

The riding boar—not a piglet, but not quite a full-grown hog either—came barreling out the stable and charged down the dirt track, passing the burning house at a full gallop.

Emperor. A gift from the famous badger knight Sir Konrad the Courageous himself.

Emperor's sleek brown fur blurred as he charged and he lowered his head, showing off a pair of newly sprouted tusks. Little nubs, maybe, but Emperor was proud of them, and Nathan was too. He loved Emperor, who had saved his life on the road more than once.

Now, Emperor smashed straight into the side of Smiling Spike. A rapid ramming. A porcine cannonball. Smiling Spike went flying, quills flailing, and shattered the fence under his weight. He plopped into the flowerbed.

Nathan ran to Emperor, Esther close behind. No saddle, no bridle, no tack—he'd never ridden like this before, but there was no time for anything else. No choice either. He gripped Emperor's furry flank and pulled himself up, then offered a paw for Esther. By now, the other mercenaries—the Laughing Company—had overcome the surprise of seeing their master getting hurled aside by a boar's charge, and sprang closer, weapons flashing.

Esther took his paw. "My mother—"

"Maybe we can get to her—maybe not." He hauled her behind him. Emperor snorted at the weight—but he was one strong pig. "We'll rescue her, though. Eventually. That's a promise."

An arrow hurtled past them, thudding into the burning house.

"Alive!" Smiling Spike cried from where he lay. "I need them alive—if they perish, I'll skin the beast who wielded the blade! Skin him and salt him myself!"

"Emperor—go!" Nathan cracked his heels.

But Emperor was already running. He knew exactly what to do.

Hooves drove into the earth. They ran around to the front of the country house, past the garden and the wagons—and there was Yelena, clasping the bars—with a squadron of pike-beasts around her. Her eyes were pleading, begging as she pointed into the distance.

She wanted him to escape with Esther. She wanted him to protect her daughter.

And he could do that. He had to.

He turned Emperor toward the road, and the gallop sent them hurtling along past the fields and into the distance.

Something slick on his shoulder. Esther's tears.

Nathan cried too, a sudden wetness settling down his snout,

blurring his vision.

He blinked the tears away.

The dream had been a warning, sent from the Supreme Rodent. A warning and he hadn't listened to it. But that would change. Things would be different this time.

Nothing more that he loved would be burned away.

+++

He finally ended their ride in Glückenhoff, the nearest village. It lay at the foot of the Glück Mountains, a little collection of tall alpine structures with thatched roofs and spring flowers bright in the window boxes and around their doorsteps. The town made its living from the mountain—shepherds taking up their sheep to graze on alpine meadows —and Nathan rode Emperor past such a flock on his way into town. The beasts of Glückenhoff gave him the occasional glance, but they knew wealthy rats dwelled nearby in the Essen's estate and said nothing about it.

But how long did they have until the Laughing Company came asking questions? And how much secrecy would the townsfolk give them?

They needed to stop, to rest—to plan. Nathan spotted an inn with adjoining stables and rode Emperor inside. The Merry Mountaineer—that was its name. It would do.

He helped Esther down. She still clasped the crossbow, hugging it like a little kit with their favorite stuffed toy. "Esther?" She didn't say anything—just cried silent tears. She was stunned—by shock and sadness.

Nathan let her stand in the middle of the dusty stable as a plump hedgehog approached. He wore an alpine hat topped with a little feather—it seemed absurdly small on his huge head. "Looking to board your piglet, then?" He sniffed slightly—would he not let him in, considering that they were rats?

Well, the gold of rats still spent. "What is your name, sir?" Nathan asked.

"Gustav, young master."

Young master? Well, why not? Nathan was dressed as a noble-beast and accompanied by the Court Rat's daughter. He dug into his satchel. "Pleased to meet you. I, ah, actually need more than just stabling. If you could buy saddle and tack for my piglet here." He drew out a pouch and started counting. Imperial marks. "Only the finest. Give him water and corn. Good yellow corn, if you please." Two stacks of coins for the hedgehog. "That's for the expenses, and here's another for you—the other half when we leave."

"Right." Gustav was still looking at Esther. "Is she—is she all right?"

He sounded concerned—worried. As anyone would be when they saw a crying child.

Maybe they could trust him?

"We've had—we've had some bad luck." Nathan straightened up. "We'll get some food—what's the best fare inside?"

"Barely soup, I'd say. My wife makes it fresh." He shook his quills. "That's the Court Rat's daughter, isn't it?"

Esther wiped her eyes. "Yes. I am. And my father will see you rewarded for your kindness."

He bowed his head and let them pass.

They went into the inn, Esther wrapping the crossbow in Nathan's traveling cloak—just in case. A good crowd enjoying a late lunch. Beasts thick around the tables, slurping soup, dipping pretzels in jars of grainy mustard, and listening to the sounds of a small band in a central stage. Squirrel minstrels, a hurdy-gurdy and a fiddle working in time, entertained the diners. Perfect for them—there were plenty of places to hide.

Nathan had Esther sit at a table in the back, well-shadowed, and got two bowls of barley soup. Already, this little outing was taxing the amount of marks he'd saved up. What could he do when they ran out? Steal more? He'd done his fair share of that before. It was wrong to steal, of course. Yelena and Eleazar, his own parents, expected better—but it might be a matter of survival.

He set a bowl before himself and another for Esther. She was crying again. Nathan took a slurp. It didn't taste like anything. "Esther?" He said her name quietly—it was all he could think of to do.

She looked at him, tears forming runnels through her pale fur. "She didn't have to warn us. She shouldn't have tried." Talking about Valencia. She looked down. "I never thanked her. I should—I should have told her I loved her. I always thought she was going be around and—and I never told her—" Her head settled on the table. The tears thickened. "My mother—I was rude to her this morning. I didn't want to do my studies. I lied to her—"

He left the table. Instinct—he couldn't just sit there while Esther cried. Nathan went around to her side of the table and put his paw on hers.

Her claws linked with his. She stopped crying.

Esther looked up, her red eyes blinking.

"We'll get your mother back," Nathan said. "We'll rescue her. And Valencia—I—it's not fair. But we're going to have to move fast. I'm going to need you with me. Can you do that?"

She nodded.

"All right." He returned to his seat. "Please, um, eat your soup." It felt wrong to tell her what to do. She was as close to nobility as a rat could be! And always so confident, so bold— the one who would tell him what to do. But Esther picked up the spoon and slurped soup, just like he did. "Your father—they attacked because of your father, I'm sure of it. Smiling Spike's a mercenary. Your father's enemies hired him."

"My father's enemies?"

"Does he have any?"

"He wouldn't tell me about them." Esther paused. "There's Von Stahl, of course." Septimius Von Stahl—the Emperor's Intelligencer. A weasel spy master. He and Nathan had clashed before. "But I thought he was out of favor."

"He's cunning, though." And cunning counted for a lot. But money did too. "Mercenaries don't fight for free—even if Smiling Spike takes a lot of joy in killing. Somebody hired them. Does Von Stahl have money?"

"I don't know."

"What about your father? Was he working on some grand plan? Something that someone would want to stop?"

"I don't *know*." She clenched her spoon, and her whiskers quivered.

Nathan stopped himself. This wasn't going anywhere. "I think we need to find him. He'll tell us what happened, and he can rescue your mother. They put her in a cage, they were hauling her away—they must be taking her somewhere." He tried to brighten up, tried to put more confidence in his words. "Your father's very powerful. He's the Court Rat! He must be able to help."

A slight nod from Esther. "That means we have to go to Erminium."

"To the Feast of St. Cuthbert after all." Nathan brought the bowl to his lips and drained what was left. Warmth cascaded down his throat—a comforting feeling. "We're going to get her back, Esther. We'll reach your father. We just have to be brave for a little more."

"I don't know if I can," Esther said.

His whiskers shook now—a different kind of nervousness.

His voice softened. "You're the most fearless beast I've ever met."

She looked at him and wiped her eyes on her sleeve.

They finished up their soup as Gustav returned, his alpine cap held in his paws. He stood by the table, tapping a foot—waiting for Nathan. Oh yes—his payment! Nathan dug into his satchel. Another stack of marks. Nearly the last he had. He set them on the table and Gustav swept them up.

The hedgehog smoothed back his quills. "Thank you, young master. Your piglet's waiting in our finest stall, with saddle and blanket and all the rest. He's got a fine meal in front of him."

"Thank you," Nathan said.

But Gustav remained, still swaying. He reached into his pocket. "There's something else." A scrap of parchment, set carefully on the table. "I was given this, to give to you. That's all I'll say."

"Who gave it to you?"

"That's all I'll say." He repeated the words, clicked his quills, and puttered away.

Nathan hastened around to the side of the table, hoisting up the parchment. Cold sunlight from the window gleamed through, giving the paper a warm shimmer. No words—only a picture. A cat's face, with pointed ears, sitting atop a triangle. All sketched in rough charcoal. Nathan squinted at the parchment, but Esther suddenly smiled—the first sign of anything close to happiness that she'd shown since the awful attack on her house.

"The cat's Sweeney." She tapped the picture. "And that's a mountain. Big Glück, I'd say. Biggest of all the Glück Mountains and the closest to the village."

"You can tell all that?"

"Sweeney and I used to trade pictures when we were bored during my father's meetings. We got very good at deciphering each other's work."

This was good news. Sweeney was an accomplished soldier, a Gallowglass from the north of the Misty Isles. He'd served time in several mercenary companies himself before signing on to protect the Essens. It probably seemed like a much easier job, with far less action—until today. But more than that, Sweeney's arrival meant that Nathan didn't have to be in command. He could let an adult, a veteran of this sort of thing, direct him and Esther—and protect them.

And yet, that was a little disappointing too. He could handle himself. He'd done it before, after all.

That was just pride speaking, though. They needed help— they had to find Sweeney, which meant getting up Big Glück Mountain.

The door creaked open. Nathan stashed the parchment and looked up. Esther followed his gaze and stifled a gasp.

Three of the Laughing Company had entered. The fox, Reynardine, his big lizard friend Draco, and another—a frog. The strangest frog that Nathan had ever seen. Quite small, coming only to the waist of Reynardine and Draco, and clad in a dark, ragged dress from which dangled countless chains and straps holding assorted bottles, vials, and flasks—all clanking as she moved. But her color—her skin a brilliant orange striped with black, and her webbed fingers a shimmering blue—was something else. She looked like she'd bathed in paint.

Draco yawned, showing teeth like daggers. "You really think they went in here? That they didn't go dashing straight for Erminium?"

Reynardine yipped. He wore an eye-patch now—a band of black silk. "They are children, my friend. They would not stray. We just have to find them—and you leave the squeakling maid to me, yes?"

"Shut up, the both of you." The colorful frog went to her full height. "If you had done your jobs in the first place, we wouldn't be here." A Sunstone Archipelago accent. Her eyes scanned the room—only a matter of time until they were found.

"Oh-ho—Contessa Vivaldi's famous temper!" Draco cried.

"I'll drip poison in that big mouth of yours as you sleep." Contessa Vivaldi—though she probably wasn't a real countess—hopped up to the bar—going for a better look.

"Esther, we've got to go." Nathan ducked down, trying to stay in the shadows. Esther had pulled aside his dark cloak, revealing the crossbow—resting it on her knees below the table. Her paw settled on the crank. "Esther—no!" Nathan slid in front of her. "We kill one and the other two will be on us. I'm decent with the dagger, but these beasts are killers. They'll get us for sure."

Her eyes stayed on that fox—but her paws stilled. "Then how do we get out?"

A fair question. Nathan glanced at the far wall. There, a back door, leading to the alley outside. They could take that, make their way around to the stable, and get out of here. But the trio from the Laughing Company were already searching the Merry Mountaineer. The crowd could help hide them, but everyone was sitting around their tables, guzzling beer in elaborately decorated steins and enjoying their lunch, leaving the way clear. Reynardine and the others would find Nathan and Esther soon.

Unless everyone was out of their seats.

"I've got it." Nathan hopped from his seat. "Get ready to move." He palmed his last coin and scrambled to the stage by the central pillar, where the band of squirrels played under a decorated wreathe. The hurdy-gurdy player, a gray squirrel with massive eyebrows, squinted down at him as Nathan hoisted up the coin. "Excuse me, sir? Could you, ah, play something exciting?"

"I would say all of our ballads are exciting," the squirrel muttered.

This wasn't going well. "Something that will make beasts

dance, then?" Nathan placed the coin in the basket at their feet. "Please?"

The squirrels glanced at each other. The gray flexed his fingers, looked at the ceiling and breathed in air—and then stomped his foot down as he unleashed a blistering series of rapid notes on his hurdy-gurdy. The fiddle joined in and the drum too.

"It's the Glückenhof Jig!" A little owl fluttered happily from her seat and slammed both talons on the floorboards at the first notes.

Other beasts followed. They bound up from their tables, couples joining together as their feet drummed an excited rhythm and the music played. The whole of the inn became a sea of dancing and merriment. The Laughing Company soldiers were lost, surrounded by townsfolk stomping their feet and clapping their paws in time to the merry notes that filled the Merry Mountaineer.

Perfect.

Esther stared at the dancing. "Sometimes you have to use what's around you," Nathan said. "Now, we'd better get moving."

They scampered to the exit, back into the cool spring air.

Time to go and climb a mountain.

+++

Though, as it turned out, a technical wonder helped them make it up the mountainside instead. A sort of carriage, set on a clockwork track, carried them up along the slope with the grinding hum of precarious machinery. A funicular, it was called. The carriage was big enough to contain Nathan, Esther, and Emperor as well—though he didn't like it. He snorted as the cart moved under his hooves, shaking his head at the groaning of gears.

"Easy there." Nathan patted his muzzle, working his hands

through Emperor's bristly fur. Outside the carriage, stately pines, and jagged cliffs, still marked with a few bands of snow, passed by. "How much longer, do you think?"

Esther sat in the front, working the levers—they'd snuck in while the usual driver went to take a break for bread and sausage. "We're nearing the end of the track. This big plateau." She looked back at Nathan. "We used to go up here, ride a sleigh over the snow. Or just enjoy the view."

"Sounds amazing." Nathan clasped the bar as the track leveled out. "Were you going to go this winter?"

"Maybe." Esther looked away. "Father is—is quite busy these days."

And indeed he was. Often away from his country house, doing the business of a Court Rat in Erminium. It must be hard for Esther—growing up mostly alone, with no youngsters her own age around, and even if she could meet some at court, she'd always be a squeakling to them. And now this tragedy—but she was still staying strong.

He hadn't been lying when he said she was brave.

The funicular reached its end with a final creak, stopping on a grassy plateau about halfway up the mountain. A spectacular view. The mountain meadow ended in a sheer drop. White sky beyond, and the jagged slope, and then the green lands below. Glückenhof was a sizeable splotch, with a road winding away, and another dot further up—leaking tiny puffs of smoke. Was that the Essen House?

Emperor burst out of the carriage. "Emperor—wait!" Nathan dashed after the piglet, who galloped into the meadow, hooves kicking above the mountain flowers as he raced about in a happy circle. Joyous oinks came from Emperor's muzzle as he gave up on running and plopped on his belly, then rolled over—saddle bags and blanket flapping as he spun onto his back and kicked his hooves at the clear sky.

Nathan couldn't help smiling and laughing at Emperor's delight. He glanced at Esther. She was smiling too.

They reached Emperor. "There we are." Nathan took his reins and gave it a tug, bringing him back to his feet. He straightened up the boar's tack. "You see? The little ride wasn't so bad."

A Northern accent came from a copse of trees at the edge of the meadow. "Glad you think so, lad—it's one of many we'll have to take."

Sweeney.

He came walking out of the brush like he had dwelled there forever—a forest spirit emerging into the light of day. The wildcat, his brown striped fur nearly matching the branches, wore a blue and black tartan sash running from shoulder to waist, and a matching kilt. A poleaxe with a blade the shape of a sickle moon sat casually on his shoulder—just another branch in the forest.

"Sweeney!" Esther cried his name and sprang across the meadow, loping through the grass, and flew into his arms.

"Easy there! Easy!" Sweeney laughed as he set Esther down, showing off his fangs in a happy smile. "You'll knock this poor cat over." He waved to Nathan, who led Emperor over. "And there's the Rat on the Road. It's you that brought her here, I think."

He looked at his shoes. "Well, ah—they captured Yelena. They took her away in a cage. And—and—"

"They murdered Valencia." All the joy vanished from Esther. "And Eduard—a beast we hired to help with the garden. You didn't know him, I suppose…"

"Oh…" Sweeney sighed, his ears going flat. "Valencia—she was nothing but kind. I could see how much she loved you, Mistress Esther. I am so sorry." He leaned on his polearm and didn't look like the determined Gallowglass. Instead, he seemed like an old cat who needed something to support him. "I should have been there. I failed you, Mistress Esther. Failed your whole family. Your father too."

"Where is he?"

"They took him. Captured him. Same as your mother, now." He mewed—a piteous sound. "Imperial soldiers—Ermine Guard. The Emperor's personal soldiers. They attacked the counting house, hauled him away in chains. Treason, they say."

"My father would never—"

"What they said, Mistress Esther—and Eleazar feared the worst. He knew that if they were coming for him, they'd seize his family as well. I was about to fight the Ermine Guard— probably send a good half-dozen of them screaming into the saints' heaven before they butchered me—but he told me to flee. To come here and make sure you and the Lady Yelena were safe." The mew came again—long and keening and sad. "And I failed, Esther. I failed."

"No." She took his paw. "It's not your fault. My mother and father are both alive. We can find out what happened—the nature of this false accusation. We can clear his name and get him released." She looked at Nathan and he nodded. "That's a fine course of action and that's what we'll do."

"That's what we'll do." Nathan smoothed down his whiskers. "How do we do that, Sweeney?"

Sweeney's ears flicked up, expectant. "Ah—well—I'm not entirely sure. I'm a soldier. I know the arts of war, not of intrigue. Eleazar, he always managed his business well. He'd speak of it, sure, but only so that another set of ears would hear his thoughts."

So Sweeney wouldn't help them. Wouldn't tell them what to do next.

That was okay. Nathan could think. Out of his depth? Certainly. But what choice did they have? "We must go to Erminium. They're taking Yelena there—and Eleazar's already imprisoned. We have to find out what happened." He crossed the grass, tail swishing behind him. "Sweeney, who was Master Essen visiting? Who was he talking to—any friends, maybe, who could give us a better idea of what happened?"

Sweeney paused. "There is one, aye. But you won't like it."

"Who?" Esther asked.

"Your old enemy, young sir. Septimius von Stahl."

CHAPTER 2. RAT MASQUE

The road to Erminium teemed with danger. Every crossroads inn, every band of trees or watering hole could harbor spies from the Laughing Company or whoever had hired that band of killers in the first place. Had Smiling Spike spent scouts ahead, chasing after them? Would the old beaver innkeeper or the passing band of hedgehog monks give up their position in return for a friendly smile or a few coins?

Nathan played it carefully, giving false names, sticking to the backroads, making sure that Esther kept her hood up to hide her face.

But the fear remained.

After two days on the road, they reached Erminium—but it didn't make Nathan feel better.

A massive city, akin in size to the great Free City of Katzenberg in the Dark Forest. But where Katzenberg had opulence, Erminium had grandeur. Broad avenues, washed by spring sun, alive with fancy carriages and wagons fresh from the countryside. Stately buildings, composed of somber marble. And everywhere, statues. Of Emperor Ferencz von Wessel III, of past emperors, of knights, warriors, and saints. They stood on boarback, on goatback, or on foot—hoisting up swords, relics, torches. An army of stone watchers, looking down from their pedestals, watching everything.

Erminium was the seat of a vast empire and wanted you to know it.

Nathan sucked in breath as he looked at the great city from Emperor's saddle. Behind him, Esther and Sweeney hopped out from the wagon of a rabbit merchant who had been nice enough to give them passage into the city. Neither of them seemed particularly awed. After all, they had been here before.

"It's, ah, rather large," Nathan said.

Esther shrugged. "But not so difficult to navigate. Come on —the Ermine Palace is just up ahead." She started across the cobbles.

"Wait!" Nathan squeaked as he swung down from the saddle. "Esther—we can't just walk in!"

"Why not? I will demand my father's freedom and justice for what our enemies have done. The Emperor will—"

"But that's just it. We don't even know who our enemies are. They may have spies in the palace." He swallowed. Telling Esther what to do felt wrong. Telling her not to go and rescue her parents felt even worse—but he had to keep her safe. "The Laughing Company will arrive soon. They wanted to capture you, remember? You're one of the targets. So we'll have to do this smart." He looked at Sweeney. "Do you think that wise, Master Sweeney?"

"Wise enough," Sweeney agreed. "Come on, then. We'll find an inn near the Ermine Palace. Then we can do our planning."

A chance to plan. To catch his breath. That sounded nice enough.

And he did want to see some of the statues. Was there one of Sir Konrad the Courageous, somewhere in that army of stone figures? Even if there wasn't, some of the others—eagle knights and skull-masked saints—did look appealingly fearsome.

Sweeney led them further into the city and to an upscale inn, the Ferrethaus, with an adjacent stable for Emperor. The kind of place that catered to wealthy merchants and lesser nobles who couldn't find a place in the palace itself. And speaking of the palace, there it was, rearing up behind high walls just across the broad avenue. The Ermine Palace. A towering, sprawling complex of vast structures, a walled world. Only towers and battlements and roofs protruded from over the walls, letting commoners catch just a glimpse of the imperial royalty within.

Somewhere in there, hidden in a dungeon deep below, Eleazar and Yelena Essen suffered.

Nathan paid for their rooms in the Ferrethaus and for a meal to take in the common room—a sort of Grand Sable pancake stuffed with meat and powdered with paprika. Strudel for dessert. Good food, but not cheap—and the coins he had in his purse grew fewer. Esther tucked in with gusto that her mother would call unbecoming of the Court Rat's daughter, and Nathan matched her bite for bite. They smiled at each other.

No need for table manners here.

"Nathan!" Esther pointed behind him. "Oh, Supreme Rodent —some good luck. Look who it is!"

Gentle music. A lilting voice. He spun around and there was an old friend plying the minstrel's trade. Croaker—a slim treefrog, his limbs a brilliant green. His fingers worked their way over the strings of his lute. He sang well as he hopped his way through the room, pausing to extend his feathered cap to this table or that, always bowing, always in motion. And the ballad he sang—

The Ballad of the Rat on the Road.

Nathan's ballad.

Heat sizzled to life under Nathan's fur. His whole life—his orphaning, his time on the road, his battles, and dangers—all set to rhyme. Esther stared at him as the ballad went on.

Should he be proud? Not when there was so much mythology mixed with the truth—and especially not when the inn's guests might notice that the subject of the ballad was right there, sipping apple cider.

Croaker spotted them a moment later, recognition flashing bright in his brilliant crimson eyes and then he bounced over—finishing the song with a flourish and a joyous chord. Applause filled the room as Croaker bowed—and then sat at Nathan's table.

"Nathan of Nestovich! Should I tell them that I've just finished singing about you, my dear boy?"

"Better not, Croaker. Do you think they'll recognize me, based on the song?"

"I think not. The Rat on the Road, Bold Sir Squeaky, is a tad more—hmmm—impressive."

What did that mean? "Impressive?"

"In a different way, perhaps." Croaker settled down and slung his lute behind him on its woven strap. "Then again, perhaps you should embrace your fame. You needn't pay for a meal again, if you don't wish it. Beasts will be falling over themselves to say that they spent a moment in the company of Nathan the Rat, the Orphan Prince of Tock." Then some of the brightness flickered in his eyes. He'd noticed Esther—and the sadness in the shake of her whiskers. "Something's wrong."

Nathan told him—quickly.

"Ah. That is—that is terrible."

Sweeney flicked his ears up, expectant. "Can you help us, troubadour?"

"I'll tell you what I told, Nathan, long ago—I am a mere chronicler of adventure, not an adventurer myself—"

"Please." Esther looked at him. "Please, sir."

His webbed fingers stilled. His red eyes looked at her and he sighed. "Oh, Blessed Beasts. What a fool I am. I believe my ballads. Every time."

"So you'll help us, then?" Sweeney asked.

"Ah—yes. Yes, I will." He was convincing himself. "You need to gain entry to the Ermine Court, yes?" They did—and to find Septimius von Stahl, who might know more about what had happened to Eleazar. "Well, you're in luck. Tonight, there is to be a masque to celebrate St. Cuthbert's Day—a grand costumed party. The palace will be swarming with notables from across the Grand Sable Empire, all of them masked. Getting in might be difficult, without an invitation—but as it happens, I've been hired to serenade the masked creatures, and I could bring you with me through the servant's gate."

That seemed simple enough. "Thank you, Croaker." Nathan grinned at his old friend. "You see? You're a bit of an adventurer yourself after all."

"No, no—don't thank me yet." His finger tapped the table. "Getting in is only part of the trouble. I don't have invitations for you, so you'll have to be careful. The Ermine Guard—the Emperor's finest—will be on patrol, of course, and if they find out that you got close enough to pet old Emperor Ferencz von Wessel's fur without an invitation, they'll take your head— and mine too. Master Eleazar's enemies will be about as well, whoever they are. And it's not like I can bring you to Von Stahl, or that you can even trust that venomed fuzz sausage or—"

"No." Esther smiled suddenly. "It's perfect."

"Perfect?"

"A masque. Everyone will be in costume." She was beaming now, enjoying her scheme. "Unless the guards are going to pull off masks and see who's beneath, we'll be perfectly hidden. Of course, so will Von Stahl. And my father's foes."

Perfect. Esther was brilliant—another example of her matchless mind.

"What's the theme?" she asked. "All the masques have a theme. I attended quite a few of them as the Court Rat's daughter. Nature Spirits, Winter Night characters, the

Silversands Kingdoms. What's this one's theme?"

Now, Croaker smiled. "Oh, Nathan—you're going to love this."

He squeaked. He probably wouldn't.

"It's your story, Nathan. The theme of tonight's masque is to be the adventures of Nathan the Rat."

+ + +

A full moon over Erminum. Big and yellow—a great wheel of cheese. Made to shine upon gardens and imperial dining rooms. Perfect for a masque. But Nathan certainly didn't feel perfect. Not when he wore an absurd costume—and one based on himself in the bargain. Esther and Sweeney had stopped by a tailor shop where Eleazar had gotten most of his clothing done, and the wizened shrew who worked there was only too happy to create outfits for them all.

But only Nathan got the full treatment.

A scarlet doublet. Striped pantaloons. A great black silken cape—a version of the outlaw cloak that he'd worn in Katzenberg. An enormous, ridiculous ruff that choked his neck and itched like it was lancing his neck with a thousand claws.

Finally—worst of all—a mask based on his own head, topped with the helmet he had worn on the tourney in the Katzenberg. The features, a big smile, fake whiskers, and round red cheeks, didn't look anything at all like him.

At least he didn't have to put on the mask until he got inside. He tucked it under his arm and led Emperor by the reins, following his friends as Croaker brought them through the servant's gate and into the back of the palace. Here, a few servants in their white uniforms with gold and silver piping darted about, some running to the kitchen or the worker's chambers in the palace and others down the discrete little passage that brought them into the palace and the gardens beyond.

Esther grinned at Nathan. "Embarrassed?" She looked wonderful—as always—in a costume based on the knife-throwing skunk performer Rosa Fumes. A black and white mask, a lemon-yellow gown, and a set of costumed knives slung in her belt.

"Absolutely," Nathan agreed.

"You ain't alone in your discomfort, laddie, if that makes you feel better." Sweeney had been garbed as the Demon Skunk —a monster that appeared only in certain Nathan of Nestovich stories. A snarling skunk's head atop his own, flags of false flame formed a wild crest, and a great fluffy tail bigger than his own. "Croaker! Can we stash the piglet here?"

"The Imperial Stables." Croaker pointed to an extensive structure up ahead. "He'll be right at home."

They walked to the stalls. Some, the ones near the front, housed simple riding goats and sheep, now agitated by the newcomers. Further on, grander creatures ate fresh, golden hay from silver troughs, and sported ribbons in their fur. Hierarchy amongst the riding animals. Nathan found an open stall and ushered Emperor inside. He reached out, petting the boar's muzzle and accepting a lick. Emperor knew him, even under a mask.

"Ah, there's Marquessa!" Esther waved to the stall across from Emperor's. "A mouflon." A delicate creature with dainty, lean hooves, black and white stripes across her muzzle, and horns that curved slightly at the top—drawn by an elegant calligrapher's paw. "That's her Imperial Majesty's riding animal. She let me ride her around when I was smaller."

Marquessa gave Esther a polite chirp.

"So what now?" Croaker asked.

"Now?" Nathan wedged on his mask. He looked out at the world through eyeholes—a version of his own face. "Now, we go to the masque."

That sounded confident and heroic. Like something Bold Sir Squeaky would say.

They walked past Croaker, who was tuning his lute, and took the winding servant's path. The garden—that seemed to be where most of the guests were. Von Stahl too, perhaps. The path led through a little hedge, the music and conversation of nobility coming through the greenery, and then the path ended, and they had arrived at the edge of a veranda with the garden beyond.

This was the home of the House of Wessel, and there seemed to be no limit to how much grandeur, how much wealth, could be crammed into the gardens, the palace, the fountains, the statues, and the menagerie beyond. Moonlight shone on a series of fountains, forming a shimmering, leaping stream away from the broad veranda, into a garden that looked as if a skilled and careful artist had been painting with topiaries, flowers, and hedges. Guests in a riot of costumes, all from Nathan the Rat stories, wandered amongst the finery, taking drinks from servant's trays, and making a hum of refined conversation.

Right in the middle of the veranda, Emperor Ferencz himself sat on a sort of gilded, wheeled throne, and stared blankly at the party. Along with the Ermine Guard—a half-dozen tall, snow-white ermines with huge, towering hats and massive halberds—a vast assortment of courtiers and servants surrounded Emperor Ferencz, who occasionally waved a feeble paw to make a servant bring a wine glass or some pulped fruit to his toothless mouth.

He was dressed as Nathan as well.

Nathan swallowed. What were they going to do? Where was Septimius von Stahl in all of this?

"I think we need to split up." Esther—taking charge. Sweeney growled. "I know, I know. You don't like it. But we need to find Von Stahl fast and we've got a better chance if we divide our forces. Why don't you stay here, in the middle, and if either of us needs help, you can come running?"

He seemed to like that notion as much as he liked everything else—not at all. His whiskers deepened his frown. "Don't take chances. Neither of you. And don't stray far."

"We won't." Nathan curled his tail close. "Esther, maybe you could go inside? To the parlor area? I think I'll take the garden." More shadows in the garden. More danger, perhaps—and he really wanted to see the Imperial Menagerie. "If that's acceptable to you, I mean?"

She was already looking back at the palace. "I wonder if I'll be confused. Mistaking someone dressed as Nathan the Rat for the real rodent." Then she squeaked. "No—I doubt it. You're too unique. Have fun looking at the menagerie." She headed out, bouncing up the broad steps and through the wide glass doors to the waiting palace.

She'd be all right. She was capable—and more at home at court than Nathan ever could be.

Sweeney seemed to be worried for Esther's safety as well. Fear flickered in his amber eyes as he watched her go. He gave Nathan a final nod and went to stand near a teardrop-shaped topiary, leaning on his poleaxe and looking like a statue of a Demon Skunk.

Nathan hastened down, weaving around the fountains—pausing to dip his hand in to make a quick splash—and then walking to the great cages of the massive animals, brought from all over the world, that made up the emperor's menagerie. Fewer guests around here. They walked together in clusters, talking quietly, and pausing to look at gilded cages.

A cape buffalo in one, a hulking massive, wise beast with sad eyes under heavy curling horns. It looked through the bars, occasionally reaching down to snag a bite from a silver barrel of hay. Beasts could come and stare at the buffalo and be amazed—but it could never leave those bars.

Something sad about that, to be famous but still trapped.

A small beast, around his size, brushed past him. Silvery gray fur. A servant's pale uniform.

"Sorry—excuse me!" Nathan called out. True, the serving girl had nearly bumped into him, but his parents had always told him to be polite. A quick nod from the servant, the white uniform already fading into the shadow of a hedge. Nathan looked back at the cape buffalo, who chewed hay and looked back with its huge, dewy eyes.

Like it was the one feeling sorry for him.

He needed to start talking to the other guests, seeing if Septimius von Stahl lurked under any of those colorful masks— but something was wrong. His paw went to his belt, where his dagger—his real dagger, not part of his costume—waited.

It was gone.

The serving girl had plucked it right from his belt. Nathan had spent enough time around excellent pickpockets to recognize a master of the trade, and this serving girl was one —but she'd made a big mistake. Picking something that would obviously be missed.

Also, she'd chosen to pickpocket him.

He let his paw fall to the side—casually—and walked to the next cage, which held a giant crocodile from Silversands. It lounged lazily in the muck, still as a log. Nathan made himself just as still, then casually glanced over his shoulder. Looking back at the cape buffalo—except instead, he examined an intersection in the hedges—a leafy corridor leading to little alcove with a gazebo. Out of the way of the rest of the party, shadowed.

A perfect thieves' hideout.

He yawned, turned around, tugged at his ruff, and started back. Walking casually with his tail trailing behind him. Past the turn, matching a passing couple of laughing stoats to disguise his footsteps—and then stopped. Hidden by the hedge. He braced himself, squared his shoulders, and leapt out. Making a run into the gazebo.

The serving girl—the thief—sat on the bench, holding his dagger. A rat kit, about his age. That silver fur, mixed with charcoal splotches, catching the moonlight, and a similar shine in her dark eyes. Two ears, quite large—one missing a chunk. She sprang up at his arrival, spinning the dagger around. A combat position.

Perhaps confronting the thief wasn't the best idea.

"I'll shout to the guards." A plaintive squeak in his voice. No —be threatening. "Tell them there's someone pickpocketing the guests. I bet they won't like that."

"Then I'll tell them you don't have an invitation." She smiled. "I know you don't. I would have found it when I picked your pocket."

"Zoya, Zoya—please." A quieter voice, from further in the gazebo. A black and brown mouse—fully grown and yet as small as the kits—stepped into the moonlight. "No need for threats. He's one of us, I think." She clicked her teeth. "A very *famous* one of us."

Zoya gave Nathan a sniff. "No—he's not—that can't be the real —"

"It is." Nathan gripped his mask and pulled it up, revealing his own face. "I'm Nathan of Nestovich. The Rat on the Road, from the ballads, and the stories. Now, could I please have my dagger back?"

"What do you think, Zipporah?" Zoya hoisted up the Winterborn blade, giving it a slight spin. "Can we trust the famous Nathan of Nestovich?"

"He told the Mole Lord where the raven outlaws had their camp, as I recall."

"No—that's not—that didn't happen." Nathan sighed. "I'm

here for a reason. Trying to help someone, my friend—" No—don't say Esther's name. They might be like him—squeaklings, the world would call them—but they could still be enemies of the Essens. Maybe they could just leave each other in peace? "Why don't we strike a deal? You give me my dagger back, I'll go on my way, you can resume picking pockets, and neither of us bothers the other. How does that sound?"

The mouse—Zipporah—walked closer to Nathan. "Is that why you think my daughter and I are here?" she asked. "To pick pockets?"

Daughter? Adopted—had to be. "That's what you did to me..."

Zoya squeaked indignantly. "We're here to help. All rats. All mice. We are here to help them all."

"And you're doing that by stealing my dagger?"

Zipporah smoothed back her whiskers. "The boy has a point. Give him back his little knife, Zoya."

"Mother—" Zoya's tail thrashed.

"Do it, my darling. He's not our enemy." She went to her tiptoes, making herself just a little taller than Nathan. "But I want you to ask yourself a question, Bold Sir Squeaky—world famous Rat on the Road. Do you know that your kind are in danger?" Danger? More than usual? "No—you were content to put yourself in the middle of famous stories and then live in comfort with the Court Rat of the Grand Sable Empire, were you not? To be the one rat celebrated, while the rest are despised." She reached back, taking the Winterborn dagger from Zoya. "Ah, but you are a child. I ask too much of you."

A child? No. He was more than that. "If rats and mice are in danger, I want to help." He hesitated. "But I do need to help my friend as well. I'm looking for Septimius von Stahl—the emperor's spymaster. Have you seen him? I know everyone's wearing masks..."

"We've seen him." Zoya chattered her teeth. "But why should

we tell you?"

"Zoya, my darling—enough!" Zipporah squeaked—strangely loud for such a small creature. "He said he wants to help. Why don't we give him a chance?" She slid a paw into her coat, a patchwork mass of different dull colors that blended in with the shadows. Papers rustled and then she squeaked triumphantly. "He we are. Von Stahl's invitation. We picked his pockets earlier tonight. He's inside, I believe. Dressed as you. Watching the tableau vivant."

"The what?" Nathan asked.

"You'll like it, Nathan of Nestovich." Zoya winked. "It tells your story—it will appeal to your pride."

"No—that's not—" He sighed. Zoya was infuriating. "I'm going." Nathan slid the dagger back into his belt. "I'm going to find him. If rats and mice are in danger, please tell me—I'll see what I can do."

Zoya looked like she was about to utter an insult but paused, her mouth half-opened. She brushed back her ears. "Best of luck to you, then, Nathan of Nestovich. If we need you, we'll find you. And next time, keep a better hold of your valuables."

He walked away, embers sizzling beneath his fur. This mother mouse and rat daughter were a complication he didn't need. And what were they talking about? A great danger to his kind? Well, if they wanted help, they could ask him once this business was done. Right now, he and Esther had troubles enough.

+++

He found her back in the entrance, sipping a glass of sweet wine and talking with a clutch of ladies in the court. They had costumes of other characters from Nathan's tales—some real, some imagined. A willowy hare wore the shimmering golden fur of the famous swordsmonkey Artemesia De Leon, and carried a prop rapier as well. A mink had a false swan's head, composed of carved wood, white silk, and real feathers set atop her head. What character that was, Nathan didn't know.

"Well, I think the Court Rat's daughter is a particularly interesting character." Esther swirled her glass. "It was her idea to send out the Messenger Moths, you know, and she saved Nathan's life in the Grand Clocktower in Tock."

The rabbit garbed as a monkey snapped open her fan. "And what version of the Nathan story is she in, my dear?"

"Ah." Esther paused. "The best version!"

"Is that so? Well, Lady Fumes, it seems your little knight is here." The monk pointed to Nathan.

Esther gave them another dignified smile. "You'll have to excuse me. We have more adventures to plan." She broke away as they tittered and walked next to Nathan—her voice dropping. "Did you discover anything?"

"I think Von Stahl's inside. Dressed as me and watching something called the tableau vivant."

"Sounds promising," Esther agreed. "Nathan, do you know that, as far as I can tell, I don't appear in *any* versions of your story?" Her red eyes flashed. "It's not fair. A rat hero is amusing. That can be tolerated. But the Court Rat's daughter? Oh no. That's too far. She has to stay in her chambers, giving her favor to a heroic Sir Squeaky—or she simply isn't in the tale at all."

"Well, a lot of the people who write Nathan of Nestovich stories are fools."

She smiled at that, and her pale teeth shone in the moonlight. The embers under Nathan's fur rose to fires. "Well-said. Let's find Von Stahl."

They slipped through the wide doors and entered an expansive parlor. A table laden with a feast in one corner— including a vast pastry rendition of the Battle of Tock, with walls and battlements of icing-drenched cake, and warriors and knights made from dates, fruit, and cookies armed with blades of spun sugar. The diners had torn chunks free from the walls and devoured many scrumptious soldiers.

Was there some cookie representing Nathan? Had it already been eaten?

Across from that, on the polished marble floor, several performers crafted a tableau vivant—a sort of living sculpture. They had two performing voles, one on top of the other, forming a towering, monstrous bear. A small hedgehog served as Nathan, hoisting up a sword wrapped round in red and orange paper flame, as other beasts stood frozen in terror or battle.

It was quite a sight.

Esther smiled. "He doesn't look anything like you."

"Neither does he." Nathan pointed. A thin ferret, clad in stately black wearing a mask of Nathan's face. He lurked at the end of the table, examining the dessert. "That's Von Stahl, I think."

"Then let's say hello."

They crossed the polished floor, skirting the edge of the tableau. Von Stahl reached to the tower in the center of the dessert, where a marzipan owl—the dessert form of the terrible Semyon—perched. Von Stahl plucked the owl free, making marzipan crumbs rain down. He looked up, dark eyes behind his mask. Staring at Esther and Nathan.

Be polite. His parents had taught him that—but they hadn't told him what to do when he faced off with an old enemy wearing his own face. "Hello there, sir," Nathan said. Von Stahl looked at him. He pulled his mask up, revealing his real face. Nathan beneath Nathan. "You remember me, I'm sure?"

Von Stahl looked at Semyon's marzipan head and then at Nathan. "And that's Essen's daughter with you, I suspect?"

"Very smart," Esther agreed. "Where is my father? My

mother? Who hired the Laughing Company?"

A low whimper. Von Stahl's whiskers drooped. "Let us begin, my dear children, with a more obvious question. Why, in the name of all the Blessed Beasts, would I agree to help you?" He pointed to Nathan. "You ruined me. You released the plans for the printing press that have now filled the world with pamphlets and political treatises and books that make my job all the more difficult. And furthermore, I truly dislike you, Nathan of Nestovich. I hate the fact that I must wear a copy of your face over my own because that is the theme of tonight's masquerade." He folded his slim arms. "Answer that question first."

"You helped my father." Esther selected a date from the castle and popped it into her mouth. She was calm—her voice clear. An equal to Von Stahl.

"A mistake. And one I won't repeat."

"Are you worried that you'll be arrested as well? Then why help him in the first place?"

"Because, little Lady Essen, beasts like your father and I do not hold grudges. We concern ourselves with grander things."

Nathan smiled. "So why bear a grudge against me? What does it get you?" He waved his paw at the tableau. "I'm the hero of the story, remember? So perhaps going against me is unwise." Try and sound confident—to sound like the Rat on the Road.

The ferret looked at the marzipan owl, crumbling in his fingers. "Hmmm." He bit off Semyon's head. Powdery marzipan ran down. "Well, we do have a mutual enemy. He launched the attack on your family, Mistress Essen, without warning. Now he has your father, your mother, and he's very keen to capture you as well. All for the crime of siphoning imperial funds to fund the Hoppite Rebels in the Dark Forest in their war against the Winterborn."

Esther's red eyes grew wide. "My father would never—"

"He did it. I helped him." Von Stahl shrugged. "All that cursed merchant squirrel had to do was pay a few bribes, bring the evidence before his friends in court, and get the emperor's fingers to hold a quill and sign the order. He left me alone—he doesn't trust me but believes I might be useful. But the Essens had to go."

All the amusement and artifice vanished from Esther. She stepped closer. "This squirrel merchant. Who is he?"

Von Stahl popped the rest of the owl into his mouth. Considering what to do. Turning his enemies against each other —that had to be appealing. "Titus Tarr."

"I don't know the name. A lord?" Esther asked.

"No. Nor a prince, nor a baron, nor even a burgher. He is a merchant. A business-beast. He may be granted a title later, as he's loaned so much money to the Ermine Court—but for now he is simply a beast with enormous, unfathomable wealth."

Enough to hire the Laughing Company.

"Why did he turn against my family?"

"I do not know. Something to do with the Hoppites. I don't understand it. The Hoppites are a way to destroy Winterborn interests without dirtying our own paws and yet Tarr wants them crushed—again, I do not know why."

More mysteries.

More danger.

"We could go and see?" Nathan suggested. That would mean going back to the Dark Forest. Back into war. "We could see how he's trying to stop the Hoppites. We could help them." It was foolish—idiotic. The kind of storybook decision that would put him and Esther into greater danger. "And we could stop Tarr for good."

Von Stahl considered it. "I had the same thought. I am going there as well."

"We'll work together, then?" Esther asked.

"I suppose so." Von Stahl seemed far from pleased. "Your parents will be safe here. They're in one of the more comfortable dungeons, and I'll have my allies in the palace watching them." He twirled a whisker as he thought. "I shall seek answers in the Dark Forest." He gave them both a final sniff. "It's best we don't travel together."

"To keep this Tarr fellow guessing?"

"Yes—and because I still dislike you."

Nathan matched his smile. "We'll find you in Thistle Town. By the way, excellent choice of costume."

A crunch of Von Stahl's teeth on marzipan. He returned Nathan's face to his own and walked away into the party, passing straight through the tableau vivant. A discrete brush from his shoulder upset the voles, and they tumbled down with panicked chirps, the false bearskin covering them as they crashed onto the tiled floor.

Esther squeaked. "We can't trust him, can we?"

"Not at all. But now we know what to do. Go to the Dark Forest, talk to the Hoppites, find out what this Tarr follow wants —put a stop to him. And free your parents." He tried to smile—to be hopeful. Esther deserved that. "Let's get to Sweeney and—" He stopped.

A serving mouse with silver fur darted across the parlor, slipping unseen amongst the guests.

Zoya.

He sighed. Tugged at his ruff. "I better make sure she doesn't get into trouble."

"The serving girl?"

"A pickpocket. I met her and her mother earlier. They said they're trying to help all rats and mice. Looks to me like they're just a pair of thieves—but I should check." He looked again at the dessert architecture—now just a tasty ruin.

Was that what his adventures had become? Fodder for cooks and diners?

"I'll find her and meet you and Sweeney outside, all right?"

Esther nodded. "Just be careful, Nathan. We'll be going on the road soon—and I need the Rat on the Road with me."

She was proud of him. She liked him. He beamed, his whiskers shaking and hurried off.

He wouldn't let her down.

+++

Zoya was a clever pickpocket—matching the Runts of Katzenberg in skill—but Nathan managed to track her. Dressing as a servant was a wise decision. For the nobility of the Ermine Court, a servant was all but invisible. But once Nathan had marked her, he could follow. She weaved out of the stately rooms and the grand hall with elaborate suits of armor standing guard. Their weapons looked nice and dangerous, but he didn't have much time to examine them.

He followed Zoya.

She stopped by a set of double doors, scrolls carved into the wood above, then looked back. "Nathan of Nestovich."

For all his efforts, he'd been spotted too. "You shouldn't be over here. Head back to your mother—or better yet, just leave this place before you get caught."

"Appointing yourself my savior?" Zoya rested a paw on the closed door. She kept her voice low, but still full of venom. "You needn't trouble yourself. Go back to your little quests and adventures. My mother and I will manage. Maybe you can find another bear to fight?"

She was getting everything wrong. Hurling herself into danger and insulting him at the same moment. His whiskers shook. "I'm not—I'm trying to—"

She squeaked and darted back, motioning for Nathan to follow—just before the door slammed open.

A mailed paw reached out, grabbed Nathan's doublet, and hauled him in. The iron grip was like the jaws of predator, biting down without a hint of hesitation or mercy, and then Nathan's polished shoes were sliding across the marble floor, and he was hurled onto the ground as the doors banged shut behind him— the click of a coffin lid.

This time, Zoya wasn't to blame. Nathan's own foolishness had gotten him here. He hadn't bothered whispering and someone on the other side of the door had been listening in.

He looked up. He was in a library. Shelves lined with books —the expensive, old-fashioned sort, that had been made by the laborious work of paws instead of printing presses. A wolverine in brigandine and greaves had hauled him in. Clearly a knight, with brilliant white fur the color of fresh snow and scarlet eyes. Pink ears jutting out and a bastard sword on his belt. No costume for this warrior.

Nathan stood, adjusting his mask. Kept it on. Best that the knight think him some princeling or page dressed as Nathan the Rat. "That was—that was quite rude, sir." His heart drummed madly. Stay calm. They didn't know. Not yet.

"It's rude to lurk outside closed doors and listen." The wolverine looked to the chair at the back of the library. "What do we do with him, sir?"

"Bring him closer, Sir Volkbert." A cold and dry voice.

Volkbert placed a paw on Nathan's shoulder—but he shook it off. A princeling would be arrogant. Nathan walked over himself. Don't be scared, even though jagged ice stabbed at his heart. Be indignant. "I wasn't eavesdropping." He raised his voice, looking at the beast in the chair. Masked, just like he was —though this creature bore a mask resembling a skull looming from a pale hood. The Nameless Saint. What the Blessed Beastworshippers expected to see when they died. What sort of skull? Hard to tell. A furry tail emerged from behind.

A squirrel tail.

Was this Titus Tarr?

"I wasn't spying," he repeated. "I just wanted to go in. To look at the books."

"Do you like stories, Nathan of Nestovich?"

He flinched—no, the Nameless Saint was just calling him by his costume's name. "I love them, Master Saint." He didn't have to lie about that.

A slight click of teeth somewhere behind the mask. "I can see that, in your choice of costume."

"You picked a grand subject as well, sir. But I don't believe the Nameless Saint makes an appearance in a Nathan of Nestovich story."

"No—but Death appears in all stories, does he not? At the end?" He left the chair, closing his book and walking closer. Not particularly big or particularly small. If it wasn't for the skull mask, he would be entirely unremarkable. "I am the richest beast in the Grand Sable Empire. I can purchase whatever I desire, and yet I like stories too. Do you want to know why?"

Maybe he did know. Maybe he was threatening Nathan. He was Titus Tarr—that was certain.

"Why?" Nathan's own voice had grown serious.

"You can make them whatever you want. And if the story is good enough—if it matches what beasts already believe—then it's as good as being true."

"I'm not sure about that." Nathan knew truth—what had happened to him in the Dark Forest—and fiction. Other beasts were probably capable of figuring that out themselves. "Is that you want to do—write stories that beasts believe?"

"Stories can grant power, Nathan of Nestovich." Tarr leaned closer. "I have wealth, and that grants me some power—but not enough. Soon, though, very soon, I will have all the power I want." His eyes flicked behind him. "And those who stand against me will suffer."

He looked over his shoulder. Sir Volkbert stood there, paw on the pommel of his bastard sword. The white wolverine looked fearsome indeed, with a muzzle full of teeth and firm grip on his blade.

But the squirrel—skull-masked and plain, ordinary and yet so full of menace—was worse.

And there was no one around to help.

They had to suspect and were seeing what he would do. After all, they might have received word from Smiling Spike and the Laughing Company that Nathan and Esther had escaped. A page or princeling—or most young beasts—would apologize, become frightened.

He wouldn't do that. Even though a hollow opened in his gut and his tail twisted on the carpet.

"If you go against the Essen Family," he chose his words carefully. "You go against Nathan of Nestovich. And you will lose."

Titus Tarr's paw reached out. Settled on Nathan's mask. He pushed it up, slowly, making the band drag against Nathan's fur. "Nathan of Nestovich." He whispered the words. Oh yes—he knew. How many rats would there be in the Ermine Palace? "That is all I needed to hear."

The door slammed open. Something creaked, shifted—and then a rapid clattering. Fluttering and flapping too.

Books descended in a leatherbound avalanche. One banged against Nathan's shoulder, covers and pages flapping as it hit the ground. Sir Volkbert snarled, a burbling, hateful curse, and his grip vanished. A hefty tome had walloped his head, others thumping his shoulders and landing on his belly. Behind him, Zoya pushed at the bookshelf. She couldn't topple it, but she could unseat the countless books inside.

How many rats in the Ermine Palace? At least one more.

"Nathan—hurry!" Zoya cried.

He ran, dashing toward Zoya and the library door. Sir Volkbert would recover soon and then draw that cruel bastard sword and follow.

Outside, across the hall. Back toward the vast parlor and the tableau vivant. Behind them, Tarr's voice rose to a chattering squeak. "They are agents of Essen! They threaten the emperor! They need to be stopped!" Oh no—all the guards—including those terrible ermines—would hear that. They'd be closing off exits, trying to capture him, Sweeney—and Esther.

She was outside, next to Sweeney—on the veranda. "Nathan." Zoya, tapping his shoulder. Insistent, with a worried squeak in her voice. "We'd better slip away. My mother's going to be enraged. I was supposed to spy on Tarr. Not anger him."

"Sorry about that. And thank you—for saving me." Why had Zoya done that? Back in the gazebo, she had seemed more annoyed with Nathan than anything.

Zoya shrugged. "Well, I guess the ballads are right about one thing—you are polite." She made a quick bow. "Farewell, Nathan of Nestovich."

They split up, just as a rank of Ermine Guards entered from across the parlor.

Nothing for it. Nathan ran. Dashed through the parlor, ripping his mask free—that felt good, at least. Wind in his fur as he scampered amongst the guests. Tall white hats and gilded halberds, emerging to give chase.

He scampered to the side—crashing straight through the tableau vivant. Upset the voles, who tumbled down, yet again, and leapt past the actor playing himself. "Sorry!" Nathan shouted over his shoulder as he sprang out—back into the cool evening air.

Up above, fireworks flashed to life. Thunder and brilliant colors. Searing hot coal red and yellows that matched the sun, bursting and drifting down. Sudden light washed over the garden and the great beasts in the menagerie roared, honked, and hissed.

Esther and Sweeney were already running, matching Nathan's speed. "You found Tarr?" Esther asked.

"Oh yes," Nathan fought for breath. "He's—he's almost entirely unremarkable. But he did sound scary. I'll say that."

They hurried to the fountains, the reflecting pool matching the glow of the fireworks above. Shimmering lights, dancing water, statues catching the fire in the sky—they were running through a land of magic spirits. The ornately uniformed guards charging after them fit in perfectly. One ermine, a scar crossing the white of his fur, loped ahead, taking the lead of his fellows as Nathan and his friends made for the servant's path through the hedges.

Sweeney slowed, spun around. "Don't trifle!" He roared as he swung his poleaxe down. "Don't trifle with a Demon Skunk!"

The Ermine Guard parried the blow, catching the haft of the poleaxe on his halberd—but it gave Sweeney time to close in, to pull back his head and strike. Ramming his skull into the ermine's pale-furred face.

The crash of a firework up above blared out the crack and the ermine dropped onto the trail, his fancy halberd rattling to the ground.

Esther's parents had done well when they hired Sweeney.

They ran on, and there were the stables—with Emperor inside. But Emperor could only carry one. And they needed to leave fast.

"A thousand apologies, Mistress Esther, but we're going to have to steal some mounts. You'll need to ask the emperor for forgiveness later, and I know your mother and father won't approve." Sweeney led them inside, Nathan running past Emperor's stall. The piglet seemed much more energetic than the old ruler who bore his namesake, thank the Supreme Rodent. "Pick something fast. This riding goat will do for me."

"I have the perfect mount in mind." Esther scurried past Nathan, to the stall bearing the empress's chamois—Marquessa.

Nathan could hardly believe it. "You're going to steal the empress's riding goat?"

Esther looked back with a grin. "We're outlaws now, aren't we? Might as well enjoy the benefits."

No time for her to put a saddle on the chamois, who bowed her dainty head and nuzzled Esther joyfully. Esther swung onto the back, gripped her neck, and urged her into the aisle, ahead of Nathan and Emperor.

Fearless, as always.

Nathan cantered after her. Sweeney waited outside, sitting awkwardly on the back of a hulking brown ram. It had already been saddled, and he clutched the reins in one paw, swinging his poleaxe at the Ermine Guards streaming into the servant's entrance.

"Confounded sheep!" He tugged at the reins, making the ram skip its way back, leaning to the side and bleating piteously. "I'd rather walk. Rather crawl!"

"Sweeney—this way, sir!" Nathan called to him, stirring Emperor to a gallop.

At least their mounts knew what to do. Emperor darted ahead, and Esther had Marquessa racing alongside. The chamois danced toward the waiting gate, moving with the sort of speed that belonged to creatures with wings. She outpaced Nathan in the space of a breath. Sweeney rode hard behind them, cursing and jabbing out with his poleaxe to hold back the Ermine Guard. Until his ram's hooves did what feet could not and raced through the gate and back into the street.

Into the maze of Erminium.

Towering buildings around them. Wide avenues. More fireworks flaring up, cascading down in shimmering rain. Was there anywhere to run?

Nathan looked at Esther. She'd galloped ahead, then pulled hard to the right. "This way—down here!" Dashing down an alley between the inn and a sprawling cathedral. "I used to hide from my tutors and nursemaids in these streets—I know them well." She grinned back at Sweeney. "You never could find me, unless I wanted to be found."

"You were a right little demon, mistress!" Sweeney called back. "Caused your parents and I no end of grief—but I'm glad you learned such sneaky lessons."

Very glad—because now they could escape.

Though with only more mysteries as their reward.

+++

They left Erminium at dawn, pausing at a tiny village for supplies. Marquessa got a new bridle and saddle and a pair of blue coverings for her horns—Esther picked the color—which would hopefully disguise her from any prying eyes. Of course, two rats traveling with a cat weren't exactly inconspicuous. Nathan made sure they kept to the shadows and the backroads and put up the hoods of their cloaks whenever they passed travelers.

The Grand Sable Empire would be after them now, but worse than that was Titus Tarr. The Laughing Company had already snatched up Eleazar and Yelena Essen. Now, they had nothing to busy them apart from getting Esther as well. They'd be on their trail and their earlier failure would only make them more hateful, more willing to reach new and dreadful heights of brutality.

Nathan and his friends went east. Away from the peaceful, ordered lands of the Grand Sable Empire, with its neatly arranged checkerboards of farmland and clean, stately towns linked by paved roads, and toward the curtain of trees waiting in the distance.

The Dark Forest.

Nathan's home.

Very close to his old village. The color of the trees in early summer, the way the clouds thickened in the morning and parted to a brilliant blue in the middle of the day, and the accents of the beasts they passed—all familiar. Memories came back. They were like splinters buried deep under his skin, and now they flared to painful life.

He could have balanced across that fallen log or swung from the low-hanging branch of that old tree, his father warning him to be careful. Or he could have sat in that moss-covered depression, enjoying the softness, reading one of his knightly adventure books until his mother ordered him home for dinner.

"Nathan?" Esther asked him as stopped at an old inn near the edge of Thistle Town—the place his father would sometimes bring him when he sold his tailored garment. "Are you all right?" They sat at a table in the sunlight, facing the quiet street.

He looked at her—paws clenched on the reins, red eyes bright with worry. Worried for him.

"Yes. Absolutely." He forced his whiskers not to shake.

The sun gleamed on the old building behind them. It was covered with moss and leaned slightly to the side like a teetering drunkard. Sweeney had gone in to see about getting them a meal and a place to stay for the night. Just a little further down the road, Thistle Town waited.

When Nathan was little, the place had seemed bigger than

the whole world. Now, he saw it for what it was: four rows of little buildings facing a grassy common that would fill up with stalls and goods and sweet-smelling food come market day. A place where you could get shoes made or some bread baked, and nothing more than that.

He looked back at Esther. "Ah—we're near Nestovich. Or, the ruins of it, I suppose."

"Oh, Nathan." She closed her eyes. "Do you want to visit it, maybe?"

"No." He stopped. "I don't know. Maybe." But the matter was out of his paws. "We've got more important things to do, don't we? Like finding the Hoppite Rebels and Von Stahl."

"True enough," Esther agreed. She brightened a little, her ears wiggling. "Ah—look at this!"

Sweeney emerged, bearing a tray containing their meal: rich brown bread and honey, some crunchy apples, and a fine wheel of pale cheese alive with spices. Nothing fancy, but the sort of grub that stuck to your ribs and made traveling easier. He set it down as they dug in. No worrying about napkins or table manners here. They scarfed down the food with the sort of hunger shared only by travelers who didn't know how long it would be until their next meal.

"Decent country, this." Sweeney pointed to the trees and the village. "I grew up in a place somewhat similar, far, far away. No frippery. No schemes. No intrigues to worry your head about." He looked at Esther. "You could make a fine life here, you know."

"What would I do?" Esther asked. "Make candles? Milk sheep?"

"You'd be safe." Sweeney sighed. "It's why your parents hired me. I've failed them, and I don't want to do the same to you. This Titus Tarr fellow—I remember hearing about him during my time in the palace. Just overhearing things. No one trades secrets with the bodyguard." His whiskers shook, ears flicking back.

"He's ruthless. More than that, he's got the sort of power you only have with wealth. Moving against him like this—I'm not sure it's smart. I could leave you and Master Nathan here, find some safe place for you, sneak back to Erminium. Try to free your parents and we could—"

"Run away? Are you saying we run from Tarr?"

The cat looked even more miserable. "You'd be safe."

"I don't want safety." Esther had bitten a large lump of cheese. She swallowed. "I want revenge. Titus Tarr has attacked my family. He burned my home. He murdered Valencia—who never treated the world with anything but kindness. I want him destroyed. I want his plans brought to ruin, his fortune wiped away, and his power shattered. That, to be perfectly clear, is our goal."

It sounded absurd. Two kits and a cat bodyguard, plotting against the most powerful beast in the Grand Sable Empire after the emperor himself. But there was nothing but red iron in Esther's eyes.

"Will you help me?" Esther asked.

When Nestovich had burned, Nathan had wanted revenge—but he was more afraid, more focused on survival, and broken with sadness than anything else. Esther hadn't lost as much, of course—but she was braver than him.

"Of course," he said.

Sweeney nodded. "Aye. I'm with you. It's just that I haven't grown so old without learning the virtues of fear."

"Understood." Esther smiled—a girl once again. "Can you pass the honey, please?"

Nathan did, as a distant crunching noise drifted over the meadow. Like the Supreme Rodent was chewing. Nathan looked into the sky. Dust, rising in plumes. It would be coming from marching boots, matching the beat of a drum. An army on the move.

Winterborn? Imperial? Or the Hoppites?

In any case, the sound of marching feet and the clank of armor were as familiar to the Dark Forest as sunlight in spring. Nathan put up his hood and motioned for Esther to do the same, just in case—but these soldiers weren't here for them. They had come for battle.

There was war in the Dark Forest yet again.

CHAPTER 3. LET THE BATTLE WAGONS ROLL

They entered Thistle Town and found the marks of the Hoppites everywhere. Banners of red and white, showing a great, pale goose with outstretched wings, dangled from the balconies of the few two-story buildings, and fluttered from flagpoles in the cool spring breeze. The citizens were out, waving whatever cloth they could find with a pale or crimson color, and cheering the Hoppite cause. Merchants offered their wares to soldiers and locals alike. An arriving army or a market day? Both were good for business.

Nathan dismounted from Emperor, leading the piglet down Thistle Town's shabby main street. He looked back at Esther, who still sat on Marquessa. "Do you see Von Stahl anywhere?" It seemed a rather futile sort of search—finding a scheming ferret in a haystack.

Esther scanned the crowd and pointed. "No—but there's a puppet show!"

Sure enough, a small booth offered puppetry on the street corner. A small cart, with a faded striped curtain, faced an assembled, attentive audience of kits, hoglets, cubs, and hatchlings. Nathan was too old for such entertainments, but he still glanced at the action as the curtain slid back and the first puppets bounced their way across the scene.

"All little creatures must be wary!" The puppeteer's voice

boomed out from below as a paw emerged, each finger tipped with a scrap of wide-eyed fluff representing a young beast. "Mind your parents. Heed the rules. For these are dark times— and the Carrion King is about!" Their other arm appeared, this one topped by a grim monstrosity.

A black clad monster, in a filthy gray cape made from a tattered handkerchief. A staff tipped with a shining black stone —fresh from the river and polished so it caught the spring sunlight. The head, perched at the top of the cape, was a carved wooden skull. It snapped its jaws open and shut with the menace of a monster.

A rat's skull?

Perhaps. It was hard to tell. Most creatures looked relatively similar with all their fur and flesh stripped away—which made hatred of rats and mice even more absurd.

The young audience cheeped, squeaked, and growled in amused terror as the Carrion King chased the five fingers back and forth. The chase went over brush composed of grass and dirt and trees made from twigs. The puppeteers knew their business. It was a good chase, bringing out lots of applause as the Carrion King hopped onto the pointed roof of a windmill and scanned back and forth for the youngsters hidden below the sails.

Sweeney, walking alongside his goat with his poleaxe leaning on his shoulder, joined them and stared at the show. "What nonsense is this?"

"The Carrion King, apparently." Nathan pulled an apple from his saddlebag and let Emperor snap it up. "A new villain." He looked at Esther. "Do you think he's a rat?"

"It's possible." Esther's whiskers shook. "He's horrid."

He received a villain's end as well: toppling down from the roof of the mill and crashing to earth while the young creatures cheered. The Carrion King puppet slipped away and his skull flew up, spinning before the curtains before dropping down in the booth. A monster, defeated.

The Carrion King must be a new addition to the ranks of demons, dragons, sorcerers, and bandit kings that fell to the blades of heroes. Perhaps, in some future story, he would pit himself against Nathan of Nestovich? Not the real one, of course. Nathan had enough troubles without dealing with the Carrion King.

But that was only the introduction. The curtains slid back and revealed an entire scene—a broad courtyard, and a painted background of towering castles and grand palaces. Erminium, created by someone who had never visited the city. A trio of robed monks, each fitting on a finger, huddled together in holy argument at the center of the little square.

"And now, ladies and gentle-beasts, a very special tale—one that all of Thistle Town must know as it joins the ranks of free cities in the Dark Forest." This had to be the story of the Hoppites. Nathan leaned closer, ears flicking up. "The story of Jan Hoppensen. Priest. Preacher. Holy Goose—who saw the corruption and greed of the Church of the Blessed Beasts and sought to free the Dark Forest from those chains!"

A goose puppet flashed in from the right of the stage. White wings stretched out, neck curled—making the scheming monks cower as he flapped back and forth. The audience cheered. Nathan's heart thudded a little faster. Freedom for the Dark Forest—what was that, if not a worthy cause?

"But the monks and priests cared not for freedom and so Jan Hoppensen met his end."

The little finger monks lurched up, wrestling with the goose as the next prop jutted up from the bottom of the booth. A wooden stake, composed of a carved stick. They forced Hoppensen on and his wings stilled. Paper flames emerged from the bottom. Paper smoke descended from the ceiling.

Jan Hoppensen burned.

The narrator gave him a honking voice. "Alas! My goose is cooked!"

This had happened years ago, before Nathan was born. He'd never quite learned the details. It seemed rather typical. Someone tried to stand against great empires and paid the price.

"But heed my words." Hoppensen's wings flapped as the paper flames coursed higher. "The goose may burn, but eagles, hawks, and falcons shall take wing from my ashes, and they will bring freedom to the Dark Forest!" Another impassioned honk and the paper flames covered him completely. The narrator returned with his booming voice. "And there they are, my friends—the Hoppites, who have fought the Grand Sable Empire and Winterborn Dominion both, and never known defeat!"

Nathan turned to the street, now cleared, as the locals of Thistle Town made way to welcome the Hoppites. They emerged from the eastern side, marching in disciplined rows and pausing to offer a wave or catch the spring flowers tossed in their direction. Not exactly a heroic army of shining knights—but that sort of thing only existed in the storybooks anyway.

These were hard-bitten soldiers, mud on their boots and dust on their tabards. Their red and white goose banners dipped in the sunlight. Halberds and maces rested on their shoulders, but plenty of harquebuses too.

Paw-cannons. One of the secrets of their victory.

The other came rolling behind the infantry. Battle wagons, composed of rough wood and pulled by dray goats and speckled hogs. Their wheels churned up the dirt road, working through the mud like kitchen knives carving up pastries. Windows and slits had been formed in the middle of the petite wagons, perfect for aiming a crossbow or paw-cannon. With these wagons, the Hoppites could stand against armored knights.

They could stand against anything.

A little sparrow, a round leather cap topping his red-feathered head, hopped up and down next to Nathan. "Look there! It's General Bunzika!"

General Jan Bunzika. One-Eyed Bunzika. He rode on a bay goat, reclining in the saddle like it was a comfortable couch. An ancient rabbit, fat thick under fading tawny fur, clad in a jerkin agleam with medals and weaponry. His whiskers drooped, his ears drooped, and his remaining eye was half-closed and seemed about to shut completely. A dark patch covered the other eye. But General Bunzika still waved a thick paw and cried encouragement as he rode along.

"Yes, yes, my friends! A free Dark Forest! A better future! We will never stop fighting!" General Bunzika boomed out the words, waving his fist from the saddle.

An old rabbit who had swallowed a magical potion that gave him back his youth.

"Nathan." Esther pointed to the figure right behind him, marching along besides another battle wagon. "Is that—is that your friend?"

Nathan stared at the pine marten, now wearing Hoppite colors. Dark brown fur, disheveled and stiffened with mud, and a yellow patch on the fuzz of his neck. Shining eyes. He wore a kettle helm and carried a harquebus on a strap over his shoulder, along with the longsword on his hip.

"Lucky Niko." Nathan whispered the words.

He should have been expecting it. The Supreme Rodent made sure that he and Niko's paths had crossed countless times during his previous wild adventure through the Dark Forest. He was back in the embattled woodland—why shouldn't he and Niko meet again?

+++

The Hoppites made camp just outside of Thistle Town. A neat enough military encampment, with the wagons arranged into a protective barrier along the edge. In battle, they would be placed into a rough fortification—a wagon fort—that could stand against any army. It seemed bizarre, that these splintery wooden creations could hold back Winterborn Ice Riders and Grand Sable knights—but it had happened, and perhaps it would happen again.

A tired squirrel sentry met Nathan, Esther, and Sweeney at the edge of the camp. After mentioning the name of Niko Nikaros, a messenger went to the general's pavilion to summon him. A little later, he arrived. Running across the grass, a huge smile on his face—an oversized kit, happy to see his friend again.

"Nathan of Nestovich! Oh, Blessed Beasts—you look well!" Niko swept Nathan up and spun him around, laughing—and then set him down and composed himself. He slumped slightly, the smile going slack and impudent. "As I told you once before, I'm not the sort of beast who likes to say 'I told you so,' but, Nathan, my little Lord Rat—I told you so."

"About what, Niko?" Nathan smiled back. He couldn't help it —Niko's delight was infectious.

"That you'd be back on the road soon enough. And look at you now! In fine raiment. The hero from the stories—the Rat on the Road." He snapped his teeth happily. "You know, I've mentioned that I know you to every beast I come across. I've gotten more than a few free drinks in exchange for a Nathan Story."

Esther squeaked indignantly. "All made up, of course."

"Of course." Niko seemed to notice Esther and Sweeney for the first time—his whiskers quivering as they settled on Sweeney, who had deepened his usual scowl to something even more hateful. All his good humor faded away. "You've brought your friends, Nathan. You aren't simply running away and looking for adventure, are you?"

"I was considering it, when I was with the Essens—but no. I'm afraid we're all on the run. And we need help."

"My parents, sir, are in danger." Esther bowed her head—the

Court Rat's polite daughter yet again. "Titus Tarr, a merchant prince, has moved against them. All because my father sought to send funds to your comrades-in-arms. We would know Tarr's purpose, and so we ask for an audience with the general."

"Ooh." Niko grinned. "Of course. He's going to love you."

Sweeney stepped past Esther and reached Niko. They were about the same size, but the marten seemed to shrink a little—the furry sausage becoming a fuzzy potato. "If you're thinking about any of your tricks, Nikaros." Sweeney hoisted up a paw, the claws flashing to sudden life. "Anything that would mean ill for these two young creatures, then you'll find me far less friendly. Do you understand that?"

"Oh yes." Niko bobbed his head. "Yes, indeed." He unspooled —going tall again. "And I would never do such a thing. Who do you take me for?"

Nathan didn't bother answering.

Niko led them to the center of the camp. They passed the Hoppites, who seemed to be like most soldiers Nathan had seen. Tired, dirty, going through the practiced rhythms of cleaning their weapons, gambling, and trying to sleep on worn bedrolls in the gentle sun. Most armies were the same, no matter what banner they happened to fight under.

At the center of the camp, a great checkered pavilion stood open to the sunlight, next to a table bearing a map of the surrounding forest held down by rocks. General Bunzika sat there, lounging in a faded chair like an aged grandfather, and squinting at the map with his good eye. He sipped from a tankard of peach schnapps, the clear liquid running over his fur, and wiped his muzzle on his arm.

An old soldier who cared nothing for niceties.

"Niko Nikaros!" Bunzika slammed the tankard on the table. "Who have you brought me?"

Esther approached and curtsied. "Esther Essen, my lord."

"General, if you please." He arched his ears. "That, alone, is a title I've earned." The general took another sip of schnapps and drew his tongue over his lips. "You are Eleazar Essen's daughter, yes? He sends you to see his investment in action. Well, why shouldn't he? We are earning our support, are we not?" He didn't know that Eleazar Essen had fallen from favor—that his support was about to vanish. "But why did you come? I thought you Grand Sable So-and-Sos already sent somebody."

"Septimius von Stahl?" Nathan asked.

"No, not him." So someone else was here? Someone promising Bunzika much needed help? Nathan looked at Niko, who shrugged. This was maddening. They were playing a game where they didn't know the rules—and they were losing. General Bunzika looked at Nathan with his good eye. "Say, I think I know who you are. You're that funny little rat in the stories. What are you called—Nelson of Nessenheim!"

"No, it's actually, ah, Nathan." Correcting the general—this was going terribly. "Sir, we've come to warn you—to help you."

"A warning, eh, Nelson? About Winterborn Armies on our heels?" General Bunzika laughed. "I know, little one. I know. We'll smash them tomorrow. And you want to help me. Do you have gunpowder? Gold? Iron?" They didn't have anything like that. "I thought not. Eleazar must be facing difficult times indeed if he sends his daughter to check on me. Go back to your papa, little girl. Tell him that General Bunzika spends his coin wisely." He was looking back at his map, sniffing at the pale and blue-colored stones clustered in the etched forest.

"Sir." Esther squeaked—loud enough to make General Bunzika look up from his map. "My father has been betrayed. I fear the same will happen to you."

"Betrayed? By who?"

"General." That voice—dry and clear and with a remarkable lack of emotion. Nathan had heard it before, in the library of the

Ermine Palace.

He spun around to see Titus Tarr approaching.

No costume of the Nameless Saint now. Instead, the squirrel wore a suit of gray silk, a broad-brimmed hat with a gray feather in a gray band, and ring of silver—a lighter shade of gray—on his forefinger. "I heard you had guests."

He wasn't alone. Smiling Spike waited on his right, his mace swinging slightly in his paws. Contessa Vivaldi, that colorful dart frog, crept along at his left, her huge eyes dark and unblinking like great dollops of ink. Sir Volkbert loomed further back, a pale shadow.

"He'll betray you!" Nathan squeaked out the words. A mistake —he was supposed to be the heroic Rat on the Road, not some kit whining out warnings. But he kept going. Nestovich—so close to where they stood—was burning again. Esther in danger —the threat so close. He had to protect her. "He betrayed Master Eleazar, and he'll betray you. If you act quickly, you can—"

General Bunzika held up a paw. Best to be silent. Nathan shut up as the general filled his cup again. "Nelson of Nessenheim— do you have any proof of this?"

A second of silence after that. He looked at Esther. "My father —"

"Is not here, at present." Tarr settled into the chair across from Bunzika. Ignoring Nathan and the others. "He's been arrested in Erminium. Something to do with corruption, I believe." His eyes flicked up. Settling on Nathan and Esther. "You know how rats are. Conniving. Plotting. His daughter blames me. They've followed me, trying to clear their father's name. Laudable. Perhaps."

"The Hoppites are friends of the rats, Tarr," General Bunzika said. "Watch your tongue." But he wasn't turning on Tarr. He was drinking with him, ignoring the danger. "Mistress Essen, Tarr brings his gunpowder to help us against the Winterborn.

You bring nothing. You tell me rumors that Tarr will betray me, but you have no evidence."

"Von Stahl." Her red eyes shone ruby bright. "Septimius von Stahl will tell you."

"Where is he?" Bunzika asked.

"He—he said he would meet us here," Nathan said.

"A spymaster lies. It is in his nature." Tarr accepted another cup and Contessa Vivaldi filled it for him. "The fact that he lied to you is quite unsurprising. Now, I suggest you find some safe place to wait out the battle."

Smiling Spike leaned closer to Nathan—another of his mad grins playing across his face. "It promises to be quite dangerous."

Niko stepped closer. "Back off, Spike. You even look at the boy and I'll carve that stupid smile off your face."

"Niko Nikaros." Spike flexed his quills, clicking them together. "I've got a whole army with me now. The Laughing Company. We've got warriors from across the world—born killers all. I'd love to have you join. There's still room, if you'd like." He was needling them, amusing himself. "Or maybe the famous Rat on the Road would like to give it a try. What do you think about that, Sir Squeaky? A repeat performance of our little dance on the Katzenberg canal?"

"You mean when we beat the quills off you?" Nathan asked.

That should shut him up.

"Enough." Bunzika slammed a fist on the table. The stones, cups, and tankard shook. The rabbit might be old, but he had strength still. "Niko, don't pick fights with the Laughing Company. We are friends here. And you—Mistress Essen. I am grateful for all your father has done for our cause. Stay close. The Winterborn are coming and you'll be safest at my side."

Not a bad idea. They could protect the general from Tarr, at least.

Or they could try. Tarr seemed to already have plans in motion—and what could Nathan and Esther do but be thorns in his side? A momentary annoyance that he was soon to remove.

Tarr looked up from his cup. His eyes settled on Nathan. The same coldness, the same nothingness—like staring into two pools of dirty water. Then he was looking past Nathan, at another rabbit who dashed in with her ears flicked back, a paw fastened to the flail dangling from her belt.

When someone moved like that through a military camp, battle wasn't far away.

"Captain Ursula Uttz." General Bunzika straightened, splashing out the remnants of his schnapps. "Speak."

The rabbit, her fur the color of gingerbread, snapped off a salute. "Our scouts have spotted the Winterborn, sir. They are emerging from the woods in a large body. Infantry in the middle, behind a column of armored bogatyr, while the Ice Riders—"

"The Ice Riders on the flanks, yes." Bunzika pulled himself free from his chair, grunting a little. He had to push a paw against the table, levering himself free. "Their generals play the same old song every time. It gets a little monotonous—if I didn't enjoy beating them so often. Arrange the wagons, Captain Uttz. You chose the battlefield well. The Little Karp on one side, the ruins of the old Striped Barony's castle on the other. We'll drive them to us."

Niko hastened to the old rabbit's side. A pet going to his master. "And you'll go to the baron's castle, sir? Won't you?"

Bunzika's ears flattened. "I will be in the wagon fort, with the soldiers."

"General—if you fall in battle, we all lose." It was strange to see Niko like this. Devoted to a cause when he had previously cared only for himself. But General Bunzika—garrulous, wily, courageous—had clearly won him over. "You're a father to these beasts—and we need our father." Nathan glanced back at

Sweeney, whose eyes had flashed open. He seemed surprised. An impossibility, but there it was, as clear as the whiskers on his face.

"Guide us from the safety of the ruins," Captain Uttz added. "Please."

A snort from the general. A sigh. "Fine." Bunzika offered a paw to Esther. "Essen, you should come with me. We'll join the children of the soldiers, the families—the weak—and watch the battle progress." He muttered to himself and stumbled from his chair. Captain Uttz caught him and led him away, the old soldier grumbling with each halting hop.

Leaving them alone with Tarr and his hirelings.

Tarr picked up General Bunzika's fallen goblet. He righted it and looked at Esther. "What exactly do you want from me?"

It was the first time the two of them had faced off. Cannons roared in Nathan's heart. Esther seemed so small, so vulnerable, even with Sweeney standing protectively at her side. Nathan went there as well, staring at Tarr. He couldn't be scared. Not now, when so much was at stake.

He was Nathan of Nestovich after all.

"What do I want?" Esther asked. "Answers. Why did you have my parents arrested?"

Tarr shrugged. "Your father was in my way. He had to be dealt with."

"I'll give you a chance to let them go. To abandon this rivalry. Your beasts killed my nursemaid, but perhaps you didn't want that. I'll let you go and punish only the guilty."

Smiling Spike grinned. "The little squeakling girl wants to make threats! What a grand—"

A raised paw from Tarr silenced him. "I don't want to negotiate. I have no reason to do so. And yet, I shall offer you a word of warning. Because of your youth, I suppose." He leaned across the table, his face close to Esther. "You have nothing. You are a child. If you prove meddlesome, I won't simply remove you. I will destroy you. And your friends. Just like your nursemaid. Do you understand?"

As cold a threat as any Nathan had heard. He looked at Esther—who simply stared back. "Soon enough, you *will* want to negotiate. Or beg, to be precise. And I don't think I'll listen when you do."

Trumpets sounded in the camp. Feet pounding on the grass. The Hoppites were moving to war.

But it seemed that battle would break out right here.

Smiling Spike gripped his mace, and Contessa Vivaldi's webbed fingers settled around some gleaming jar dangling from her belt. Sir Volkbert flashed pale teeth and clutched his sword. Nathan reached for his dagger, tensing his arm. He'd have to strike fast.

Sweeney growled. "Esther." He put a paw on her shoulder. "Come along. We're bound for the castle."

They went away, leaving Tarr at the table. Still clutching General Bunzika's goblet.

+++

The ruins of some old Striped Barony castle, one of many left behind from past attempts to conquer the Dark Forest, seemed a decent enough place to witness the battle. General Bunzika didn't like it. Nathan watched him from a perch on a ruined tower where he, Esther, and Sweeney had settled. The old rabbit looked out at the green meadow stretching below them, servants, aides-de-camp, and the children of the soldiers darting about like bees in a hive, and he grumbled and swore and slammed his fist on the table. He wanted to be at the front. To see battle.

"No wonder his beasts love him so," Nathan said.

"Even Niko." Esther looked at Sweeney. "You seemed surprised at that."

"Aye—that I was." Sweeney drew something out of his cloak —a spyglass of polished bronze. "You see, years ago, Lucky Niko Nikaros and I served together. A mercenary company, called, rather inappropriately, the Fortunate Few." He looked at the clear sky and its few puffs of cloud. "It was I, Niko, the famed swordsmonkey Artemesia De Leon, and an old frog named Sir Thomas Mulberry."

He seemed wistful—which was quite odd. For all the time that Nathan knew him, Sweeney never deviated from various expressions of rage. But he was sad now, as he reminisced about his old friends.

"We were young and we were foolish. We would fight for good causes and we'd be paid handsomely to do so."

"What happened?"

Sweeney snapped the spyglass to life. "War has a habit of poisoning even the finest of causes. Take a look down there yourself, before the battle begins."

Esther went to the edge of the tower, placed her elbows on the battlements and peered down. She made an introspective squeak—then gave the telescope to Nathan. He balanced it carefully—another wonder that the Essens had purchased—and blinked. The grass, from far away, now looked as if he could reach out and touch it. Supreme Rodent! He had never seen anything like this. But no, he couldn't be awed. He had to look at the situation. To best help Esther.

He directed the spyglass to the section of the field where the Hoppites had assembled. They were building their wagon fort, rolling everything into position as movement came from the trees. The wagon fort was birthed in plumes of dust as wheels rattled and the Hoppites maneuvered cannons, culverins, and harquebuses into place.

A fortress of wood and gunpowder.

Nathan brought the spyglass down, to the middle of the camp. There was the gingerbread rabbit, Captain Uttz. She moved about the wagon fort, waving her paw. Shouting commands, no doubt, though distance made her silent. Then, the cannons thundered, the booms echoing across the meadow as white clouds of smoke burst out like fast blooming flowers across the greenery. Nathan stifled a gasp. The battle had begun. Sure enough, a little bit further up, the Winterborn troops had just made their advance from the cover of the trees.

Bogatyrs, armored in all the glory of their empire. Blue and white banners, bearing the icicle icon of the Winterborn. Green riding goats and white-furred warboars, caparisoned in the colors of their noble houses. The barrage had caught them in mid charge, leaving knights collapsed on the grass like trampled toys, useless armor split and sundered, and the stains from pieces of beasts turned the grass a terrible shade of crimson.

He closed the spyglass.

"What's going on?" Esther asked. "It looks like—it looks the Winterborn charge didn't work."

"You don't want to see." Nathan gave the spyglass back to Sweeney. Esther had seen only a little horror in her life, and that was enough.

Esther folded her paws, her tail coiling—but she didn't disagree. "How's our friend Tarr doing?"

Sweeney snapped the spyglass to the life and swiveled around, looking back toward Thistle Town. "Still in his camp with the Laughing Company and the Grand Sable troops. Looking right pleased with himself. But they're not moving against the Hoppites, that's for certain." Then he stopped. A pleased purr stole from his lips. "Nathan, lad, have a look at that hillock over there." He passed Nathan the spyglass and pointed. "In that cage. Is that—"

Another look. Once again, the feeling of seeing something far away right before your eye. How the Supreme Rodent must feel when he gazed down at earth.

On the hill, a little island amongst scraggly trees and tall grass, a gibbet swung from a post. A cage of twisted iron, just big enough to hold one beast.

And that beast, lean and ragged, was a ferret forced into a bow by the cruel bands of iron.

Septimius von Stahl. They'd found him at last.

He closed the spyglass. "It's Von Stahl. Tarr must have caught him—"

"And put him in that cage." Esther started for the steps leading down from the tower. "It's near the front lines. The Winterborn could simply ride out and claim him. The Emperor's Intelligencer—he'd be a fine prize. Tarr gets rid of an enemy and makes friends with the Winterborn in one move."

"Esther—Nathan—" Sweeny yowled. "What are you doing?"

"What Tarr said." Esther grinned. "I'm being meddlesome. Follow us and we'll rescue him." She was halfway down the steps and jumped, landing neatly on the grass. Marquessa looked up from her grazing, bleating happily as Esther swung into the saddle.

Nathan followed her down. "Sorry, sir!" He called up to Sweeney, who was already starting down the steps himself.

Esther was their queen, and he was happy enough to follow her example.

+++

An easy ride brought them across the meadow. A good distance between them and the battle—but not enough for comfort. The cannons of the wagon fort still roared out their dreadful song, the echoes drifting across the green. The battle was far to their left, the gibbet drawing closer as their mounts galloped, but a look over Nathan's shoulder showed him everything. The Winterborn crashed hard on both flanks of the wagon fort, their banners waving and their arrows and crossbow bolts humming down as their infantry tried to advance.

But the wagon fort stood strong—firm as a rock in a river. The Hoppites had to be using the wagons as cover, swinging their flails, and jabbing out their pikes to stop the Winterborn troops from smashing through. All the while, their cannons and harquebuses crackled and boomed and reaped a grievous harvest. Even from far away, the burning gunpowder smell, sulfurous and cruel, thickened the air.

Rotten eggs and spilled blood. The smell of battle.

Esther had drawn her crossbow from Marquessa's saddlebags and slung it over her shoulder. "Are the Hoppites winning, at least?"

"It looks like it," Nathan said. "But I'd wish us further away. Let's grab Von Stahl and go."

"And how should we do that?" Sweeney asked.

He hadn't exactly thought about that—hadn't time to do anything but ride.

Esther considered it as they rode closer. "Smash the pole, tilt it downward." She grinned as Marquessa galloped under her. "Drop the grateful Von Stahl into our eager arms."

Sweeney yowled. "This is what comes from going to war in the company of children."

They neared the hilltop. The gibbet drew closer, a dark mass of iron against the cloudless sky.

Sweeney cupped a paw to his mouth and shouted. "Von Stahl! How are you?"

They had reached the bottom of the gibbet. The cage dangled from a stout pole driven into the earth. A grim piece of work,

where a prisoner could be left to starve until they fed the flies—
a few of which already buzzed in lazy circles around rusted iron.
At least it offered a decent view of the surrounding countryside
—though that provided little comfort to the beast trapped
inside.

And that beast was Septimius von Stahl. He managed to twist
around to stare at them. He barely fit in the gibbet, his limbs
poking out through the gaps in the iron bars, his head tilted
down as if on a broken neck.

"Is that Nathan of Nestovich?" Von Stahl blinked his dark
eyes. "Or am I dreaming?"

"It is, sir!" Nathan waved to him. "I suppose we've come to
rescue you."

"I rather wish I *was* dreaming." He sagged against the bars.
"Well, get on with it, then. Get me out of this accursed cage!"

"Absolutely," Esther agreed. They dismounted, nearing the
base of the pole. Sweeney put his foot against it, and Esther and
Nathan pulled.

It was like trying to tug down a tree. The pole had been driven
too deeply into the earth.

"What are you doing down there?" Von Stahl asked. "Is it
working?"

"Patience, you sneaky sausage!" Sweeney shouted. "We'll get
you down." He stopped suddenly, his ears flicking up. "Hold on. I
think something might be coming." He pointed down the hill.

Blue and white shapes, riding fast. Ice Riders—the terrible
Winterborn light cavalry. They were far away, but their goats
could close the distance quickly. Already, their pale goats
pounded across the grass—an encroaching curtain of white.
Sunlight gleamed on short bows and sabers.

They were coming fast.

Tilting the pole wouldn't work.

"Maybe I could put a bolt through the lock? Then you could drop down—you'd survive the fall, I think." Esther hoisted up the crossbow. "The lock's about the size of an apple. And the range isn't terrible."

"What if you miss?" Von Stahl asked. "And hit me?"

No—they needed something else. Nathan swallowed. He knew what to do.

He swung from the saddle. "I'll climb up and get him down." The words stole out. He hated them as he heard them—but then Esther smiled, and he smiled back. "Better to save your bolts for more suitable targets."

"Right." He went to the edge of the pole, gave his paws a wiggle, and held on. Squirrels alone hadn't mastered the trees. Rats could climb just as well, and he had practice. Back in Nestovich, he'd scampered up and down the old bent elm next to their cottage, and he'd made it up the trees outside the Essen House as well. But those had branches, and places to rest your paws. This didn't have anything.

He started up.

A stout pole, at least, with a few cracks where he could dig his claws. He worked his way up. One paw over another. His tail dangled below him. Wind came from the direction of the battle, bringing the sulfur tang to boil up his nostrils. Stirring his fur and making his ears wiggle.

Like the Supreme Rodent had crouched low and was breathing on him. Trying to turn him into dandelion fluff, flying away.

Except rats didn't fly.

"Nathan!" Esther shouted to him from below. "You're all right?"

"Fine!" He called back. His paws ached. He gasped as he kept going. A little more. The spring sun beat down. He should have tossed his cloak aside. An ache in his muscles, like he'd been wrestling with a mountain. But the top—it was so close. He was at the cage now, and his foot could settle on one of the bars. Give him a chance to catch his breath.

Von Stahl looked at him. "Shall I take a nap while I wait for you to set me free, Nathan?"

"Maybe I'll just leave you in there." Nathan panted. He brushed back his whiskers. "If you don't shut up."

Sweeney called. "How much longer? They're nearly here!"

He looked down. The Ice Riders had reached the base of the hill now, riding hard. Sleek goats, their hooves pounding below them and kicking up grass and dust. Arctic hares sat in the saddles, their pale fur shining like crystals in the sunlight —matching the gleam of their lethal curved sabers. They wore intricately embroidered robes, sashes, badges, and capes as elaborate as their fuzzy, extended moustaches.

Esther sent a crossbow bolt flying out in their direction, but the Ice Riders rode on.

He had to hurry.

He gripped the bars of the cage, pulled himself up. A final tug and he was there—perched on top of the pole like he was a bird about to take flight. Von Stahl looked at him, arrogance vanished and replaced with fear in his shimmering black eyes. The lock to the cage lay further down, but what good would that do? Von Stahl would simply topple down to the top of the hill.

But the cage—that might save him.

He freed his dagger. Winterborn iron, with an icicle etched on the pommel. A gift from a bogatyr, perhaps a year ago. It had served him ever since.

The cage dangled from a simple hook, attached to the pole by a stout spike driven into the rough, splintery wood. He worked the blade against the spike. The dagger slipped in his paws, nearly dropping, and he caught it, stabbed it again—kept working at metal and wood.

The cage creaked. Von Stahl squinted against the sun above. "Nathan of Nestovich—what are you doing?"

"Setting you free." The blade caught, the tip cutting between the spike and the sun-blasted wood. Nathan squeezed the pommel, twisting it to the side. Hard to pop it free with Von Stahl and the cage's weight pulling the other way—but he could weaken it, shifting the spike so it failed to gain purchase. The cage would do the rest.

Wind rustled past him, making his ears and fur dance. The whole of the world seemed to shift, and he tensed his ankles—breath ragged, weak. He could hear the metal and wood, almost hidden by the wind. Nathan and that lock might have been the only things in the world. Another jab. Another push. It had to be done.

He couldn't let Esther down.

The cage creaked. The joints shifted—and then the cage was dropping, the momentum flicking the pole back. Splintery wood gave way and a terrible squeak left Nathan's mouth. His claws shot out, fighting for purchase. Gripped a length of the pole, held fast, and he shuddered as one of his feet—thank the Supreme Rodent, only one—and his tail dangled below him.

The cage hurtled down. Struck the top of the hill. "Nathan!" Von Stahl wailed out, crying as the cage reached the slope of the hill and began to roll. Bouncing as it careened through the grass, racing down the hillside with the speed of a galloping boar.

Bringing poor Von Stahl with it.

Nathan forced his eyes away from the cage. Back to his friends. Esther and Sweeney stood together, their riding beasts clustered behind them—facing off with the advancing Ice Riders. Esther's crossbow hummed again, and Sweeney had his poleaxe at the ready, threatening anyone who came close with that lethal half-moon of iron. The foremost Ice Riders stayed further back, waiting to cluster in a mounted mass.

When they'd charge.

They were trapped. What were they going to do?

But something else was putting dust into the air. Nathan squinted. A battle wagon, two rams galloping hard at the reins, came racing up the hill. Niko was inside.

Coming to save Nathan again.

"Niko!" He shouted, but the wind and the distance stole away most of his words.

Niko brought the wagon to the top of the hill. "Nathan!"

He hoisted up his paw-cannon and it thundered in the direction of the Ice Riders. The beasts inside the wagon worked bigger cannons, which chorused together, driving away the Ice Riders—or at least forcing them from the hillside.

Niko called to him. "Jump down, Lord Rat! If you want Von Stahl, we've got to move fast. He'll roll all the way to Katzenberg soon enough!"

"Jump?" It wouldn't be jumping—it would be letting go—and dropping. "Niko, I don't think I can—"

"No choice, my friend." Niko's eyes shimmering as he stood on the drover's seat. "You jump or those Ice Riders claim us all. It's a simple enough proposition." He held out his paws. "Do you trust me, Nathan of Nestovich?"

He did. There was nothing more to be said.

He forced his paws free and down he went.

Wind tore at him. His tail flapped behind him as thunder boomed close on the hillside. His cloak billowed, flapping up like broken wings, and then he plopped onto something soft. Niko's lap. Though only for a second. He rolled off that and dropped right onto the grass.

Soft earth, at least. A small mercy.

He looked up at the sky. Breathing seemed impossible. Esther's face appeared above him—a slight smile. Relieved and amused. Emperor next to her. Leaning down, sniffing with his muzzle—and then dragging his thick, slobbery tongue across Nathan's face. Goopy saliva clung to his fur and skin.

He sat up.

"You're all right, Nathan?" Esther took his paw and helped him up. Her voice came from far away.

He should say something appropriately casual and heroic. "Um—yes. I think so." Then he squeaked in pain as he got into the saddle. Oh, this wasn't working.

"Then ride, lad!" Sweeney pointed down the hill. "Von Stahl's getting away from us and there's no telling if the Ice Riders will make another charge."

He straightened in the saddle. More bruises. He winced and gripped the reins. Where was Von Stahl? He squinted against the sun as he started to ride.

The cage had reached the bottom of the hill and now bounced along, carried by momentum. A bizarre wagon pulled by no animal, rolling its way to nowhere.

"Look at Von Stahl go!" Niko laughed. "You want to grab him?"

"He's on our side, this time," Nathan said. "Sort of."

"The shifting fortunes of war." Niko cracked the reins. "Follow me."

They went down the hill, all of them riding together. Dust and grass flying from their hooves and the wheels of Niko's battle wagon. A wild voyage, the wind cutting about them, gunfire and explosions roaring away in the distance, and Von Stahl yipping and shrieking as he tumbled along. Despite Nathan's bruises, the savagery of the battle close by, and fear that made him clutch the reins hard enough to hurt his hands, it felt fine to ride, to race, and to speed across the open meadow.

The battlefield was a terrifying place—but it could be exhilarating too.

+++

Niko's wagon, first to leave, neared Von Stahl's cage first. The battle wagon rattled its way ahead of Nathan, Niko cracking the reins as the rams surged across the grass—a pair of fuzzy ships on a green sea. Hard to see Von Stahl. Nathan strained his eyes as he kept up the gallop. The iron bands of the cage caught the sunlight, diamond bright for a moment as it flew up, and then it was dipping down, heading toward a spur of moss-covered stone jutting up from the earth.

A terrible clang—the Supreme Rodent striking a gong—and the cage split open.

"Von Stahl!" Nathan shouted and tugged in his reins.

For a moment, the ferret was airborne. A furry sausage transformed into a javelin. He sailed along, his formerly fine clothes rustling, before plunging into the earth.

Thankfully, into a waiting expanse of mud.

He carved his way through it, casting up sprays of muck, limbs flailing—gouging away with his muzzle like a plough. Then, finally, momentum left him completely, and he stopped. Von Stahl lay collapsed in the muck, suddenly still.

They rode around him, slowing their various riding beasts and the battle wagon. Emperor panted , oinking excitedly— grateful for the break in his run. Nathan looked down from the saddle. Septimius Von Stahl simply lay there, still as a tree root apart from the rising and falling of his chest. Was he all right?

"S-sir?" Strange, to be checking on a beast who had been a sworn enemy—who had tricked him, betrayed him, and made common cause with killers. "Are you all right?"

Slowly, a mass of mud masking his face, Von Stahl looked up. His eyes blinked open. Little orbs of bright obsidian in a mass of earth. "I—I was the Imperial Intelligencer." He made it to his knees and raised mud-caked paws to wipe clean his mud-caked face—to no effect. "I had power. I had prestige. I dressed in fine clothes and drank wine and sat upon silken cushions." Each word grew in power and ferocity. He was on his feet now, shaking his fur. Chunks of dirt rained down. "And look at me now! Look at me now! Oh, Blessed Beasts—what you have done to your faithful ferret!"

Esther leaned down from the saddle. "Sir, I think it was Titus Tarr that—"

"Oh no." Von Stahl pointed to her. "It all started when you visited me at the masked ball. Tarr and I had an arrangement. Shaky, perhaps, and well-spiced with possible future betrayal—but it was an arrangement. Then you made me your ally, and he found out, and now my life is cages, mud, and discomfort! So much discomfort!"

"There can be more discomfort." Niko was reloading the harquebus. A complicated procedure, but he seemed to manage it well enough. "Why don't you get in the wagon, Septimius, and we'll find a safe place for you to hide? A nice, sheltered hole, far from danger."

"Right. Yes." Von Stahl started toward the wagon. "That sounds lovely."

Nathan relaxed in the saddle. They had Von Stahl. They'd beaten Tarr. They could ride away and—

An explosion came to life—bigger and more terrible than even the cannon blasts that had volleyed from the wagon fort near the meadow's edge. Emperor squealed in worry and Marquessa danced a nervous tarantella. Nathan spun around.

Smoke poured from the side of the wagon fort.

Several of the vehicles lay sundered, the chunks hurled across the grass. Movement as the Hoppites dashed about, rushing to plug the gap. Another wagon slid in, but the Bogatyrs were already crashing their way through, the sunlight catching their armor as they surged in. It was like breaking the shell of a nut. You only had to crack it once, and everything inside was yours.

Those poor Hoppites. The one strength they had against the Winterborn—gone.

"What—what happened?" Nathan managed.

"Gunpowder, set to blow." Sweeney's goat reared up and he brought it under control. "A good amount of it, I'd say. Blew a hole in the Hoppite fort. It'll sink them, sure as any ship."

Niko stared across the meadow at the defeat. His eyes looked different. Nathan had seen him angry before—it was one of Niko Nikaros' natural states. But this was a unique sort of rage. Flecked with sadness in the way his eyes widened and then closed shut, and then his paws clenched tight around his harquebus, and he sucked in torrent of air through sharp, clenched teeth.

"Betrayed." He twisted the reins, angling the wagon toward the ruined castle. "We were betrayed."

And it was obvious who had done it.

Titus Tarr won again.

They rode back across the field as Hoppite troops moved back—retreating in good order at least. Nathan watched them as he galloped after the wagon to the castle. The Hoppites leapt into their wagons, paw-cannons thundering behind them as they rolled back—the knights galloping after with swords and axes swinging. From this distance, it was like watching constellations in the night sky that had suddenly decided to go to war.

"Esther!" Nathan called over to her as they neared the ruined castle. Emperor's hooves struck down, but the piglets chest heaved. All this riding about was tiring him. Not that Nathan felt much better. "What are we going to do now?

"I don't know!" Esther shouted back as more cannons and gunfire rippled across the field.

"Why did he do it?" Nathan cried. "Why betray the Hoppites? Why work so hard to make them lose?"

"I don't know, Nathan!" She looked over her shoulder, glaring at him. Her red eyes gleamed huge—and sad. "I don't know why Tarr's doing what he's doing or how to stop him or how to free my family. I don't know how to do much of anything." She looked away, riding ahead.

Oh, Supreme Rodent. He'd said too much. She was angry, frustrated at him. And she had a right to be.

They reached the edge of the ruined castle, where General Bunzika and the more vulnerable Hoppites had clustered to wait the battle's outcome—which was now a clear and grim defeat.

The former Hoppite fortress was like an anthill that had caught an ember. Hoppites loaded the wounded, the young, and the old into waiting wagons, heeding the commands of officers as the Winterborn thundered closer. More guns thundered away to cover the retreat, or just to add extra doses of sound and chaos to the battlefield. Children wailed. Beasts snorted, squealed, and bleated as cracking whips and reins stirred them to frenzied movement.

Niko leapt from the wagon, leaving the miserable Von Stahl squatting in the back. "Tarr!" He shouted at the retreating Hoppites, drawing his sword. "Where's Titus Tarr?"

Nathan hopped down from Emperor, leading him by his reins and following Niko. Esther and the others waited behind. "Stay there!" Nathan called to them. "Let me see what happened."

And Esther shouldn't get any closer. Not with Tarr and his mercenaries up ahead and the Winterborn closing in.

"Niko!" It was the rabbit captain, Ursula Uttz. She led four other rabbits, carrying a thick bundle between them. Their ears drooped. Their fur disheveled and ragged.

Nathan had known enough of grief to recognize it in others.

Niko looked at them and the sword dropped in his paws. Angling toward the earth. "Is that—"

A silent nod from Uttz. "Soon after the gunpowder charges shattered our line."

General Bunzika. It could be no one else.

"No." Niko stepped closer, moving toward the bundle. An old quilt, spattered with stains, the kind that kits would wrap around themselves on cold nights—that was the burial shroud of the greatest military mind in the Dark Forest. "He was—he was old, I know. Old and blind and tired. But there was fight in him. There was always fight in him—"

"I don't think it was fate alone that sent him to the Nameless Saint." Uttz looked at Nathan. "You said the merchant, the squirrel, would betray him. I think you were right."

Contessa Vivaldi. The poison dart frog confidant of Tarr. She'd jested about poisoning her friends in the Laughing Company. Could she have done that to General Bunzika? A little drip of poison into his goblet, which Tarr himself had picked up from the table in the Hoppite Camp?

Niko looked at Nathan. "I need to be with him." He sounded guilty. "I never had a father. Not really. Not until I met him."

"He was a father to all of us." Uttz waved on the shabby funeral cortege toward a waiting wagon on the other side of the ruined castle. "And now we are orphans."

Niko Nikaros trailed after them. He had changed—and it was a good thing. After living a life only for himself, he'd found a cause he could believe in and fight for. Nathan had gotten to see that fight, just for a little—until the cause collapsed.

Tarr's fault again.

"Nathan!" Sweeney shouted from the edge of the ruins. His riding goat stirring below him. Von Stahl had joined him, awkward on the rear of the saddle. "The Winterborn—they're riding in. Get on that boar of yours and go!"

Of course. They'd lost, but they weren't defeated. They could fight again. Still beat Tarr.

Nathan hurried across the fallen stones and tufts of grass for Emperor—until a gunpowder blast tore into the wall above him. He pulled back. Stones pelted down. A gray rain and a waterfall of dust. Emperor squealed in pure panic and raced toward him. Nathan managed to grip onto the reins, holding the boar in place as his hooves drummed against the patchy earth. Choking dust, roiling smoke. What saint-worshippers would call the breath of demons, spilling out over everything.

The collapsed wall formed a stony, jagged hill. Stopping Nathan from joining his friends.

"Nathan!" Esther's voice, cutting through the chaos.

"Go!" He shouted back. Could she even hear him? "I'll figure something out! I'll find you later!" Sweeney would make sure she left. He knew better than to risk the life of Esther Essen.

Pale shapes cut through the dust. Could Nathan reach Niko and the Hoppites? No—their wagon was already rolling away—and galloping goat hooves were closing in.

The Ice Riders had reached him at last.

He drew his dagger. Stood protectively in front of Emperor, who snorted and shook his little tusks. The Ice Riders galloped through the gap on their white goats, all swirling scarves, sashes, and sabers, and cantered in a circle around him. Kicking up more dust, laughing as their ears flicked up and down. A mass of warrior hares, delighting in their catch.

One rabbit, an enormously fat iceberg sitting on the saddle of a magnificent goat, held up a paw and they stopped. He pointed with his saber. "Nathan of Nestovich," he said. A familiar voice.

"The Rat on the Road?"

"Little Petro?" Nathan asked.

"Ah! You remember me. And I, of course, remember you." He shouted to the other Ice Riders. "Look at that, my brothers! The most famous rat in the world."

Who they had just captured.

CHAPTER 4. LORDS OF WINTER

Little Petro brought Nathan to the outskirts of vast Winterborn encampment—where the Ice Riders set their tents and let their goats graze the thick green grass. That night, as a golden spring evening settled cool over the Dark Forest, they celebrated their victory with vodka, wild songs, and joyous boasts that echoed around the dancing firelight. If they cared at all that subterfuge had won them the day, they didn't show it. A victory was a victory, and they wanted to celebrate.

Nathan was right in the middle of it. Surrounded by Ice Riders who cared nothing for shedding blood and less still for the murder of a rat kit.

He sat by the fire, seemingly forgotten, as the Ice Riders swaggered, danced, and boasted their way around the camp. Emperor lay on the ground next to him, a fluffy brown lump, and Nathan would occasionally give his stomach a pet or scratch him under the chin to keep him calm. One Ice Rider produced a fiddle and sawed cruelly at the strings, making a noise like a dying goat. Two hulking hares broke into a swirling dance across the fire that quickly transformed into a brawl. They tumbled together on the soggy grass, ears flicking up and down as they hammered each other. How long until they noticed him? How long until they decided that butchering a rat kit would be the one thing to make this night better?

Ignore them all. Watch the dancing sparks and burning logs. The mottled shadows of crumbling wood and the hot orange glow of coals. All the wild music and dancing, the brawls and boasting, the danger, was far away.

If he stayed very small and quiet, maybe they'd ignore him too. Then he could find some way out of this mess and make it back to Esther's side. She needed him, her, and Sweeney both.

And he'd failed them as Tarr won again.

A hefty hare plopped down next to him. "Nathan of Nestovich!" It was Little Petro. So much for staying hidden. Little Petro's large ears, each sporting a single silver ring, jutted upward in excitement. "Enjoying the festivities, little rat?"

He wasn't so little—though the water buffalo in Emperor Ferencz's menagerie would seem small compared to Petro.

He gave Petro a polite smile. Always be polite—his parents had left him with that. Though being polite to an Ice Rider warrior who had captured him after a brutal battle seemed more than a little strange. At least he could figure out the answer to the question that had been burning like the fire in front of him since his capture.

Was he a guest? Or a prisoner?

"So, ah, Master Petro, do you suppose I could ride away before —"

"Try some of this." Little Petro shoved a canteen into his paws. "Thicken the hair on your chest."

He gave it a sip—and gagged. It didn't slip down his throat—it burned. It sizzled against his neck like it would sear its way out and spill onto his belly. He'd had plenty of wine before, and even vodka, now and then, but this was far more terrible. Nathan choked, swallowed, spat. The burning remained. He looked back at Petro and forced the smile back on his face.

Petro laughed. "Hah! Now I can tell the world that I shared a drink with the famous Rat on the Road!" He accepted the canteen. "Peppered vodka. My own brew." Petro settled back, his heavy paws on the grass. His whiskers drooped a little, his ears flicking back—growing serious. "Let us not speak of grim matters, young Nathan. The battle is over, the Hoppites crushed. You live and I live. Is that not worthy of celebration?"

"I'm afraid I have more to worry about than survival, sir."

"Oh?" Petro drank his peppered vodka as easily as it was water. "Something that would explain why you rode with the enemy, yes? I am not surprised. Since I first met you with Lady Olga and young Alexi, I knew you were a rat on a mission."

Lady Olga and Alexi. Little Petro might not be a sworn foe, but the lynx bogatyr and her squire were true friends. If they knew where he was, perhaps he could get some help? Maybe even escape.

"Are they part of this invasion?" Trying to pose the question casually. Making friendly conversation about old chums.

"Her Ladyship? No." Little Petro settled back on the grass. "She is done campaigning. Returned to rule Olgagrad, which has its own problems. The serfs, the *muhziks*, are always stirring up trouble, and the White Tsarina and rival boyars are looking for ways to cut her down to size. But do not worry—that cat always lands on her feet." He yawned. "As for Alexi—Sir Alexi now—he's been given a most important assignment, which matches his high rank. He's—" He went silent. "Ah. Nathan. I think we will now have problems."

A new group of Ice Riders walked through the camp, leading their snow-white war goats. A few of them had white kaftans and ivory in the pommels of their sabers. The Grim Host. The most brutal of the Ice Riders. But the hare leading them drew every eye, for one reason.

His size.

If Little Petro was a water buffalo, this hare was a mountain. Thick legs worked below him as he hopped along. Vast rolls of fat jutted out from his scarlet kaftan and his ears stretched up above a vast fuzzy face split with a veteran army's amount of scars. About twenty rings dangled in each ear, clinking with each hop. His saber looked big enough to cut a tree in half, and he smoked a massive pipe seemingly as big as a cannon.

The humongous hare lowered the pipe to look at Nathan and Little Petro. His mouth, hidden below a moustache that drooped down to his massive waist, opened to release a gout of smoke that could have come from a dragon. "Son." He had a deep rumble of a voice—burbling up from somewhere in his huge belly.

"Father." Little Petro bowed his head respectfully.

So this was Big Petro—the famed Ice Rider father of Little Petro.

Big Petro carried a ragged bundle under one arm. He let it fall onto the fire. A red banner with a white goose, wings outstretched. A Hoppite flag. It caught the flame, the cloth rising and falling like a living thing as it burned. "You fought well in the day's battle, Little Petro." He settled to a kneel, the other hares flanking him. "Then I heard a tale I did not believe. You found a rat. You invited him to our camp. Now I see this tale is true."

Nathan stared straight back. He didn't want to be polite anymore. "I surrendered. Not that I was with the Hoppites in the first place. Little Petro brought me back." Shivers coiled under his fur as he looked into Big Petro's vast eyes. It was like trying to stare down a cliff. "Is that a problem?"

"Little Petro." Big Petro ignored Nathan. "You rob rats. You kill them, if they give you trouble. You do not drink with them."

"Father…" Little Petro's mouth opened in an awkward half-smile. "He's Nathan of Nestovich. The famed Rat on the Road, the Orphan Prince of Tock. From the stories, yes? I thought it would be fun."

One of the Ice Riders, a white-clad Grim Host warrior with a missing ear, spat on the ground. "A servant of the Carrion King!"

There was that name again. The Carrion King. Nathan still didn't know its meaning.

"I serve no one but myself." Nathan stood. These Ice Riders, so close to the ones who had murdered his parents, surrounded him now. More than eager to cut him to pieces. His heart pounded—but he wouldn't let them insult him. He wouldn't let them hurt Little Petro, who had risked everything to keep him alive. "Your son, Big Petro, is treating me honorably. Would you have him act otherwise? Or is the famous Big Petro so frightened of a little rat boy that he would shame himself in the hour of victory?"

He'd read some of those words in a particularly well-written Sir Konrad story.

Big Petro leaned down, nearly dipping into the fire where the Hoppite flag burned. "You think I'm afraid of you?"

Nathan stared back as Emperor, sensing his master's discomfort, stirred and snorted. "Um—no." He swallowed. Don't be scared. "But perhaps you should be. I've defeated worse than you."

Then Big Petro's huge mouth broke into a massive grin. His hefty buckteeth jutted like boulders below his moustache. "Son —I see why you like the little rat. He's full of spirit. I think we should tie him behind a fleet-footed goat and drag him over the fields. Or make him fight a swarm of fire ants. Or tie one of his limbs to four goats riding in each of the four directions or—"

"You won't, father," Little Petro said.

"Why not?"

"Because I won't let you."

The two hares, father and son, faced off. Both of their ears went up. Flicking skyward in the same moment, like a quartet of swords rising for a duel. Their muzzles wrinkled, paws drifting to the sabers in their sashes. All around them, the Ice Riders of two groups, Little Petro's and Big Petro's, shifted into positions of battle. The terrible sawing fiddle went on for a few more moments before drifting off altogether. No sound but the crackle of fire, the goats bleating as they clopped grass, and the gentle breathing of combatants about to fight.

Was it going to come to battle? All over him?

"Ice Riders!" A shrill meow from the edge of the camp. The hares looked up.

Hooves drummed against the dirt.

A column of bogatyrs and their entourage had paused in their ride through the camp. Sleek and noble war goats, muscle under well-combed fur. Polished armor and colorful coats of arms etched on their tunics and surcotes. Well-kept weapons—the sort with fancy names that were cared for like royal children. The Winterborn knights, a mix of Arctic foxes, white wolves, and wildcats, stared down at the Ice Riders.

One little lynx rode at their head, wearing full armor. It was Alexi. Lady Olga's squire.

"Alexi?" Nathan called the name of his friend. It spilled out—the sort of childish joy that came from seeing a friend.

"Sir Alexi now, actually." Alexi bowed his head happily, then yowled at the others. "Nathan of Nestovich is a friend. A friend to the Winterborn Empire. He rides with me." He pointed. "Get on that boar of yours, Nathan. You will be my guest."

Sometimes, the Supreme Rodent was kind. This was a way out, and it wouldn't make Little Petro seem weak before his father. Alexi was a knight, a bogatyr, while both Little and Big Petro were Ice Riders. They could not contradict the command of a bogatyr. Nathan scrambled onto Emperor's back before anyone could stop him and joined the column of knights.

Where would Alexi take him? He didn't know—but it might very well be further away from Esther. Far from his friends and deeper in danger. So maybe the Supreme Rodent wasn't being so nice to him after all.

+++

They rode east for the better part of three days. Heading toward Winterborn territory. Sir Alexi's territory. He explained it as they crested a rise through dense forest. "I'm a boyar, you see. A lord. And so I have certain responsibilities. One of which is the management of the ostrog—the frontier fortress—on White Whiskers Crossing."

A lord? Nathan had no idea. A rat orphan befriending Winterborn nobility—such things didn't happen.

Maybe Sir Alexi would think it a mistake.

Nathan pulled his cloak tightly around him as Emperor's breath came as mist. This far east, spring had yet to melt the snow. It gathered in fading drifts around the boles of towering trees and stretched out in pale blankets in the clearings.

Eastern Forest. A cold land.

Sir Alexi seemed to notice Nathan's worry. His ears tented. "Something wrong, Nathan?"

"Will I cause you problems, Sir Alexi?" He looked ahead through the trees. The column of Beasts-at-Arms, mounted knights, and Ice Riders, wound along the dirt road. Some settlement up ahead, the lights like flickering eyes through the trees. "You know. A rat at your side?"

"I'm a boyar. If they have a problem, I'll have their heads." He yowled. "And it's Alexi, you dolt—no need for a 'sir.'" The lynx stirred his goat to a trot, matching Emperor's pace. "White Whisker Crossing is just up ahead, down that road. Would you like to race? That fine piglet of yours against my little goat?" His amber eyes shone. Playful—just like he was when Nathan and Alexi and Lady Olga made their way through the dangerous forest.

Two friends in the middle of a war.

"If you insist," Nathan agreed. "Prepare to lose."

Alexi had one of his footbeasts, a stout ferret, count them down and then they were off, running together along the band of snowy trail. Nathan clutched the reins tightly, breathing hard as Emperor surged along under him. Snow flew from the warboar's hooves and he grunted happily, delighting in being able to run fast and free. They raced along as the trees faded. After that, a wide stretch of snowy ground bordering a hill, where a wooden stockade waited and beyond that, what seemed to be a squat castle made of Dark Forest wood.

The goat raced ahead of Emperor, galloping just a little faster. Alexi mewed happily in the saddle, the goat taking the slope. Nathan galloped after him toward the gate—and they rode together, each matching the other's speed. But should Nathan win? Or tie? Maybe that would make Alexi look bad? Losing to a rat and all.

He gave the reins a slight tug. Emperor slowed his pace with a reluctant snort.

The race was Alexi's. He ran into the gate and cantered about as Emperor rode in. "Ah—I win. Well done, Nathan. You could have beat me, I think."

"Perhaps." Nathan changed the subject quickly as the rest of the column approached. They had no desire to race. "So, you just rule here? All by yourself?"

"I have some advisers. And the White Tsarina sends orders that must be obeyed." A scruffy shrew groom emerged to take their mounts. "Tonight, we'll banquet and celebrate our victory —then see what comes next. You'll be my guest of honor." Alexi hopped down, more serving beasts arriving to take his cloak and hat. He waved to a hedgehog in an embroidered peasant's gown. "Show him to the guest chambers. Grant him whatever comfort he desires."

If the hedgehog had any problems with serving a rat, she didn't show it.

He was overthinking things. Filling his mind with worry when there was no cause. Alexi was his friend, and he could trust him.

But how strong could friendship be when hatred ran so deep?

To make matters worse, Tarr was still lurking about. He'd won a victory, though how could the Hoppite defeat benefit him? If anything, the Hoppite loss would strengthen Winterborn influence in the Dark Forest, which would harm Grand Sable merchants like Tarr.

Once again, Nathan was still playing a game without knowing the rules.

He looked back at Alexi and bowed—putting all the respect into it that he could. "Thank you."

Alexi simply grinned. "Wait until you see the feast, Nathan—then you'll thank me." Casual and kind—like they were any pair of boyhood friends.

+++

He rested a little from the ride, bathed in stinging cold snowmelt, and then dressed in the Winterborn finery that the servants left him. Strange garments. Nathan put on a white tunic of scratchy wool with designs of flowers and green chutes bold on the collars and cuffs, matching trousers, and—to top it all off—a dark blue cloak. His dagger, Winterborn after all, slid neatly into his belt. No one had taken it. And why would they? Here, there was no doubt that he was a guest.

A hedgehog servant with a torch led the way to the feasting hall. Up above, it had started to rain. The sort of wild, unceasing spring downpour that would stir up legions of flowers in the coming weeks. For now, it made the torch and watch fires gutter and steam and sizzled cold down the back of Nathan's neck. He stumbled in the slick snow. The hedgehog snorted in amusement but said nothing.

He tried to make conversation. "Are there many guests for the feast?"

The old hedgehog shrugged as they reached the wooden doors. Lilting music inside, stomping feet, the sound of conversation. "They come from far away." She pulled open the door. "Sir Alexi's a popular little lord."

Inside, a feast far different from any Nathan had ever attended. A world away from the refined nibbling and pastry castles of the Grand Sable Emperor's palace. Here, the minor nobles, knights, and warriors sat around rough wooden tables, stomping their feet and pounding their fists in time with the wild folk music from a trio of shrews by the roaring fire at the center of the hall. Vast plates of food—steaming bowls of stew, piles of pierogies, and stacked cabbage rolls—went round the tables, and the guests gobbled them down and spilled remnants onto the floor, where a swarm of pet hunting beetles scurried about to devour the leftovers. Peppered vodka washed every throat.

The food smelled wonderful. The unwashed beasts? Not so much.

Alexi sat at the center of the table, a white fox next to him. The fox was in mid-molt, his white fur vanished in several clumps and the brown poking through. He looked like he was a cloud falling apart.

"Nathan!" Alexi waved to him, calling over the music and the merry-making. "Come. Sit at my right paw."

Nathan joined him, stepping awkwardly amongst the dining guests. He settled down. The chair squeaked under him. "Ah—thank you."

"No need to be so polite." Alexi slammed a paw on the table. "Here—try some of this brined cheese. You'll like that. What do you think of the musicians? They're from a nearby village, down by the river. I think they fear that I'll have their homes put to the torch if they play a false note."

Nathan looked up, his mouth stuffed with deliciously pungent brined cheese. Had becoming a boyar changed Alexi? "But you wouldn't—would you?"

Alexi's ears flattened. "No, I would not."

Of course he wouldn't. "Sorry—foolish thing to say."

"No different from most of your squeaking. Now fill your belly."

He did and the food was grand. Fear and riding for three days on military rations had done a great deal to make him hungry. It must be the same with everyone around, for they ate heartily and drank just as much. One of the beetles nudged his head against Nathan's leg, wiggling his antenna in expectation. Nathan upended his plate, letting the crumbs patter to the ground, and the insect swept them up and wiggled his shell in delight. Alexi and Nathan both smiled at the beetle's joy.

The bug scurried away, lifting and buzzing past two servants emerging with more food. Nathan watched the carapace—and then he stopped. The servants. A mouse and a rat. Different clothes than the ones they wore in the Emperor's palace—different servant's uniforms—but there was no mistaking those bright eyes or that particular shade of fur.

Zipporah and Zoya Schall.

What were they doing here? Had they followed him? That seemed impossible. But why else would two rodent thieves travel across half the continent and pop up in some border boyar's frontier fortress?

He looked away. Had they spotted him? He wasn't exactly inconspicuous. The only richly dressed rat at the party.

Best not to bother them—whatever they were doing. Zipporah had said they were fighting on behalf of all rats and mice. Spying on Tarr, perhaps, like at the party in Erminium. Staying out of their way would be good. Helping them would be even better.

But their presence meant something else. Tarr might very well be here.

Those cold eyes. The death that followed him.

Nathan's belly ached and the pungent cheese stung his tongue.

"Something bothering you, Nathan?" Alexi asked. "How's the grub?"

He made an appreciative squeak.

"Excellent. And wait until you see what we've got for dessert."

The half-hairless fox stood. "Lord Alexi." He pointed to the door, now creaking open. "Our guests have arrived."

Moonlight and falling rain entered—along with Titus Tarr himself. Just as expected.

He strode into the room with Sir Volkbert at his side. The squirrel wore the same pearl-colored finery as he had before, and somehow managed to keep it clean despite the rain and muck. He and Sir Volkbert bowed deeply. When he looked up, his dark, shiny eyes settled on Nathan.

But he said nothing—and neither did Nathan.

Sir Alexi hoisted his goblet. "I welcome you, Master Tarr, master of the Tarr Trading Company, merchant of great renown, to White Whisker Crossing."

"And I am very happy to be here, Sir Alexi Alexandrovich, boyar of the Winterborn Dominon, knight of the White Tsarina." Tarr walked across, Sir Volkbert a silent, pale and armored shadow behind him. More servants entered. They carried baskets, huddling close to keep their contents dry. "Congratulations are in order, my young lord, for your victory against the Hoppites." A victory that he had engineered. "Now that the trouble is ended, might we see my agreement with the White Tsarina come to pass?"

The fox answered first. "She seems amendable. But is worried about your connections to the Grand Sable court."

"Count Lazlo." Tarr smiled back, pleasant as an old friend. "I assure you that the House of Tarr Trading Company serves but one banner—that of commerce. The uninterrupted flow of goods across the continent is all that I concern myself with. From the Grand Sable Empire across the now peaceful Dark Forest—through our new trading centers in the Free City of Katzenberg—and all the way to the Winterborn Dominion." Katzenberg—he'd set up there? "Through trade comes peace, and through peace, vast quantities of wealth for all. Why would any monarch fear that?"

So that was why he'd destroyed the Hoppites. Peace meant that commerce could continue—that Tarr could grow richer still.

He clapped his paws. "I've brought gifts. Proof of the reach of the Tarr Trading Company."

Sir Volkbert snapped his teeth at the servants, who plopped the baskets on the tables. Strange fruits, red and yellow and green. Slick with rain and gleaming like jewels. Nathan had seen a few before, but only on the tables of noble-beasts. Everyone stared at the alien fruits, growls and chirps mingling with the music.

"From the Westlands," Tarr explained. "The colonies of the Copperbright Kingdom. Those beasts know the value of trade."

He could bring those delicacies all the way here? He was fantastically rich—of course he could. But it was still a good demonstration.

A serving weasel placed one such fruit—a yellow sickle-moon known as a banana—on Alexi's plate. He poked at the skin with a claw and brought it up to his muzzle. "I am very grateful. Do you simply—"

"Grip the stalk there and twist." Nathan reached over to help his friend. He looked past the banana at Tarr as he pulled it free, tugging the fruit out of its yellow armor. Alexi's ears flicked back and his tongue jabbed out like a little berry—amazed by his friend. "Sometimes, you just need to put a little force in the right place, and everything comes apart." Hopefully, that sounded properly menacing.

If he couldn't do anything else, he could at least do that.

Tarr stared back at him, eyes cold as the rain outside.

Count Lazlo left his seat, ending the awkward moment with a friendly yip. "We shall let the young boyar enjoy his feast, Master Tarr. Join me and the others and we shall discuss the terms of trade concerning your new investments in Katzenberg. Best not to bore young Sir Alexi with such matters."

Alexi seemed in complete agreement. He was enraptured by the banana, pulling the skin back onto the pale flesh and drooping it down again and again. Trying to figure out how it worked.

What were Count Lazlo and Tarr talking about? Should he try to eavesdrop? No—not without getting caught. And he couldn't just leave his friend and host.

Instead, Nathan reached over and showed Alexi how to flex the peel downward. "Hold it like a dagger. There—now you can eat." He pantomimed taking a bite. "It's soft."

A snap of Alexi's jaws. "Yum." He devoured it in a moment. "You don't eat the peel?"

"Not unless you like eating grass and bark."

"Let's see if the beetles like it." Alexi tossed the banana peel onto the floor. Nathan considered telling him that it might cause someone to trip, but there wasn't time. "You seem worried,

Nathan. You looked like you wanted to take Titus Tarr's peel off."

"He wants to kill me, Alexi. He truly does."

"No—who would want to kill you?" Alexi mewed in dismay. "Well, you needn't worry. Stick with me and you'll be safe."

He wanted to believe his friend—but they were in Winterborn lands. And rats and mice were rarely safe where Winterborn flags flew.

Like Zipporah and Zoya.

He needed to check on them. He could tell Alexi, of course, but that would be an awkward conversation—'oh, those two rodent thieves disguised as your servants—they're my associates'—and he doubted a boyar, even one who was his friend, would take kindly to rodent spies.

"I'll stay close," Nathan agreed. "Need to grab some more food." He hopped from the table, clutching his empty plate.

"See if you can find some more bananas!" Alexi called.

Back into the haze of the hall. Nathan wandered amongst the revelers, the shrew musicians starting up a reel that made several Winterborn beasts leave their seats and start wild, high-kicking jigs on the dirt floor. One pale furred Ice Rider smacked a foot into a beetle, sending the terrified bug buzzing over Nathan's head. He ducked down as it crashed into an arrangement of vodka bottles and sent them all rattling to the ground.

Where were Zipporah and Zoya? Impossible to see them in this mess, with the low firelight making shadows dance everywhere and rain streaked with moonlight cutting in past the windows in silver curtains. He looked around, sniffing—nothing but banqueting merriment, rich food, and wet fur.

He walked into something solid and stopped. Looked up.

It was Sir Volkbert.

The pale wolverine looked uncomfortable. Pale of fur he

might be, but he was still a Grand Sable Empire knight, and he was now in the camp of his nation's sworn enemies. He looked at Nathan, his mouth open to reveal yellow fangs. Panting slightly and grunting—but it was no roar. It sounded—and this was truly bizarre—nervous? But how could a wolverine be nervous?

"Um—hello," Nathan said.

"Hello." Sir Volkbert's tiny round ears flicked back. "You call a Winterborn lord friend?"

"I've called many beasts friend."

"Like Sir Konrad the Courageous?" Sir Volkbert clamped his jaw shut. He seemed to be regretting what he had said. But his eyes glimmered.

"I knew him, sir. The stories were right about that, at least."

"Oh—that's—that's quite interesting." Volkbert fiddled with the pommel of his bastard sword.

Sir Volkbert was like him—one who loved the stories of Sir Konrad's adventures. But unlike Nathan, Volkbert had never had the joy of meeting Sir Konrad in the fur—never got to see a legend come to life.

"Yes, sir," Nathan agreed. "He is brave and honorable—he believes in chivalry. And I don't think he would ever follow around a monster like Titus—"

"What were you saying about me?" Tarr's voice from behind. Supreme Rodent! The squirrel could move stealthily. Nathan spun around. Tarr stood there, a goblet of Winterborn vodka held casually in one paw. He brought it to his lips and took a sip. No sputtering at all—just that smile. "Something unflattering, I gather. A lie, perhaps. But what does it matter when you are such a novice in the telling of lies?"

"We're going to destroy you," Nathan said. "Is that a lie?"

Tarr leaned down. "Didn't you already try?"

He had his dagger. Winter's iron, resting on his hip. Nathan could draw and slash—no, a stab. Straight for Tarr's throat. A killing blow. He could press that blade in until the blood flowed and the threat to Esther Essen and all his friends was gone. The Winterborn would be on him. Killing a guest, and one responsible for a valuable trade network to the west, would certainly be frowned upon.

But he could do it anyway.

His home would be safe. All it would take would be a single stab. Nothing that he hadn't done before, under the tutelage of Sir Konrad and in actual combat, hundreds of times.

Well, maybe dozens of times.

Or less.

"Pardon me, young sir—" A panicked squeak. A bowl of berries splashing against his tunic. Red sauce bright against the embroidered wool. Zipporah, about as big as he was, had collided with him. Clumsy—but a trained clumsiness. "Oh, will you look at that? Your finery—all stained. I'm sorry, young master—so terribly sorry."

"That's all right," Nathan said. "I'll just—"

"You'll come outside, and I'll clean you off with fresh rainwater. No argument on the matter—I must atone for my mistake." Her arm fastened on his, her eyes going hard as flint. No arguments. "Come along, this way—if you'll excuse me, sir." A bow to Tarr and she was pulling him along.

He went. It would be rude not to.

They reached the door and the curtain of rain. Zipporah leaned closer. "Good thing I was there, Nathan of Nestovich—you little fool. I won't let the rat hero get his head lopped off in a frontier outpost, that's for certain." Behind them, a growl, a crash, and a rattle of armor. Sir Volkbert had slipped on the banana peel and slammed into the table, sending plates and cutlery cascading to the floor. "Just as well," Zipporah said. "We're in a mad comedy and no mistake—and it needs its pratfalls."

Nathan was certainly taking one.

+++

Outside, Zoya waited under the sloped roof—trying her best to stay dry. Nathan squinted through the rain at her as the cold soaked his fur and ran down his whiskers. She looked indignant, with her paws on her hips and an angry twist in her muzzle, like this whole mess was his fault.

But he was trying to save her! And her mother too.

"What was he doing now?" Zoya asked.

Zipporah squeaked and shoved a cloth, already soggy, into Nathan's paws. "Trying to get himself killed."

"I was not!" A whining squeak in his words. He mopped at the shirt. "And what are you two doing, skulking about?" Skulking—that was the right word for them. "What do you think would happen if Sir Alexi caught a mouse and rat thief in his fort? Do you think the Winterborn would be happy?"

"The difference between us, young sir, is that we *wouldn't* be caught." Zipporah numbered the reasons on her paws. "First of all, nobody pays attention to servants. Secondly, we're not world famous—unlike a certain Nathan of Nestovich, the Rat on the Road. Thirdly, we're not fools who would pull a knife and try to gut Titus Tarr right in his host's house."

"He was going to do what?" Zoya grinned at Nathan. "Stab Tarr?"

"I could've," Nathan muttered.

"It wouldn't have helped. Done nothing but got you killed."

"It would have *killed* him—"

Zipporah reached into her apron. "So he dies—and what would that do, except ruin your legend? Nathan the Rat, Bold Sir Squeaky, a hero to all rodents, now a cold-blooded murderer cut down in some Winterborn midden heap? Tarr has forged weapons that can't be stopped with a blade." She drew out a pamphlet. Cheaply printed, crumpled, soggy—the sort that a good printing press could produce in the thousands. "Have a look."

He examined the front. A frightening form. A ragged, hooded cloak and a staff topped with a gray stone. A rat's skull projected from the hood. The same that he'd seen in Thistle Town, in the puppet show.

The Carrion King.

"Read it."

He flipped to the title. "A True Accounting of the Treacherous Plots of the Carrion King." The text that followed—bunched together and mingled with fearsome etchings of bones and poisons—sketched a grim tale. A monstrous king of rats—the Carrion King—preparing to make terrible war against all other beasts. Sending out rat agents to spread poison and death. To stir kingdoms to war by trickery. To kidnap innocent kittens, hoglets, pups, and cubs and subject them to terrible torments.

A hidden claw bearing a blade, held at the throat of the world.

"Lies." He gave it back to Zipporah. "All lies."

"This is Tarr's weapon." She tucked it gingerly into her apron. "Already, pamphlets like this are being passed around on street corners from here to the Copperbright Kingdom. He's got a hidden press somewhere, cranking them out. They travel with his trading company. Why? Because rats and mice are traders—it's how we survive." Like Esther's father, the Court Rat of the Grand Sable Empire. "Tarr can't build his empire of trade without destroying our people wherever he finds them in positions of power—without drowning rats under waves of hatred so that he can take their place."

And Esther's parents were the first victims of this lie.

"And as for the rest of us—those rats and mice who aren't

wealthy merchants speaking into the ears of emperors—well, we're just a stain to be swept up with the same dirty rag. Now, do you see why we're after him, Master Nathan?"

His whiskers shook. "I do." They were trying to be heroes. To save all rats and mice from treachery and lies. He had to help. "I'll —I'll bring this to Esther. Tell her about Tarr's plans. She'll find some way to—"

"She's the Court Rat's daughter," Zoya said. "Has she ever known hunger or want? Does she care about other rats and mice? About anything else, besides freeing her rich parents?"

"Zoya—my darling—hush." Zipporah hoisted a paw. "We need allies, don't we? Let him try."

"Why should we?" Zoya asked. "I don't see that he's any good."

Any good? Nathan was the Rat on the Road. A hero of story and song. "I'm—I'm pretty good." A squeak in his voice. Zoya grinned at him and twin coals burned bright in his cheeks. Oh, Supreme Rodent, this was awful! "I'll tell Alexi. I'll fight Tarr right now—"

"No, Nathan—you can't." Zipporah's tone went kind. Grandmotherly. "You need to live—because you're so famous. And Tarr's going to make that difficult." She pointed into the feasting hall, where fires burned, and beasts drank and danced. "They're going to assassinate you. Tonight."

"What? Alexi would never—"

"He won't know. His advisors cut a deal with Tarr, who has hired killers a-plenty." Her little muzzle wriggled. "Bribery opened some ears and told me everything."

"I'll tell Alexi—"

"Then they'll kill him too—and blame you for his death."

His bravado faded. It made sense—no matter how terrible it sounded. "So what should I do?"

Zoya reached over. Patted his arm—gently. "We'll find a way

to get you out." The arrogance—the annoyance—was gone. "In the meantime, you stay safe. Can you do that?"

Stay alive, surrounded by his enemies. It would take every trick he had—and quite a few that he didn't—to pull that off. "I can try," he said.

That didn't sound very heroic at all—but it was the best he could manage.

+++

He didn't sleep that night. Scurried around the encampment instead, getting ready while Sir Alexi's other guests feasted and drank their way into exhausted slumber. By the time he made it back to his bed and collapsed on top of the covers, still fully dressed, he was tired beyond belief—not to mention soaked to his skin. The rain drummed on the roof above the little cabin serving as his chambers and the fire in the corner hearth danced and flickered.

A calming rhythm. A gentle lullaby.

Like the ones his father would sing to him when he couldn't sleep.

But no—no sleep yet. He kept his eyes open. Paws crossed on his chest, head on the pillow. Still in his Winterborn garments, with the dagger on his belt.

Waiting.

Time passed. The rain fell.

His eyelids dipped. No—not now. Look at the fire instead.

Burning low. Crosshatched with orange as the coals faded.

Like Nestovich. Nothing but ruins, blackened and dead.

Footsteps squelched in the mud. Nathan had a second to get ready and slipped under the bed.

The door creaked open—silently. Three pairs of boots. Nathan stayed low, hidden in the shadows. Not hard to do. He was still small. Even for a rat. Even for a kit. Now it helped him, though dust clung to his coat and his quivering whiskers. He forced himself silent. Not even breath stole from his lips.

The boots maneuvered across the floorboards. Moving silently. A fancy pair, with twisting roses and vines worked into the leather. The thin blade of a rapier drifting down, hovering above the floorboards. Reynardine, no doubt. Next to him, thicker legs ending in short, simple boots. Mottled scales above them. Jacopo Draco. Finally, another pair. Goat fur, below loose blue trousers. An Ice Rider? Maybe they recruited him to help with the murder.

They probably didn't need to offer much.

The three pairs of feet maneuvered around the bed. Nathan stayed still. Looked right and left. One beast on each side and another at the foot. All getting into position. All saying nothing. His heart pounded. They couldn't hear that, could they?

No words at all from the trio of assassins.

Then, like some silent signal had been given, blades hummed in the still air. The noises cutting over the pouring rain outside. A rapier, some sort of rapid stabbing weapon, and something heavy and sharp crashed into the bed together.

Shredding the pillows and rolled bedding he'd hidden under the sheets.

In the dark of the dying fire, it had to look exactly like a sleeping rat.

Fabric tore. Cloth ripped. The rapier punctured through the straw mattress and reaching the floorboards, the pointing jutting out—just inches from Nathan. He looked at the needle point, shivering, and stayed silent.

Then it was over. The slicing, hacking, and cutting ended after just a few seconds.

They'd figured it out. They were capable killers—and this was an old trick. He'd picked it up from the Ballad of the Cruel Badger and it had worked just fine in that song.

But it wasn't working now.

"Sheets and pillows." Reynardine snarled. "He's tricked us. He knew about the attack." The rapier withdrew. Straw puffed into the air. "Did you tell him, Vadim?"

"Not I!" A raspy voice from Vadim, the Ice Rider. "I swear on St. Antonias, I would never—"

"Reynardine, Reynardine—cool your blood, brother." Draco's boots shifted. "We can cast blame later. Right now, there's one question: did the little rat scurry away? Or is he still here? The pillows under the blanket trick bought him some time, true enough—but if he fled, the Ice Riders outside would have spotted him. And if he's still here..." The floorboards creaked. The lizard knelt, eyes shining. "He couldn't have gotten far."

Nathan twisted around to see the lizard's face, right below the bed. His forked tongue flicked in and out.

Time for the second part of his plan.

He rolled away, out of reach of Draco's grasping claw. Dusty brown nails gripped his shirt, but Nathan pulled hard and made it out from under the bed. Then he was dashing across the floor, tail flailing behind him, and lunging out for the fire. A single stick, left in the hearth—one end jutting out like a chunk of bone from a half-eaten haunch of boar, the other smoldering in the dying fire.

Still ruby red and burning.

He pulled it free and spun around. Sudden heat against his whiskers. A toss and the burning chunk of firewood landed on the bed.

Reynardine faced him. The fox had acquired a new eye-patch —one of delicate lace, the whiteness of snow, which contrasted boldly against his flame-colored fur. He probably thought it made him look handsome and rakish.

Now, a snarl curled back Reynardine's teeth to reveal yellow fangs, and he hoisted up the rapier for a cruel stab. "Now, my little rat, I shall finish what I started." The haphazard torch burned behind him, sending up flickers of greasy smoke. Oh, Supreme Rodent—would it work? "Then I'll find that white-furred she-demon and send her to join you."

"Be a little hard to find her, sir." Nathan winked. "With just the one eye."

A yowling, snapping rage. Reynardine pulled back his blade—just as flame stretched across the ripped mattress and pillows in a decent blaze.

And tasted the gunpowder that Nathan had carefully stored inside.

He'd pilfered it from the fortress's armory. They had barrels of the stuff laid out behind an old cannon set in a rickety tower. Nathan had carefully filled a bag, hiding it deep under his tunic and cloak to stop it from catching the rain, and ran back over the mud to his chamber—avoiding Ice Rider patrols and drunken guests as the night deepened. Shivering all the way, from fear as well as the cold. No way he could explain this to Sir Alexi if he was caught—and the guards might just toss him to Titus Tarr, who would give him to his hirelings and their blades in an instant.

The explosion made it all worth it.

It tore apart the bed, casting an eruption of choking smoke, simmering fragments, and burning straw into the still air. The thunder clawed at Nathan's ears and left ringing remnants.

Jacopo Draco caught the worst of it, the blast smashing him against the wall hard enough to crack the wooden planks. The Ice Rider—Vadim—vanished behind the cloud and Reynardine tumbled down, falling onto his face. Enough to kill them? Nathan could only hope.

No time to waste.

He grabbed his black traveling cloak—his Runt cloak—and dove through the door. Out into the rain. One thing about Reynardine and Draco: they didn't travel alone. The rest of the Laughing Company must be close by, backed up by Ice Riders. All eager for his blood.

Nathan hurried across snow and mud. Pulled up his hood. Rain drummed against the brim and soaked him as his ears rang. A distant sound—a keening, lost in the numbness caused by the blast. He slipped in soggy snow, caught a pillar of a guard tower, and peered out.

The ringing faded. Wafted away to reveal his name. "Nathan!" It was Zoya Schall, standing tall in the back of a sleigh with three stout goats at the reins. A troika, as the Winterborn called it. Zipporah held the reins tight, a round fur hat perched on her head. Next to them, Emperor—saddled and ready to ride —snorted in the rain.

They'd thought of everything.

He hurried over, racing through the mud and snow. Dancing light behind him—the explosion must have set fire to the cottage, which was now burning bright. Poor Alexi. He'd invited Nathan into his home and Nathan had set it on fire. He needed to apologize.

"Nathan—behind you!" Zoya, shouting again.

Nathan spun. A dark shape, running toward him. Vadim the Ice Rider—a storm-cloud black rabbit hoisting up a cruel, curved cavalry axe. Reynardine and Draco followed him, as more shapes charged across the interior of the fort. They'd be going for their riding goats and weapons. Vadim neared Nathan in a rapid hop, pulling back the axe to strike.

Something shimmered, lost in the rain. A noise like a boot stomping in muck. Vadim twisted in his leap, a bird who lost his wings, and crashed into the half-melted snow. A kitchen dagger projected from his chest.

Zipporah hoisted another, holding it by the blade. "Move it, young Sir Nathan—Sir Squeaky must run or die!"

They didn't have to tell him twice. He reached Emperor and pulled himself into the saddle. Oinking from the piglet—both joyous and frightened. Nathan got his feet into the stirrups and clutched the reins. Shouts from behind, and more firelight. Torches. The Ice Riders and the Laughing Company would be coming after them in force.

"Where do we go?" He put Emperor to a gallop, aiming for the gate.

"The best place of all, Nathan of Nestovich!" Zipporah cried. "Away from here!"

Out through the gate and down the slope, with goats charging behind them.

On the run once again.

+ + +

They rode hard down the slope and into the forest, snow and water flying from the hooves of their animals and the sleigh's runners. Trees rushed past in a dark haze, the branches a blur. Nathan stared ahead, rain slicing at his fur, running down his whiskers, soaking his eyes. Hard to see much of anything in the moonlit downpour through a haze of trees. He peered over his shoulder as Emperor galloped ahead. He could trust the boar to stay on the trail—and not gallop straight into a tree.

He hoped.

Behind them, a force of Winterborn soldiers and Tarr's assassins. Ice Riders, racing ahead on their goats. Reynardine and Draco rode amongst them, reins clutched tight, their goats bucking, surging down the road. Snow flew amongst them, matching the whiteness of their barred teeth as they closed in.

Crossbows snapped and paw-cannons flashed to life.

"Nathan!" Zipporah's warning. "Get your head down, you little dolt!"

"I'm no dolt!" He shouted back—but the rain and gunfire stole his words.

Bolts sang through the air, humming around Emperor. Gunpowder stink too, vanishing quickly as they rode on. A branch just above the wagon exploded, sending snow-covered splinters flying. Nathan clutched Emperor tightly, pressing his belly to the boar's back.

A pained squeal. A crossbow bolt had sunk into Emperor's back.

They were going to catch him—and the Schalls both.

Unless he did something drastic.

He forced his eyes up. A fork in the road. One snowy trail leading ahead, losing itself in the woods. The other dipping down. Curling like a skewered worm. Snow shimmered on the road. Beyond that, through the forest, something flickered. An orange eye—a fire. Someone was out there, camping in the war-torn wilderness.

Hopefully having a more peaceful night than him.

He cracked the reins. Emperor squealed again—but listened. The piglet longed to please.

He rode alongside Zipporah and Zoya. The mouse mother held the reins tight, her trio of goats riding hard. Zoya stayed close to her. They had risked everything to save him—endangering their mission that would protect all rats and mice from Tarr's villainy. Nathan was just trying to help Esther save her parents.

And doing a bad job at that.

Zipporah's dark, shimmering eyes met his—then looked at the fork in the road. "Nathan—"

"I'll find you again," Nathan said. "We'll stop Tarr. Esther and

I will figure something out—all right?"

"Nathan, you buffoon, you dunce—what are you going to do?" She shouted over the crash of hooves and the sleigh over the snow. "Don't you understand? You're the key. Your story can't end here. You're what can defeat Tarr's story, and if we lose you —"

"I'm just a kit, Madam Schall!" Nathan called. "And I don't want anyone else to suffer because of me. Not anymore!"

He pulled hard to the right and charged straight down the other trail—as Zipporah's troika slid hard to the left.

They split up, forcing their pursuers to do the same.

Zoya spun around, watching him. Her eyes matched the moon, huge and terrified, and her paws stretched out like she could grab him. She seemed frightened—terribly frightened— for his safety. Nathan looked back, watching the rain fall on her fur as her mouth opened and cried his name. She was saddened, terrified—all because of him.

So he wasn't just a bother. That was nice to know.

Then the trail curled under him. Sloping down hard. Impossible to see from the road, but it twisted into a sheer drop, passable by switchbacks hacked into the hill. Nathan tugged hard on the reins. Emperor squealed like he'd swallowed a coal. His hooves slowed, stopped—and slipped.

Snow topped with rainwater. A terrible combination.

The piglet twisted. "Emperor!" Nathan held close as a hoof flung free, and then another, and then they were tumbling down together. His boots slipped free. Emperor rolled away from him, throwing his tusks in the air, soggy, snow-covered fur like a shaggy comet in the air, and then Nathan crashed into the hillside, went up into the cold, wet rain, slammed down again, and rose once more.

The Supreme Rodent was playing pawball with him.

Until he struck down a final time—and stopped.

Right on his arm.

Sudden terrible pain. Nathan squeaked loud enough for all the beasts in the Dark Forest to hear. A sheer, grinding agony in his right arm. He clutched it, the flesh raw under his fur. Torn? Bleeding? Or broken?

He tried to stand, but a burning light seared behind his eyes, and he slumped down in the snow.

Emperor was next to him. He was all right, at least. Coming up and shaking off the rain and snow.

Torches up above. Nathan looked up. The Winterborn had dismounted—the smart move—and were coming down the hill. Reynardine led them—Draco must have gone after the Schalls —and carried a burning torch in one paw and his rapier in the other. The slim fox seemed carved out of the rain and the darkness, water running down the edge of his blade as he descended carefully.

Nathan needed to run. To fight.

All he could was hold his arm. Try and stay awake.

Zipporah was right. His story couldn't end here.

Something thundered in the woods behind him. Gunfire. More harquebuses fired—blasting from the shelter of the tree in a crackling salvo. Bullets struck the Winterborn ranks. Not many of them had charged out after Nathan and the Schalls and splitting up had divided their forces still further.

They couldn't stand against the hidden paw-cannons roaring away from the woods.

An Ice Rider captain bellowed an order. Hares dropped flat or dove for cover in the snow. Reynardine himself vanished—too smart to be caught in the open.

A firm paw settled on Nathan's shoulder. "Easy there, Nathan."

Niko's voice.

"N-Niko—"

"Don't try and move, lad. Captain Uttz—his boar."

"I've got it." Captain Ursula Uttz, General Bunzika's trusted lieutenant, took Emperor's reins and helped him up. "He's a noble steed, isn't he?"

"He'll be safe." Niko had his arm under Nathan's shoulder. Lifting him up. Carrying him. "By the bones of the Saints! You've certainly gotten bigger. Keep the arm across your chest, yes? Don't try and move it. Don't worry—we've got a skilled barber-surgeon who can patch you up."

Good luck indeed that they were helping him, the Supreme Rodent had done right to cross their paths—but who were Uttz and Niko fighting for now?

Niko seemed to guess what Nathan was asking as he carried him under the trees, where more rabbits and other beasts waited with harquebuses and halberds. "We're a new army, fighting for a free Dark Forest. Captain Uttz created a suitable name. I think you'd like it, young Nathan." He winked and his eye gleamed in the moonlight. "We're the Orphans."

The Orphans. He could trust them.

He was an orphan too.

CHAPTER 5. THE PLAY'S THE THING

He dreamed of Nestovich burning again.

The same terrible flames, the smoke rising in curtains to the cold gray sky. The taste of blood, the terrible tang of iron, thick in his mouth. Nathan stood outside his house and watched the tongues of fire licking up the walls as death and slaughter filled the streets around him. More pain. More failure.

This time, something was behind him.

He turned around.

The Carrion King stood there.

The same filthy gray cloak that he'd seen in the puppet show in Thistle Town. The same dust-caked gray skull and the staff tipped with a silver orb. No villainous speeches or grand pronouncements on the worth of evil. The Carrion King just stood and watched. He was like one of the Reaping Jacks that farmers set out for merriment on Reaping Day.

And all he had to do was stand boldly in the minds of beasts and they would do the rest.

Nathan woke up with a gasp.

"Easy there, my boy. Easy." He spun around. An old rabbit barber-surgeon, spectacles perched on his nose and ears flicked backward, stood back from his cot, hidden away in a shadowy tent. Rain drummed light on the roof. "Your arm, my boy—do not test it."

He looked down. Numbness below the elbow, broken occasionally by ripples of pain that made his teeth clench. His arm had been lashed to a splint and set on his belly. He tried to move it, and the pain worsened, the barber-surgeon's ears flicking up in concern. He stopped. His arm—he'd landed on it when he fell from Emperor's back after that terrible ride through the cold and dark woods. Running from the Ice Rider horde alongside Zipporah and Zoya Schall.

The Schalls—had they made it?

He sat up. "Zipporah—Zoya—"

"We only found you, Lord Rat." Niko had pulled back the tent flap. He looked even more bedraggled than usual, snow clinging to his fur and granting him a frosty beard. His harquebus, carefully covered, rested on his shoulder. "And you're lucky that we did." He settled on a stool across from the bed. "What of the arm, Doctor Pitti?"

"A clean break. It will heal—in time." The rabbit pulled a strip of cloth free and set it over Nathan's neck. "I'll give you some instructions on cleaning it and exercising it. Until then, the arm must rest here. Rest and grow strong." He tucked the arm neatly in the sling. "Use the other."

"What if I need to use two arms?" Nathan asked.

"Then grow a third." Doctor Pitti stood and perked up his ears. "He can drink, walk about for a little, eat some grub—I recommend that he does all of that." He winked. "He's certainly got his spirits back."

Niko helped Nathan from the bed. A broken arm—he was practically a cripple. And at the worst time too. Titus Tarr was growing more powerful with each passing moment. He'd destroyed the Hoppites, made his trade arrangement with the Winterborn, and would be pulling the profits from a network that stretched across the continent—using all of it to fuel his tales of the Carrion King and inspire hatred and fear of rats.

He had to be stopped.

And a one-armed rat boy certainly wasn't up to the task.

They walked outside. Miserable spring rain drifted over the camp of the surviving Hoppites—the Orphans. They had set the cannons and weaponry under coverings by a few ragged battle wagons. All the rabbits and hares looked similarly battered, damaged, and drenched. Niko led Nathan to a campfire where Captain Uttz laid out some breakfast. Bread and cheese and cold water to wash it down.

He was hungry. He ate well.

Uttz smiled as she settled on the overturned log across from the fire. "Happy to be alive, Nathan of Nestovich?"

He nodded, his cheeks stuffed with cheese.

She laughed. "Well, here's something else to gladden you. Some of our scouts have spotted your friends and they're bringing them here." Her ears flicked to the edge of camp. "Ah—here they are now."

Two riders making their way out of the misty woods. Nathan hastily swallowed his cheese and stood up. Zipporah? Zoya? No —the sizes were wrong. They were riding closer now, bringing their mounts to a canter.

It was Esther Essen, riding tall in the saddle of her mouflon, followed by Sweeney.

They were safe. Nathan ran toward them, stumbled, which made his arm shift and bang against his belly and then he squeaked so loud the Supreme Rodent must hear him, but he was up again, and had reached his friends.

Esther leapt down. She embraced him. "Nathan!" Her arms went around his back. Nathan's heart thundered. She was so close to him—and so happy. A pair of hot coals sizzled to life in his cheeks as she nudged his pained arm and made him squeak again. She stepped back, whiskers shaking in concern, and he smiled.

She was back by his side. Everything would be all right.

Sweeney approached next, leading his riding goat by the reins. "I lost you, lad. I lost you in battle and you fell into the paws of the enemy and suffered their wrath. Just as I lost Von Stahl—no one knows where he is. It's a grave mark on a bodyguard—and one who failed twice already at protecting his charges."

Sweeney shouldn't be woebegone and weak. Not him.

"No—that's not it, sir. You—you did a good job. You always do." Nathan stepped closer. Sound happy—confident. That would cheer up Sweeney. "I was found by friends. Alexi—he's Sir Alexi now—and had another run-in with Titus Tarr." Esther's ears swept up. "I learned what's he up to. The Carrion King? That's him." He told them everything, talking quickly between slurps of cold water. "That's why he moved against your father, Esther. He knew Eleazar Essen would try to stop him."

"And now I will," Esther said. "Where is Tarr?"

A fair question and one Nathan couldn't answer. "I'm not entirely sure." Esther's smile faded. "He said something about the Free City Katzenberg. He's going to use that as a trading center, so he can send goods from the Grand Sable Empire to the Winterborn Dominion."

"Making everything part of his network." Esther stomped a riding boot in the soggy earth. "We'll go to Katzenberg. We'll stop him."

"I've got friends in Katzenberg." Tadeusz Nucks—the crime lord who ruled the city's underworld. Nathan had saved his young son Theo from Smiling Spike during his previous visit to the Free City. Nucks had promised his eternal gratitude. "They'll help."

"Excellent. We'll depart immediately." Esther stepped past Nathan and executed a regal bow to Niko and Captain Uttz. "You saved my friend's life. You will forever find a friend and ally in the House of Essen."

The two of them looked at each other. A promise of alliance with a little rat girl, who had one wildcat guard to her name—along with Nathan of Nestovich. Captain Uttz then returned the bow. "You honor us, my little pale maiden."

"And we can use your help. Especially if the Grand Sable Empire turns against us as well." Niko waved toward the ragged camp. "Send a messenger moth when you can. If you want some poor Orphans in your army, we'll coming running."

"Thank you for that," Nathan said. "And, you know, for saving me."

"Ah, Nathan." Niko gave him an open-mouthed grin, his sharp little teeth shining in the sunlight cutting through the fading rain. "Since I found you on that muddy road, my life has been much more exciting. I suppose I'm grateful for it." He waved to an approaching squirrel groom, who led Emperor through the camp. "Ah. Here's another of your friends."

Emperor. Nathan ran to him.

The piglet jabbed his muzzle in his face and licked him furiously, his whole body shaking with delight. It was grand to see him again. Nathan hugged him close and petted his fur, then tried to get into the saddle. Tricky to do with one arm, and he winced a little as he gave his wounded arm another jab. Finally, Sweeney picked him by the scruff of his neck and plopped him down with an irate yowl.

He went back to his riding goat. "Like old times, Niko. You and I and the Fortunate Few."

"Like old times," Niko agreed. "The bad old days."

"Heh." Sweeney adjusted his poleaxe. "I'm sorry about Bunzika. He was a good rabbit."

"That he was," Niko agreed. "And he lived long. May the

Blessed Beasts give us all such a life—but make sure it ends in victory."

For warriors like Sweeney, Niko, and Captain Uttz, maybe that was the best they could hope for. Then again, what was this fight against Tarr if not a war? And Nathan was a soldier—a warrior fighting for Esther, the pale maiden, as Uttz called her, that he loved.

He adjusted his coat for the rain and trotted Emperor over to join her as she started up the trail. Sweeney rode behind them. Distances in the Dark Forest seemed strange, with so many winding paths and overgrown or disused roads, but they'd reach Katzenberg soon enough.

And hopefully change the fortunes of war for the better.

+ + +

A day and a half later, they arrived in the Free City of Katzenberg. The greatest city in the Dark Forest—maybe in the world—and a home to more merchants, brawlers, entertainers, bankers, thieves, rakes, river pirates, artisans, smugglers, and beggars than even the Supreme Rodent could count. Nathan and his friends rode together through Stenchtrench, the hazy, stinking slum where he had once lived as a pickpocket, and then through the endless colorful stalls and exotic goods of Moss Market, before reaching the hulking counting houses of Coiner's Corners.

A misty spring morning had given way to a warm day, and all of Katzenberg's beasts were going about their business. Rich creatures went about in sumptuous litters, swarms of young hatchling, kit, and hoglet pickpockets plied their trade, and street merchants advertised elaborately woven golden pretzels or dancing marionette knights and demons with their yowling voices.

Nathan glanced at Esther, who was staring at everything with wide eyes. Too many fantastic sights to take in. When he arrived in Katzenberg, he had been the same way. "Try not to stare," he said. "It'll mark you as an outsider." Wait—did that sound rude? "I mean, not that you would ever—"

"I'll take care, Nathan." She patted the crossbow lashed to her saddle. "Besides, if anyone causes me trouble, I'll feed them a bolt."

She could take care of herself.

They reached Gold Garland next, a neighborhood of stately homes behind high hedges and fences—another world from the chaos and clutter of the rest of the city. Nathan led them to a neat, comfortable three-storied house of somber stone.

The home of Tomasz Nucks.

They dismounted, tied their mounts to the post outside, and reached the stout double doors. Inside, a sudden crash and a series of panicked cheeps. What was going on? Sweeney sniffed the air and gripped his poleaxe and Nathan's paw drifted to his dagger. Then the door opened, and Artemesia De Leon's fire-maned face appeared.

"Ah—young Master Nathan, Mistress Esther Essen, and old Sweeney." De Leon—swordsmonkey extraordinaire, fastest blade in Katzenberg, and chief enforcer for Nucks' criminal empire. She wore a scarlet doublet of deep red and a silken half-cape matching her brilliant orange fur. She seemed amused, and her basket-hilted rapier rested in her belt, so whatever was going on couldn't be too dangerous. "Why don't you come in?" Another crash. Another screech.

"Thank you, Mistress De Leon." Nathan gave her a respectful nod as they entered the parlor. "Is Master Nucks home?"

"Out in Tock, along with Ignatius. Arranging some deal with the Doge." They were out of town? Oh no. That meant they couldn't help. "I'm playing nursemaid to young Theo. He's with his tutor now." She led them toward the library, where Nathan had enjoyed so many good books. "It's proving to be a most exciting session."

They found Theo Nucks perched on a stool by the bookshelf. "No sums! No sums!" He wrenched down a book of Sir Konrad the Courageous' knightly adventures and sent it hurtling across the room with all the strength his raccoon kit arms could muster.

It crashed to the floor, nearly striking the slim otter in scholarly black, who chittered as he dove out of the way. "Master Theo—please!" He adjusted his round spectacles. "If you'll merely attempt the questions, you'll find them utterly simple. I promise you, I shall guide your quill so that you complete each equation with grace and ease and—" Theo sent another book hurtling toward him. It opened as it flew, its pages fluttering like a bird, and banged into the otter's belly. He plopped onto the couch and looked at De Leon, his dark shining eyes pleading for help.

"Theo. Enough." De Leon stomped a foot and Theo sat on the stool. "Leave Professor Albertus alone. Besides, looks who's here for a visit?"

"Nathan!" Theo sprang down and ran across the library floor, stepping on a few fallen books. "Nathan—you're here!"

"Hello, Theo." Nathan clasped the raccoon's paw. "This is Esther Essen, my friend, and Sweeney, our guard."

"Hello," Esther said. "Thank you so much for inviting us into —"

Theo ignored her. "Nathan, what happened to your arm? Were you fighting a monster? Another giant bear?"

De Leon helped Professor Albertus back to his feet. "I noticed that. If someone hurt you, Nathan, say their name and they die. Nucks isn't here, but this family owes you a debt that can never be repaid. I'll help you however I can."

Thank the Supreme Rodent! With De Leon on their side, they couldn't lose.

Esther picked up a fallen volume of Ermine Empire History and set it on the table. "We're searching for Titus Tarr. A merchant prince. A true villain and rat-hater."

"I think I would know if someone like that was in town—and he isn't."

"What of the Carrion King? Have you heard any stories of him?"

Professor Albertus seemed to have recovered. He adjusted his spectacles and smoothed his frazzled fur. "Ah yes. The Carrion King. A most interesting rodent character looming large in the folklore of the Dark Forest." His whiskers twitched as he looked at Nathan and Esther. Two rats. "A falsehood, of course. In my class at the University of Katzenberg, I mentioned that he shall perhaps join the rank of Reaping Jack and St. Nicodemus, though he is a far more malevolent—"

"I think he's in a play." Theo pulled a tattered pamphlet from his pocket. "Looks frightening."

They gathered around the pamphlet. *The Wrath of the Carrion King—a Romance of the Cruelty of Rats.* An image of the Carrion King himself appeared, hoisting up his staff and grinning as only a skull could grin.

"A play," Esther said. "They've turned it into a play." It made sense. Though books and pamphlets were easy enough to make, there were still some beasts who couldn't read. But they could watch a play and get Tarr's message that way—that rats were villains. "Where are they presenting this?"

"The Motley Maze." De Leon sniffed. "It's part of the Battle of the Bards—a little dramatic contest that the Jolly Jesters put on each year. That's the crew who runs the Maze for Nucks." She picked up the pamphlet. "Looks like they have the House of Hilarity. That's one of the bigger playhouses."

Esther smoothed down her whiskers. "Then let's go there and burn it down." She made the order like a general and turned to go.

"Wait!" Nathan called. If they started setting fires in the Motley Maze, it could spiral out of control. Especially if they upset the Jolly Jesters, the gang that ruled there. Tomasz Nucks would not be happy. "Let's just go and see what we can see, all right? Then we'll figure out a way to stop it."

Theo bobbed his head, as if he'd been planning strategy too. "Another adventure, Nathan?"

"Absolutely," Nathan agreed.

+++

The Motley Maze—the wild, beating heart of Katzenberg.

Gaudy pleasure halls and gambling dens flourished on all sides of the streets, clockwork bringing the exaggerated figures on the signs above their entrances—a paw hoisting up a fan of playing cards, a cavorting demon, a rearing boar—to mechanical life. Crowds streamed in and out of the establishments, all in various states of drunkenness. Many wore masks and they mingled with the countless performing acrobats, trained insects, and assorted jongleurs plying their trades on the street.

Nathan, Esther, and Sweeney joined a crowd of spectators around a trained messenger moth, garbed in the robes of a monk, who tapped bells etched with numbers to answer the most complicated mathematical questions.

Sweeney smoothed down his whiskers. "That's one smart moth. I've known kings with less sense."

"I'm feeling foolish right now," Esther said. Impossible—she was one of the smartest beasts Nathan knew. "There's so much going on. Especially with this Battle of the Bards business. Wait —over there. The House of Hilarity."

It waited at the edge of the block. The House of Hilarity had a door shaped like the humongous grinning mouth of a marmot. At least a half-dozen beasts in colorful costumes shoved pamphlets into the paws of the crowd. "The Carrion King shall stalk the stage tonight! Come and see a tale of vile skullduggery, cruel betrayal, and heroism against all odds!"

Esther had her crossbow slung over her shoulder. "I'll shut them up."

"Esther—wait." Nathan slid in front of her before she could start shooting bolts. "They're just hirelings. That's a good way to get arrested, or attacked by a mob, and the show will still go on. We need something else." What was it that Zipporah had said? To defeat a story, they needed another story. That's why she had risked everything to keep him alive.

The biggest, roundest bullfrog Nathan had ever seen walked in front of the pamphleteers. "Rubbish! Utter rubbish! Dross! Garbage! Filth!" His cheeks bulged with each pronouncement, made in a refined Copperbright Kingdom accent. The frog had fine clothes, including a lace ruff that somehow fit around his huge neck, but every garment was stained and tattered. Bedraggled or not, he was speaking against the Carrion King. A friend of rats, perhaps? Then he spun to face the audience. "Why would you attend a boring, wretched play like that— poorly written, poorly acted—when you could see a show of true magnificence? Come to the Sunshine Stage, my friends, and prepare for dazzlement and delight!"

He was just advertising another play.

Sweeney's his ears tented and he pointed. "I know that frog." He waved. "Mulberry!"

"Sweeney!" Mulberry hopped over. "Good fortune has crossed our paths again!" He went tall, and it seemed impossible that his lean legs could support so round a body. "My dear friend! My comrade-in-arms! Blessed Beasts, you look well. Guarding rats, I see?"

Esther curtsied. "I am Esther Essen, sir, and this is Nathan of Nestovich. We are pleased to meet you."

The bullfrog's bulging eyes bulged wider. "Nathan of Nestovich! Bold Sir Squeaky himself. Now there's some luck." He bowed. "Sir Thomas Mulberry, at your service. Wandering adventurer, raconteur, hero of some renown. Currently treading the boards at the Sunshine Stage."

"Mulberry and I were in the Fortunate Few together," Sweeney said. "De Leon and Niko as well."

"Poor devils. How are they?"

"Better than you, it seems. How's the actor's trade?"

Mulberry let out a dismissive belch. "As difficult and deadly as any military campaign. Come along and I'll show you." They started down the street, Mulberry waving a webbed hand at the House of Hilarity. "You've heard of the Battle of the Bards? An annual to-do in the Motley Maze, of epic proportions. Every week, a new contest is put on by Lucky Lucia, the Fennec Fox leader of the Jolly Jester Gang. The winner gets a fine monetary reward and the promise to keep performing, so they can pass on a portion of their proceeds to the Jesters. The loser faces Lucia's wrath." He snorted. "A new genre each week. The last was poetry. The failed poet was hurled into the Big Karp River. By catapult. He hasn't been seen since."

"And this is the week for plays?" Nathan asked.

"Precisely, my dear boy." They turned a corner, approaching the Sunshine Stage. This one bore a stylized sun above the entrance, with a torch that could be lit inside once the real one set. "And I find myself wondering what it will be like when a catapult sends me airborne." They walked inside.

Not exactly a grand theatre. The Sunshine Stage had a collection of chairs, a few of them tattered and patched, facing a set of dusty blue curtains currently pulled back to reveal a set and actors. The backdrop showed a snowy scene, the actors in front taking their positions amongst fallen prop swords, a limp suit of armor, and the wooden silhouette of a warboar.

Nathan recognized two of them. "Rinaldo! Rosa!"

They looked up from their scripts. Rinaldo the Wrinkled and Rosa Fumes—a minstrel toad and a knife-throwing skunk. A smile split Rinaldo's mottled face—for just a moment. But Rosa bounded down happily, her black-and-white tail waving through the still air as she sprang up the aisle and rested a paw on Nathan's shoulder.

She had been the first one to show kindness to him after Nestovich burned.

"Nathan of Nestovich! How are you?" She winced at his wounded arm. "Still getting into mischief, I suppose." A nod to Esther and Sweeney. "Mistress Esther, Master Sweeney, it is good to see you again as well. I see Sir Thomas Mulberry found you. Have you come to see the show?"

"What exactly are you performing?" Nathan stared at the warboar. It seemed a little smaller than a true warrior's mount, the tusks a little less developed—but very familiar. And the city in the snow—he'd seen that too.

Wait a moment. This was his story!

"*The Tale of Nathan of Nestovich*!" Mulberry cried. "A story of daring, good humor, adventure—a brave rat boy, a most unexpected hero, pitted against loathsome foes. Rinaldo, with some alterations, will play the titular role." What? Rinaldo would play *him*? "I shall be Nathan's loyal companion, Niko Nikaros, reimagined as a handsome, debonair bullfrog with a fantastic singing voice. And to make it even better, we have a true genius crafting the sets and the marvelous effects that will delight every member of the audience."

"And who would that be?" Esther asked.

A terrible crash came behind the curtains. Then a clockwork monster—a terrible mixture of skunk and dragon, the size of a wagon—descended from the rafters. It crashed to the floorboards, its mouth opening and unspooling pantomime fire made of orange and red ribbons in every direction.

"Wretchedness! Foulness!" A familiar form, stooped and gray-furred emerged onto the stage. "Never mind. A few adjustments—just a few adjustments—and all will be well." A possum bearing an apron laden with tools and mechanisms, including several small sets of spectacles on different chains.

The Great Flammarion. Famed inventor of Tock.

He turned around, looking at the newcomers for the first time. "My old apprentice, Nathan of Nestovich, if I'm not mistaken. The saints must have dreamed up this coincidence." The dragon skunk's head came free, creaking as it rolled over the stage, and then dropped into the audience.

"Master Flammarion!" Nathan hurried down the aisle. "How are you?"

"I have had better times, young Nathan." He let out an irate screech. "After spreading the printing press far and wide, one would think that my genius would be rewarded. Instead, I am cursed. A thousand imitators have cropped up, the inventor's field is overcrowded, and my financial skills are, unfortunately, rather lacking. Hence my current employment."

"Managing theatrical magic for the Sunshine Stage," Rinaldo said. "Or trying to."

Nathan took a step back and joined Esther. They looked at the stage, the actors, the bits and pieces of their pasts scattered everywhere like they'd been casually tossed out of a toybox. Another pang rippled up Nathan's arm. He clutched it. Esther's eyes flicked to him, red and bright with concern.

He wasn't a character in a storybook—but maybe he needed to be.

"This could stop that Carrion King play. If it wins the contest —if it's good enough—we can stop Tarr's plans in Katzenberg." Nathan adjusted his sling, hiding it under his black cloak that he'd gotten in Katzenberg last year. "We'll help them, Esther.

We'll make their play great. We'll win the Battle of the Bards."

On the stage, the giant clockwork skunk suddenly reared up and swung its claws down, bashing them into Rinaldo and sending him to the ground in a croaking heap.

Esther sighed. "We've got our work cut out for us."

+ + +

A few hours until opening night and things were a mess.

Artemesia De Leon had come by, bringing Theo and Professor Albertus. The otter academic, who taught literature as well as logic and reasoning, sat across from Nathan in the front seats of the theatre and worked with him on the script. Meanwhile, Flammarion scrambled his way across the stage to get the set and mechanical devices ready, making raspy hisses at Theo, who dangled from the ceiling on a rope to test its strength. Mulberry strutted about and warmed up his singing voice with deep croaks. Discarded props and costumes lay scattered on the stage, the ingenious effects flashed to life without warning, and the script was—to put it mildly—boar crap.

"Why do I have to face the audience and tell them exactly what I'm thinking for four paragraphs?" Nathan asked. "Isn't it obvious?"

Albertus accepted a cup of tea from Sweeney, who came bearing drinks and snacks on a tray. "It's called a soliloquy. A common theatrical device. How else would the audience know what you are thinking if they are not explicitly told?"

"What about by what I do?"

He let out a little chirp. "I'm afraid that's not how stories work. However, you are correct that it goes on far too long— and this metaphor where you compare courage to a midwinter sunrise on a cloudy day is pointless. Shall we remove it?"

"Yes, please."

His quill scratched away. Progress, at least.

Esther came by, bearing a mass of prop swords in her arms. "How's the work going, sirs?"

"Quite well, actually." Albertus beamed at Nathan. "The lad possesses an amazing amount of creativity. His suggestion of having Nathan the Rat defeat the dragon by riding a cannonball into its mouth is inspired."

"Nathan's always reading stories," Esther said. "I'm not surprised that he's mastered the art."

Sizzling heat cooked Nathan's cheeks yet again. "Thank you—but we still have a way's to go."

"Well, Ana's here. She got your message." Esther pointed to the entrance. "Let's see if she can make our plan work."

They left the scribbling to Professor Albertus and headed up to the aisle to the rear of the theatre.

Ana waited there, her arms folded, looking at the mess on stage with the same expression that she wore when planning daring heists: partly calm, partly amused, and always calculating. A squirrel pickpocket—leader of the Runt Gang that had adopted Nathan when he'd first visited the city. She clasped Nathan's paw and gave Esther a hug as another mechanical crash split the theatre.

"Ana—hello!" Nathan's whiskers shook—it was good to see her. She wore a black dress now and a white cowl. "I missed you."

"Missed you too, Nathan. And it's Sister Ana now."

"You've taken Holy Orders?" Esther asked. It seemed unbelievable for Ana to go from criminal to holy beast.

Ana shrugged. "The Runts couldn't play pickpocket forever. I made some deal with an old priest in town, turned his church into an orphanage so we could get some respectability." Her fuzzy tail drooped. "There are so many orphans these days. Somehow, I've ended up in charge of things. I run the church, keep them fed, and seek donations." A wink. "The old way."

So she was still stealing and probably teaching her charges to do the same, just like she did to Nathan. But she was also helping the abandoned children of the Dark Forest. What could be saintlier than that? Nathan had completed his studies as a guest on the Essen Family's fine estate and played in a meadow. It was easy to see who had done more.

"So, I hear you've got a job for me?" Ana walked past the seats, examining the stage. "What is it?"

"We need you to get us an audience." Esther pressed a stack of pamphlets into Ana's paws. "Nun or not, I have a feeling your charges put their paws where they shouldn't. Now they can serve the forces of righteousness. Take out some coins—then put these in."

"Sneaking out your advertisements?" Ana widened her eyes. "You think that'll pack the house?"

"We have to try," Nathan said.

"That you do, but St. Ana's Orphanage needs donations. I'll be requesting some in return for our service." Ana accepted the stack of pamphlets and settled into a chair, facing the stage. "Now let me see exactly why I'm risking the lives of my children."

Her children? Bizarre to think about, but it was true. All those orphans were her charges, and Ana was risking everything to look after them. She'd grown up fast. Nathan stood next to her, his paws dangling at his side. A prize, pampered beetle next to a wild and fearsome scorpion.

Rinaldo had taken the stage. He wore shimmering costume armor and hoisted up a banner embroidered with a rat's head— Nathan's head. A false rat's tail made of cloth and rubber dangled from his rump.

"Alas!" He puffed out his mottled cheeks. "Alas—what a terror has befallen my people? What ill fortune? What misery? Is there no end of woe that we rats must face? Forsooth, my heart sinks heavy in my chest like a sailing ship weighed down with stones, and cannonballs, and trees, and various other heavy things, and it is sinking—"

Ana blew a raspberry. Rinaldo glared at her, his eyes hateful below their ridges.

"We're working on the dialogue," Nathan said.

"It's not just his words." Ana looked from Rinaldo to Nathan. "He's supposed to be you?"

"I guess so."

"Hmmm." Ana folded her paws. "It's all wrong. He doesn't have the spirit you have, Nathan."

"The spirit?"

"I don't know. I can't capture the feelings with words." She stood. "But there's only one beast in here that can play Nathan the Rat, and he ain't the toad on the stage." Ana tucked the pamphlets under arm. "You tell him, Esther. I got the feeling that he'll do whatever you ask." She gave her tail a shake and started for the doors and the sunny streets. "I'll bring the children by tonight. They'll be expecting a good show."

"Goodbye!" Nathan waved to her as she slipped out into the streets. Was she right? Should he really play himself? "I don't think I could—I'm mean, I'm not an actor. I've never even been on a stage before." He gripped his wounded arm. "What if I mess it up?"

Esther had been listening carefully. "You've faced far scarier things, Rat on the Road. But you don't have to do it, if you don't want to."

"Right." He looked back at Rinaldo, who was waving his prop sword against the claws of the clockwork skunk emerging from stage left. "I'll get back to writing. But we'll be ready, right? For when the audience comes?"

"We'll have to be." Esther smoothed back her whiskers, her

red eyes blinking—shimmering with fatigue and worry. "The show must go on."

+++

As night fell, the crowd gathered outside the Sunshine Stage. Nathan and Esther peered through the double doors of the theatre and looked at the cobblestones under the moonlight. Time to see if working with Sister Ana had paid off.

A single look showed that it had.

The line went down the block. A vast assortment of Katzenberg creatures—plump beaver and marmot merchants in their silks and finery, muddy nautical otters from the dockside district of Shackshore, and a mass of chattering hatchlings, kits, and cubs who had to be Sister Ana's orphan charges—all clustered together by the lights of colored lanterns, talking and snacking as they waited for the doors to open. It looked like half of Katzenberg was here to see *The Tale of Nathan of Nestovich*.

Would they like it? Was the play ready? Nathan's heart worked a rapid drumbeat in his chest.

Esther pointed. "Look there. The guest of honor."

A group of wildly dressed beasts strolled together, the crowd parting before them as they neared the theatre—and they looked like performers themselves. Their clothing was made of madcap checkered and diamond patterns. Brilliant pink, blue, and silver worked with gold thread shone on their elaborate capes and pantaloons, and each beast bore a mask. Some had bulbous noses, others were ovoid and flanked by butterfly wings, but all the masks had the same elaborate gaudiness of their garments. The beasts were armed too, with cudgels, rapiers, and long daggers on their belts and backs.

The Jolly Jesters.

Lucky Lucia, the Fennec Fox who had to be their leader, wore a bejeweled domino mask. Her huge ears drooped with multicolored earrings. "Come, friends—let us fill our cups with entertainment and see what joys it brings!" She waved a paw, and the Jolly Jesters strolled to the head of the line.

No one complained. They were the masters here.

"Do you think they'll like it?" Nathan asked.

"We'll have to wait and see." Then Esther gripped Nathan's paw, her fingers like iron. "Look who else is here."

Difficult to see them in the crowd, but Esther pointed and then there was no mistaking it. Sir Volkbert, the white-furred wolverine, a pale cloak over his armor. Next to him, her brilliantly colored skin glistening, stood Contessa Vivaldi. A pair of smoked glasses rested on her broad nose, hiding her dark eyes—even though the light was fading.

"My crossbow's in the back." Esther straightened up and closed the door. "I'll fetch it."

"No!" His voice squeaked. "They'll—they'll kill you."

Her eyes went grim. Nestovich burned again. He couldn't let Esther come to harm.

"I mean—we have to protect the show. If you hit a wolverine or a frog with a crossbow bolt on the street, the City Watch will sweep in, and that'll be it for our play. And the Carrion King's show? It'll still be there, and it might very well win."

Her red eyes blazed. But she nodded. "We'll watch them. We'll be ready." She started back as the old hedgehog ticket-taker went to open the door. "Come on. Let's get to our places."

They slipped back through the theatre as the doors creaked open and the crowd filed in. Down a passage, their shoes clicking on the scuffed floorboards, and then they were backstage, in the wings, hidden by the faded curtains—looking out over the expanse of wood where the drama was soon to take place.

Everyone backstage had a job. Rinaldo and Rosa prepared for their entrance. Nathan used his good arm to pass the toad his lute while Esther gave Rosa a harp. Flammarion scurried across the stage to check his machinery. Sir Thomas Mulberry hopped his way to the edge of the stage to take his place as narrator, while Sweeney tugged the ropes to open the curtains.

Then the curtains slid back, curious applause rippled through the theatre, and the play began.

"Welcome, welcome all!" Mulberry's voice boomed—the trained, confident voice of a veteran actor. He made a sweeping bow. "Cast aside your worries and your cares. Journey with us through the realm of story and legend—the Tale of Nathan of Nestovich." He waved his webbed hand to the stage. "Behold! Two travelers, wandering through a land broken with war. A pair of humble troubadours, seeking their fortune in the Dark Forest."

Rinaldo and Rosa dutifully played their instruments, and each did a little jig as they walked. The wagon moved along grooves worked into the stage, following their progress.

Then they stopped. Rosa's eyes flicked up and down. She was waiting for something—which didn't happen. "Hark!" Rosa called. Still nothing. "Hark!" She repeated.

Something was wrong.

Mechanisms in the rafters creaked. Flammarion worked his machines.

A little stuffed baby rat dropped down. The best thing they could get to represent the baby Nathan. Huge glassy eyes, a knit face, all set in a bundle. It bopped Rinaldo on the head and he stumbled—tripped on the prop wagon and landed on his back. Oh Supreme Rodent—this wasn't supposed to happen. The play was going terribly! Nathan bit his lip and Esther cringed.

Then laughter filled the theatre. Ripples of applause.

Nathan looked at Esther. She smoothed down her whiskers. "They seemed to like it."

They needed to. They needed to like his story, true or false, instead of the tale of the Carrion King.

"A rodent infant!" Rinaldo rolled over and picked up the rat baby. "The Blessed Beasts have put a baby rat in our path! My dear Rosa Fumes, what is to be done?"

She picked up the Nathan dummy and gave it a sudden toss —then hurled a few throwing knives into the air. They hummed around the prop baby and thudded into the stage, getting more applause. That, at least, was all according to the script. "Let us raise him!" She picked up the baby and started juggling, adding a few knives to fly and shimmer along with the bundled rat. "Let us train him in the arts of cunning and war. Let us make him a great hero, who shall guard the Dark Forest against all who would do evil."

"Yes!" Rinaldo cried. "Let us do that!"

This wasn't how it had been. It was the Rat on the Road's story, Bold Sir Squeaky's story, the Orphan Prince of Tock's story. Not his. But this was the story being told.

More applause. Nathan and Esther hurried out, helping ready the next scene, as Rinaldo bounced backstage to change costumes.

The next scene went well—and the one unfortunate, accidental pratfall only made the audience laugh more. Nathan and Esther watched from backstage, and he mouthed the words that he'd written alongside Professor Albertus. Rinaldo, on his knees and wearing a fuzzy hood, now played Nathan as he learned how to wield a sword from Mulberry. Rosa appeared next, costumed as a cruel skunk conqueror in a dramatically flowing cape who gave a long speech about his evil plan to conquer the Dark Forest. Sweeney stood behind her, holding a spear and looking menacing. Rinaldo promised to stop him.

"The Dark Forest will never be conquered!" he cried, and the audience cheered.

The curtains closed and Rinaldo hopped his way off stage,

joining Nathan and Esther. His pebbly legs faltered, and he leaned against the wall for support. "How was I? By St. Julian, it is powerfully hot out there."

"You were wonderful," Esther said. "You too, Master Sweeney."

He came in, holding his poleaxe. "I was? Well, thank you for your kind words."

"Now, the skunk dragon will make its appearance, and..." Rinaldo gasped. "Oh—Good Heavens." He dropped to his knees. Nathan ran to him. Rinaldo croaked and vomited—unleashing a great torrent of greenish goop. A chunky, filthy flood. It spilled onto the floorboards, spattered the curtains, and a fat dollop landed on Nathan's cloak. Esther stepped back, Sweeney swinging his poleaxe into a defensive position. Oh no—what now?

Flammarion dangled down from the rafters on a rope. "Rinaldo!" The toad was on his back, breathing heavily. Flammarion hopped down and searched his body.

His paw emerged, holing a tiny needle. A little line of silver, scarcely visible. "Poisoned."

On the stage, Rosa was going into her monologue. Nathan peered through an old prop mirror set further back, which let him look past the stage and into the audience.

Contessa Vivaldi sat in the front row.

They had been watching her, but how could they have prepared for something like this? Poison was delivered through cups or meals—not a needle. But Vivaldi—and Tarr—had been planning to do just that.

Rinaldo was sick. He could barely stand, let alone perform.

Titus Tarr was going to win again.

"Never—never mind." Rinaldo coughed and sputtered. "I've still got some strength. The show must go on. Just get me on my feet and—"

"Rinaldo—please." Esther squeaked. "He can't do it. We need —we need to end the show. I don't want anyone else to get hurt."

More applause. The scene on stage was about to end.

Nathan closed his eyes. Wait—could he—could he go up there? He didn't want to go on the stage. Seeing his story turned into this madcap play was bad enough without actually being in it. But if he didn't do it, if his story wasn't delivered to everyone, then Titus Tarr would win, Esther's parents would remain in chains, and rats and mice all over the world would suffer.

Nestovich, again.

He gripped the fuzzy hat from Rinaldo's head and pulled it free. "Rest," he said. "I'll take care of it."

Esther squeaked, louder than the applause outside. "But Nathan—that frog—"

Sweeney was already stepping back, gripping his poleaxe. "You leave her to me and De Leon."

That would have to be enough. Nathan gave Esther a quick smile. Then he scampered onto the stage.

The curtains went up. Gasps filled the audience. The footlights burned in front of him, heat growing under his fur. His wounded arm throbbed as his throat dried up. What was the line? He couldn't remember it now. Whispers filled the audience. Lucky Lucia was up in the Sunshine Stage's box, her huge ears perked as she leaned closer.

"I'm—ah—I'm the real Nathan." He stammered out the words.

It sounded miserable. They'd laugh at him. They'd boo. They'd pelt him with rotten vegetables.

He looked offstage. Esther was there, giving him a big thumbs-up.

"I'm the real Nathan." Nathan raised his voice. "And I'm here to fight for the Dark Forest!" He raised his dagger, and a few sets of paws clapped together in unsure applause.

Mechanical creaking from the side. The Skunk Dragon descended, making a terrible groan. Its mechanical jaws opened, and tongues of cloth flame danced out. Nathan ducked below them, weaving back and forth. Some cloth brushed the fuzz on his head, but he kept going. Reached the neck and gave it a jab with his knife, just like he'd seen Rinaldo do during rehearsal. The head popped free with a click. A vast spray of fake blood—mashed berry juice—spurted out.

It drenched Nathan, mixing with the toad puke.

The audience gasped. Good—they were enjoying the show. Everyone loves a dragon.

He spun back to the crowd and hoisted up his dagger in victory. More applause now. "This foul fiend is defeated! Heroism has won the day!" The audience cheered—but he needed something else. Something that wasn't in the script.

He lowered the dagger. The applause faded, replaced by more awkward silence.

Then he spoke.

"Rats—rats can be heroes too. That's what my story teaches. Not that we're all heroes. Some of us can be villains, I suppose." No, that made it sound like rats were bad. "We're normal—just normal creatures. That's what we are." But was that right? Rats had their own traditions, their own faith. There was so much that made them unique. "Well, we do some things differently, but that doesn't mean—"

"Nathan!" Esther hissed. He looked at her. "Tarr!" she whispered. "Tell them about what Tarr's doing!"

That was it. "I do know this." He made his voice louder now. Let it carry through the whole of the theatre. "Rats want to live in peace. That's all we want. And beasts who preach hatred, who try and turn the Dark Forest against us—they want power. They want to rule—and we'll stop them." Again, he jabbed his dagger at the sky. "Because the Dark Forest will always be free!"

Again, there was silence. The beast shifted in their seats. What was wrong? They were looking at the box, where Lucky Lucia watched the play.

Waiting for her decision.

Lucia stood and leaned down. "A character who changes actors at the climax. The real Nathan the Rat taking the stage. An impassioned speech on behalf of rats, which comes out of nowhere. A clockwork dragon skunk." She stretched her tongue, her dark eyes gleaming. "A most unusual play. A most original play." Then she hoisted her paws. "And that uniqueness makes it one of the most wondrous plays that I have witnessed in all of my time in the Motley Maze!"

She applauded, and the rest of the crowd did too. The cheering echoed off the walls of the theatre. Nathan sighed deeply, the relief coming cool as Rosa, Mulberry and even Rinaldo—who had recovered and cleaned himself up—came out for their bow. They clutched hands, faced the cheering crowd, and bowed as one.

The play was a hit.

+++

Afterwards, long into the night, the players celebrated. Mulberry arranged a feast from one of Katzenberg's finest eateries, and they gobbled yellow and orange cheeses alive with fiery spices, rich breads with boar butter, and an assortment of pastries stuffed with fruits and custard for dessert. Sweet Argent wine washed it down, and Nathan sipped some along with cold water. Sweeney, Mulberry, and De Leon headed out into the night on some errand, leaving the others to celebrate and enjoy the echoes of applause.

Soon enough, Rinaldo had his lute going and gentle music

filled the Sunshine Stage. Rosa joined Flammarion and they danced together, lean possum tail and striped skunk fur moving to the tune.

Esther tossed Nathan a napkin. "Your whiskers."

He wiped them away. He was messy—and Esther noticed.

Then she offered her paw. "Care to dance? I'll mind your wounded arm."

"Um—" Nathan started, but her hand was on his and then they were up, shoes clicking on the floorboards of the stage. "Thank you." Her eyes were so wonderfully bright. "For helping me on the stage. I was so scared."

"I had a feeling you could manage it. As soon as Ana mentioned it, I knew it was the right thing."

"You did?"

"You're brave, you know. And I'm grateful to have you by my side." She let go of his arms. "You're like my brother, Nathan. The brother I never had."

She was so nice to him. So—wait—*brother*?

Something cold coiled in his belly. His whiskers drooped.

"Nathan? Is something wrong?"

"N-no." His good arm fell limply to his side. A brother. A good friend. That was all. What was wrong with her? She was so smart—hadn't she realized that he didn't want to be her brother? Or maybe—maybe that's what she wanted, how she saw him, and all his wishful thinking wouldn't do anything to change her mind.

The theatre doors slammed open—a mercy. Anything was a mercy after the pummeling Esther had dropped on him.

He stumbled away from her and faced the door.

Sir Volkbert walked in, a thick rope tying his arms to his side and a growing bruise below his pale fur. Sweeney strolled behind him with his poleaxe extended and prodding the wolverine's back—jabbing out every so often like a prankster's poke to make Volkbert shuffle along. Mulberry, a hefty mace with faded gold worked around the spikes, strolled alongside Sweeney, and there was Artemesia De Leon, fingers resting casually on her rapier's basket hilt.

The Fortunate Few, together again.

"Look what we caught!" Mulberry hopped in front of Sir Volkbert and patted his fuzzy cheek. "Should have stuck to the snow, Mr. White Fur!"

"I'm a knight," Volkbert said. "I expect to be treated with respect, as the rules of chivalry command—"

"You might be a knight, laddie, but I'm not." Sweeney swept his legs with the haft of the poleaxe—making Sir Volkbert tumble down like a discarded toy. His armor rattled and his fuzzy limbs splayed, his little ears flicked back. De Leon's rapier hummed out—metal lightning—and froze just above his pink nose.

Mulberry puffed out his cheeks. "You're in a spot now, Volkbert, and no mistake."

Supreme Rodent—were they going to kill him? It certainly looked that way. They were mercenaries, warriors, and though they had new jobs that had softened them a little, their blades were still sharp and ready.

"Knights in fancy armor." De Leon's rapier drifted lower —aiming for Sir Volkbert's throat. "You think yourselves invincible. When all an opponent must do is find the weak point, and give the gentlest of pushes—"

"Wait!" Esther and Nathan called out together. He looked and her and fell silent. She was the leader here. "I want to talk to him." She walked over, squeezing between Mulberry. Nathan followed. They stared down at the unfortunate wolverine. "Why do you serve Tarr?"

"I'm an albino beast in the Grand Sable Empire. Everyone considers me a Winterborn traitor." His tongue lolled, his eyes sad. "But not Tarr."

"And look where such service has brought you," Mulberry murmured.

"May I kill him now?" De Leon asked.

"No—wait." Esther knelt now. Her face close to Sir Volkbert. "Where's he printing his pamphlets from? Where's his press? Is it in the Empire?"

Volkbert showed his teeth. "He has allies everywhere. He has a trade empire with more power than any flag. You'll never beat him."

"Then what does it matter if he loses one printing press?" Esther folded his paws. "Please. He has my parents."

Volkbert's eyes went to Nathan. "You really knew Sir Konrad the Courageous?"

What? Why ask that? "I didn't lie when I told you I did." Nathan wrinkled his nose. "He protected me. He did what was right. If he was in your shoes, sir, he'd help fight against Tarr."

The answer seemed to change the wolverine knight. His little tongue protruded through clenched teeth, and he sniffed deeply. He seemed like he was trying to stop himself from whimpering, to force whines out of his voice. Then he spoke, very quietly. "The Abbey di Ecco."

"The what?" Sweeney asked.

"In the Sunstone Archipelago. Isola di Ecco—Ecco Isle. The Abbey there. Tarr talks of it often."

That's where his press must lie. The birthplace of the Carrion King.

"Thank you." Esther patted his paw. "Keep him bound. Put him backstage for now—we'll buy a wagon, and he'll go with us." A smart decision. Sir Volkbert doubtlessly knew more about

Tarr's operations. "We'll leave at first light. Go to Kostamare and find some sleek vessel to take us through the Sunstone Sea. Then we'll find Tarr." She squeaked—a determined, definite noise. A book being closed. "And we'll beat him again."

"Aye, Mistress Essen." Sweeney put formality into the words. He wasn't talking to the young kit he protected—he was talking to his commander. "It will be done."

The beasts of the Fortunate Few nodded. Mulberry and Sweeney hauled Sir Volkbert to his feet while De Leon went to talk with Flammarion.

They had much to plan. One battle had been won—the war was still waiting to be fought.

+ + +

As strange a convoy as any that had crossed the busy roads to Kostamare rolled along in the morning sunlight. Sweeney and Mulberry trotted along first, weaponry jangling from the saddles of their goats. Then Esther on her mouflon, which pranced daintily over the mud without staining her hooves. A wagon rolled along next, Artemesia De Leon sitting casually inside while Flammarion managed the reins. Sir Volkert, trussed up, sat in the back.

And then Nathan, on Emperor. Looking at Sir Volkbert, who was leaning against a sack of potatoes they'd thrown in the wagon for supplies.

"What was he like?" Sir Volkbert asked suddenly. "Sir Konrad, I mean?"

What to say? That Sir Konrad was foolish? Ridiculous? Unbelievably brave and unstoppable in combat? Or at least he was until age had confined him to his manor estate. Nathan knew the answer. "Honorable." He looked down at the road, Emperor's feet leaving a trail of mucky hoofprints. "He would never have served someone like Tarr."

Volkbert's dark eyes shone sadly. "I loved reading his chivalric romances."

"Me too."

"The battle with the otter pirate queen, the hyena bandits—"

"The dragon's reign of terror?"

"I love that one," Sir Volkbert said. "It's why I wanted to be a knight in the first place."

And real life, as Nathan had so often learned, wasn't like the stories at all.

"Nathan!" Esther's voice. Nathan perked up. They'd talked to each other over the ride, but it hadn't felt right. *Like a brother* kept ringing in Nathan's ear, and Esther seemed to know that something was bothering him but couldn't figure out what it was. And it was foolish. They had so much else to worry about.

But his heart still hurt.

"Up ahead. Look." She pointed to a sign, half-overgrown with moss, but Nathan could read it without even seeing all the old letters.

Nestovich.

He'd passed by this sign many times on his way back from Thistle Town, where his father sold his tailoring. Nathan would be in their old wagon that always leaned a little to the left, nestled amongst all the goods they'd purchased at the market. He'd have an old book, tattered and purchased from some bankrupt noblebeast or abandoned monastery, and look up to stare at the sign. Home would be coming soon, and the warmth of the fire, his father's bad jokes, and his mother's keen questions about how the day had gone.

That would never happen now.

"Nathan." Esther held her paws together. "Do you want to visit it?"

"Yes." But could he really do it? Could he tread on that earth again? "No—I don't know."

"I'll go with you," Esther said quietly.

He looked at the others. Sweeney, Mulberry, De Leon, Flammarion—all were sympathetic. Even Sir Volkbert lowered his pink snout and looked equally sad. That was odd.

But Esther. She would be with him.

He nodded.

They let their convoy rest on the side of the road. Nathan and Esther dismounted, Sweeney following at a distance that was protective and respectful. Down a little gravel road and then they were there.

The town square of Nestovich.

The ruined houses had been claimed by moss, which coated charred logs in soft green blankets. Grass grew amongst their flagstones. No skeletons visible—scavengers and some kindly locals must have dealt with them. Flowers grew now, the bright sort that bloomed at the height of spring, and the sun shone where there had been laughter and joy, and then spilled blood and fear and death, and then—ever since—the purest silence that existed only in the absence of life.

Nathan walked to his house. He looked at the ruins and sank down to his knees. The sobs came, deep and terrible.

Esther ran to him and put an arm around his shoulder.

"It can't—it can't happen again." He fought back his tears. "Tarr can't win."

"We won't let him."

There were times when you really needed a friend. It was good to know he had Esther.

CHAPTER 6. A DEATH IN THE ABBEY

Nathan dug his paws into the dirt, trying to wrestle a stubborn weed free. How long had he been doing this, working in the garden in the Abbey di Ecco—working in secret in search of Titus Tarr's hidden printing press? Around a week, maybe more. And what had he done? He'd helped old Brother Ambrose, the salamander gardener, to harvest rosehip for the tea of monks and nuns, planted tulip seeds, tended the apple tree, and weeded the garden.

Many times.

At least his arm had mostly healed, though he still wore it in the sling when he wasn't working in the garden.

Maybe Esther, working as a scullery maid in the Abbey di Ecco's kitchens, was having better luck.

A shadow covered Nathan. He sat up, clutching the weed. Dirt clung to the roots and dribbled down, staining the old novice's robes they'd given him. "I see the weeds are fine opponents for you, young Simon." Brother Ambrose smiled. The salamander gardener had slick black skin speckled with yellow the color of rich mustard. Bright eyes shone below his monk's hood, which he usually wore up. Ambrose didn't care much for the sun—an oddity, given his job as the abbey's gardener. "But are you defeating the weeds or are they besting you?"

Simon—that was the name Nathan had given them when he asked for a job. "We're battling to a standstill."

"Hmmm." Brother Ambrose knelt and examined Nathan's paw. "You said that you worked in the garden of a baron's estate that had been destroyed by the Hoppite rebels." That was the story that he and Esther had been told to use. The plump quail nun had listened to Esther with a sympathetic bobbing of her head after they arrived in the monthly ship that brought supplies to the Isola di Ecco from the coastal city in Kostamare and sought work. "Is that not so?"

"Yes, sir."

"But your paws are so soft—so smooth."

Nathan swallowed. He liked Brother Ambrose, who never worked him too hard and entertained him with clever puns and jokes that a monk had no business knowing—but the salamander was smart. Far too smart. "Well, my father—he did most of the work. I'd help, when I could, but he wanted me to go to school in one of the Ratholes, a rat neighborhood in a big city. That's why he helped me learn to read." His whiskers quivered —he steadied them. "I'm afraid I've got more weeds to battle, Brother Ambrose."

"I shall leave you to your war, Simon." Ambrose went tall, his webbed hands folding. Nathan followed his gaze.

A cluster of high-ranking monks, more than a few mixing fine velvets and jeweled rings with their robes, crossed through the courtyard near the garden, heading for the church. Abbot Odo, a squat, gray-pelted mole, walked at their head with his huge paws hidden under the sleeves of his robe. His muzzle wrinkled and he wasn't talking to the other monks as he hastened along, like he was trying to complete some important errand.

Nathan should talk to Abbot Odo. If there was a hidden printing press somewhere in the abbey, Odo might very well know about it. But how could a half-crippled rat orphan seek an audience with the most important beast in the abbey? And even if he did, Abbot Odo might be in league with Tarr.

So he waited—and gardened.

Brother Ambrose looked at the other weeds and made a gentle, disappointed sucking noise at Nathan's lack of progress. "I'm needed for morning prayers, along with the others. Take a respite, my boy, and then resume your work." He paused by the well, where a bucket of fresh spring water waited, and smoothed some over his scalp. It glistened in the spring sun. "The weeds aren't going anywhere." He walked away, hunched over, his slick tail dragging behind him amongst his colorful flowers.

Morning prayers. All the monks and nuns would be there, singing away to the Blessed Beasts.

A perfect chance for a little investigation.

Nathan waited until Ambrose had joined the cluster of monks ambling into the main chapel and then darted to the garden shed that had been his home and bedroom for the past few days. Inside, waiting on a leash tied to an old shovel, was Blizzard—a snow white messenger moth. Nathan grabbed some bread, honey, and cheese that Esther had brought him from the kitchen. The cheese—a delightfully pungent cheddar—went in his mouth, along with some of the bread. The rest he put in front of Blizzard, who fluttered down and started chewing. Nathan had taken him—or her?—outside last night, letting the moth fly around the spires and cliffs of the Isola di Ecco.

When he was ready, he'd tie the little message under his pillow to Blizzard's leg and send her flying to Kostamare, where Sweeney and the Fortunate Few waited with a fast ship. They'd come to the abbey, blades at the ready, and destroy Tarr's printing press.

But he had to find the cursed thing first.

"Good moth." Nathan petted Blizzard's folded wings. Silky and soft, like moss on pale stones. "You'll be flying home soon." He grabbed his sling and hung it over his shoulder, letting his arm rest carefully against the cloth. Uncomfortable, but necessary.

Then he headed outside and into the abbey. Time to snoop.

+++

The dining hall—one of the largest buildings in the Abbey di Ecco. The monks and nuns ate every meal there, seated together at the vast tables. No elaborate tapestries or pastry castles, but it was a grand chamber, nonetheless. Right now, it was empty. Strange, to walk in a place that was usually full of hubbub as monks and nuns discussed matters of faith or traded abbey gossip. Now, there was nothing but dust and the sound of prayers coming from the adjacent church.

Nathan passed a long table, the blonde wood turned gold from the crisp sunlight coming in from the wide windows.

What was he doing? Was the printing press going to be lurking in the corner? Would Titus Tarr be under the table?

Light footsteps came from the entrance to the kitchen and Nathan froze. Should he run to the hall? Dive under a table? No—he could think of a suitable lie.

But it was just Esther.

"Nathan!" She hurried over, crossing the table and joining him. A homespun dress and apron instead of her usual finery. Crumbs and dust covered her pale fur and her red eyes looked tired. "Are you sneaking around while the monks are at prayer?"

"Um—yes."

"An excellent plan. I'm doing the same." Esther walked ahead of him. "I've used the services as an opportunity to search the monastery and snuck out during the night as well. Gone all over the island, examined most of the buildings. The dormitories, storerooms, scriptorium." She sighed. "Nothing."

"You've done all that?" It was more than he'd managed.

"I haven't even found a single secret passage. Nothing hidden in a bookshelf or a wine cellar. Have you?"

"Not really."

"There must be some. Every place like this has a few secret passages." She grinned at him. "I would have done more, but I must do my job, and the head cook is very attentive, and the work is hard. One thing's for sure—I'll never take the kitchen servants for granted ever again. My paws feel like they're going to fall off and I'll never get the flour out of my fur." She wriggled her whiskers. "What have you done?"

"Um—I've pulled weeds." Supreme Rodent—he sounded pathetic.

"All right." Esther pointed to the large double doors. "Well, there's one place I haven't been. I want a lookout to help me, and you can do that." They left the dining hall, walking down the wide halls of sun-washed stone. "How's your arm, Nathan? Is it healing? We're very lucky the monks and nuns are such charitable sorts. Who else would hire a one-armed rat to work in the garden?" Esther was in her element, talking fast, spinning schemes, bubbling with excitement. "Does that Brother Ambrose fellow suspect? The cook doesn't. He's too concerned about making a suitable pie for the evening meal."

She was having an adventure.

They passed the courtyard and turned a corner. Now, Nathan knew where they were going. Abbot Odo's chambers. It made perfect sense. Odo might have some documents, letters from Titus Tarr—if he and Tarr were allies—mentioning the hidden printing press. Another corner and they'd reach the hall where Odo's rooms waited.

Then a barking roar split the quiet of the abbey at prayer, followed by frenzied squeaks.

Nathan sprinted around the corner.

Zipporah and Zoya Schall—the mouse and rat thieves who had saved him so many times—lay on their bellies. Their tails were held firmly in the powerful paws of Brother Flavian, a massive badger who looked like a mountain in his robes. "Murderers!" He barked again as he shouted, and the doors of the church opened at the call. "Squeakling killers! They have stained their paws in the blood of Abbot Odo!"

What? Murderers? Zipporah and Zoya would never do something like that. And Abbot Odo—he was dead?

Suddenly, the hall was swarming with monks and nuns. They clustered in a circle, talking fast and filling the hall with worried grunts, growls, and croaks. Brother Ambrose was amongst them, watching everything with eyes like rain-washed obsidian. Nathan stayed close to Esther. Would they notice that these two rats were already in the hall? Hopefully not. They were just part of the audience to this dark drama playing out by the abbot's chambers.

Brother Flavian shoved Zipporah against the wall. She held Zoya close, and the mottled kit looked small and—impossible as it may seem—frightened. "I sought Abbot Odo in his chambers, after he did not arrive for morning prayers—and I found him." Flavian snapped his teeth. "Dead! Not stabbed or strangled—but still dead. Murdered by rat poison. Rat sorcery!" He pointed. "These two were in his office, standing over the good beast that they killed."

Zipporah snapped her teeth. "You don't know what you're talking about. Odo was my friend. He asked that I come, to help him—and we found him like this."

"Why would Odo ever befriend a squeakling like you?"

"Maybe you don't know your abbot as well as you think you do."

Flavian barked again. "I know thieves when I see them. You came to the island—we'll find some little skiff on the shore if we search, no doubt, and snuck in here to find the abbey's holy treasures. Maybe you were interrogating Odo, maybe he simply surprised you as you searched his office—but you killed him, and by the Blessed Beasts, you will face the executioner's axe for your unholy crime."

Supreme Rodent—no! Fear burned bright—and shame. Nestovich burned again. He couldn't let his friends suffer. "They —they couldn't have done it!" Nathan shouted.

All the nuns and monks stared at him. Oh no—he'd made everything worse. Drawing attention, putting himself and Esther at risk.

Flavian took a step closer. "Perhaps they were in league with the squeaklings already here."

"Flavian, my friend." Brother Ambrose appeared next to the badger. "Simon seems far too small to play a part in such a crime. Recall the words of St. Balthazar: 'let not your mind clasp faith so tightly that it loses its grip on the truth.' We must not let hatred and certainty allow the true culprits to escape."

"Brother Ambrose, we have our killers. Why waste time?"

"Humor me, Brother Flavian." Ambrose faced the assembled nuns and monks. "If you dispatch a messenger moth to the mainland to fetch the bailiff, they should arrive a little after sunset. In that time, we may very well decide that these two rats are responsible—or we may find that they are not. But let us use that time to think instead of rushing to judgement."

An aged ferret, her eyes milky and sightless, clicked her teeth knowingly. "Let me guess, Brother Ambrose. You'll investigate?"

"I think it will not unduly distract me from my duties in the garden, Sister Cecilia."

The ferret let out a rasping laugh. "Leave him to his work, brothers and sisters. The rat and mouse can stay locked in the wine cellar until the bailiff arrives. I'll see to the messenger moths." She faced Brother Flavian. "You will have your justice. One way or another."

The badger nodded his head, then clamped a heavy paw on the shoulders of the Schalls. "Don't try anything." He led them away, dragging the smaller creatures across the floor. The monks and nuns parted, murmuring, and making holy gestures as Brother Flavian led Zipporah and Zoya down the hall and to the wine cellar—where they would wait until a boat ride to Kostamare brought them to the executioner's block.

They passed Nathan. Esther put her paw on Nathan's arm as he looked into Zoya's eyes. She stared back—still frightened. What did a thief fear more than being caught?

He gave her a quick nod. A promise that he'd get her out of there. The best he could do.

She returned the gesture and then they were gone.

The holy beasts went about their duties—dazed and shocked. Several whimpered or cried. Brother Ambrose remained, waiting until the hallway was empty apart from him, and Nathan and Esther. Then he motioned for them to follow.

"You know those two, don't you?" Ambrose didn't look at Nathan as he crossed to the door of the abbot's chambers. "Friends?"

"They saved my life, once," Nathan said. "And they're innocent. They're thieves—not killers." Well, Zipporah had used a throwing dagger to devastating effect, but that was different. "And trustworthy. If Zipporah Schall says that she's Abbot Odo's friend, then it's true." Except that Zipporah had made a career out of lying and taught her adopted daughter to do the same. "They are innocent, sir. If you can help them—"

"I intend to," Ambrose explained. "Not for any love I bear them, but for the sake of Abbot Odo. He was a good beast and did not deserve this sort of death. I have had a—checkered past. Abbot Odo did not have to welcome me to this island, but he did. I want his true killer to face justice. You and your friend, the scullery maid, may assist me. The Blessed Beasts know that I could use the help. Besides, I think you're involved."

Esther folded her arms. "How do you know that?"

"Because there is much your little friend isn't telling me." Ambrose winked. "Isn't that right, Nathan of Nestovich?"

Then he went into Abbot Odo's chamber.

+++

He knew.

He knew—Supreme Rodent—how long had he known?

"That's not my name!" Nathan stumbled in after him. "I'm Simon of Smallheim. My father worked in the garden of a baron, but the castle was burned down by the Winterborn— ah, the Hoppites." He looked back at Esther, who gave him a sad shake of her head. She closed the door, and they were in the abbot's rooms, alone with Brother Ambrose.

And Abbot Odo's corpse.

He sat in a chair at his desk in the corner, one heavy paw in front of him, the other dangling to the side. He was hunched over, his head down between his shoulders. If not for the fact that his tiny dark needle point eyes were open and staring blankly, he might just be pausing in his work to think.

But no breath filled his chest.

He was dead.

Ambrose approached him, his webbed fingers brushing over the abbot's garments. "There's no mark of a weapon on him." He looked back at Nathan and Esther. "How did he die?"

He was asking them? Nathan stammered, but Esther spoke up quickly. "It could have been age, perhaps. Taking its toll."

"I think not. Abbot Odo was strong. I spoke with the physician here of the abbot's health when I gave the doctor herbs to ease the comforts of some of our more, shall we say, venerable members. He assured me that our Abbot was in perfect health."

"Then it was poison. It kills without leaving a mark."

"Poison's certainly a possibility." Ambrose pointed to the table beside Odo's bookshelf, well-stocked with the grand and colorful manuscripts that the Abbey di Ecco had made for generations. A small meal waited on a plate, mostly eaten. Bread, honey, and a triangle of cheddar cheese—a bite in the cheese. "Looks like he ate before he met his end."

And there was a poisoner amongst the Laughing Company. Contessa Vivaldi. If she indeed had something to do with this.

"Could there be poison in the food, then?" Esther picked up the crust of bread and gave it a sniff.

"I hope not." Nathan joined her at the plate. "I was eating that. The cheese too."

"The abbot gets his meals straight from the kitchen." Ambrose circled the room, running fingers over the bookshelves, the simple sleeping pallet, and the worn stone walls. "If someone wished to poison him, they'd have to intercept one of the novices who was bringing over his meals or sneak someone into the kitchens—without knowing which morsels would go to the abbot."

"Then how did the poison get into the abbot's meal?"

"Perhaps it wasn't in his food at all." Ambrose stepped back from the table. "Nathan, Evelyn—that's not your name, I take it."

"No, it is," Nathan said. "Evelyn of Smallheim—"

"Esther Essen." Supreme Rodent! She'd just given it away. But she looked happier now, a brisk shake in her whiskers. She curtsied. Somehow, she made a scullery maid's garments look regal. "A pleasure to meet you, Brother Ambrose."

"A pleasure to meet you as well." Ambrose waved to the

abbot. "Now, what do you see?"

Nathan squinted. "A mole." His arm ached and he patted it. "He's at a writing table." This was like someone had told him half the joke, but not the punchline.

"But what, my dear Nathan, is he doing at the writing table?"

"I don't know—he's not writing—"

Esther squeaked. "That's just it. The table is empty. Why would he sit down to an empty table?" She walked closer and leaned out—shuddering a little at how close she was to Odo's body. But her arm went to the desk and tapped it—then withdrew quickly. "It's a reading desk. He must have had something there. Some papers, maybe—but he has no quill and no ink." She looked back, and then at the window carved into the stone and brick above them, casting buttery yellow sunlight on the table. "The light is perfect for reading."

"And yet the book is gone," Ambrose said. "Taken, perhaps, by his murderer." He crossed to the center of the room, pausing by Odo's bedside where a jug of water waited. He scooped up a handful. "It may be otherwise. Perhaps Abbot Odo was poisoned and slumped into the chair because it was closest when his legs could no longer support him. Perhaps he was about to get parchment and quill before the poison took hold. But the book—the missing book—is a single paving stone in a great road. We must find others, and that road will lead us to his killer."

"Where do we find more of these paving stones?" Esther's tail snapped back and forth in excitement.

"The library, perhaps—but Sister Cecilia's busy with the messenger moths, and I'd rather get her help than a novice." Ambrose let the water settle on his forehead and run down his features. "In any case, we should leave so they can prepare Abbot Odo's body for his eternal rest." His dark eyes flashed as water dripped down past his little slit nostrils. "There's something else we can do in the meantime. Find some more paving stones. Now follow me. I'll need to stop by the garden and ask one of the novices to do the day's planting. On the way, you can tell me everything."

"Should we?" Nathan whispered to Esther.

"You should." Ambrose winked. "I'll find out anyway."

"You can't argue with that," Esther agreed.

They walked through the halls, quiet and somber now—the abbey growing still as a graveyard to suit the death of the abbot. Esther hurried to keep up with Ambrose, a shake in her whiskers. She was enjoying finding these clues, trying to piece together what had happened to Abbot Odo—and seemed to be skilled at it too, or at least, she'd made a fair prediction about the desk.

A good thing too. Nathan was flummoxed—especially about where this mystery would take them next.

+++

Brother Ambrose brought them past the gate of the Abbey di Ecco and into the rocky, wild country that formed the rest of the island. All around, the Sunstone Sea gleamed gold in the spring sunlight. The Dark Forest coast lay in one direction, the riotous port city of Kostamare closest. The rest of the Sunstone Archipelago lay in the other, scattered stones dropped from the paw of the Supreme Rodent containing great city-states and sun-sweetened countryside. A land of riches and danger.

But there appeared to be plenty of danger here as well.

Rocky hills and stretches of grass, trimmed with wildflowers, ended at sheer cliffs looking down at the roaring sea. The waves thundered against spires of stone, breaking white and bathing the air in chill mist. A few rocky slopes led down to narrow, unfriendly beaches, the stones darkened by the constant crash of the waves. Nathan and Esther had arrived at a dock on a sheltered bay on the other side of the Isola di Ecco, and the churning of the surf had been enough to make him launch his vomit over the side more times than he cared to remember.

"This way, if you please, Mistress Esther—Master Nathan." Brother Ambrose brought them down a gravel trail winding through the rocky hills, to where a strange house waited on the scrubby grass. A ramshackle collection of stacked stones formed a bulbous lump, firelight dancing through the open door. Stone walls protected a little garden from the wind. "Grobian!" Ambrose shouted as a fresh batch of seaborne air whistled around them. "Master Grobian—it's Ambrose!"

"Ambrose?" A wildcat poked his head out. Some of his fur had fallen away, one ear jutted up and another angled downwards, and his green eyes glowed—wild lanterns. "Get in here, fellow. Quickly!" He shuffled back, revealing a wild patchwork garment assembled from countless colored scraps.

How could this cat help them?

"I've brought friends, Grobian." Ambrose led Nathan and Esther inside. Grobian had a cozy enough house, beyond the stones—a kettle waited over his fire, and he set a variety of colorful trinkets—feathers, shiny stones, bits of driftwood—dangling from his low ceiling. Nathan ducked under them as he stepped inside, and Ambrose had to hunch over completely. "This is Nathan and Esther."

"Kits, eh?" Grobian plopped down on his cot and poked the fire with a stick. "I don't care for young beasts."

"That's rather rude, sir—" Esther said.

"I don't care for old beasts. Or beasts of any age. I hate every creature in this wide world." Grobian poked out his tongue.

"What about me?" Ambrose asked.

"You?" He mewed. "You, I merely dislike."

"Grobian's a sort of unofficial groundskeeper." Ambrose

settled by the fire. "He cares for the rest of the island. In return, we leave him alone."

"Which is all I want," Grobian said. "But fate apparently has other ideas."

A hermit, then. And something had disturbed him. "What do you mean?" Nathan asked. Maybe he'd seen Titus Tarr or his underlings sneaking onto the island, going into the abbey to find their hidden printing press. "Did you see a squirrel in white? Or an evil porcupine dressed as a jester? Or a fancily dressed fox, a poison dart frog, a—"

"Peace, peace." Grobian waved his paw, the claws dancing as they flickered in and out. "All I saw were rats. Two of them. A small one and smaller one." He took the kettle from its post over the fire and let it rest on a waiting stone. "They landed on a little skiff down below the cliffs. Used ropes and grapples to come in and then scaled the abbey walls."

Zipporah and Zoya. That's all he had seen. Nathan's heart sank.

"I tried to warn them, I did. About the cave demons."

"The what?" Esther asked.

"Demons, missy. They that dwell in the caves below the sea." Grobian's ears flicked up. "At night, I hear them. They've crawled up from the underworld and gnash their teeth, roaring and raging as the tide comes crashing on the rocks." His voice rose to a shrill yowl. "Don't you go down there! Don't traipse where the demons tread!"

Esther and Nathan exchanged a look. Demons? They were interesting parts of storybooks, but demons weren't real.

Were they?

"Did you see anyone else coming and going?" Nathan asked. "Besides, the, ah, the demons?"

"Nary a soul." Grobian leaned closer, widening an eye. "As

well I didn't—for the demons would surely have claimed them."

Brother Ambrose stood. "Thank you for your time, Grobian. We must away."

"You be wary of them that dwell in the dark." Grobian picked up his kettle and poured the steaming herbal into a waiting cup. "Be wary, I say." He was growling the words to himself as Nathan, Esther, and Ambrose left and returned to the rocky hills.

They stood together as the sea crashed against the cliffs. Spume rose high, shining in the sunlight—spun gold dancing in the chill air. Nathan patted his wounded arm and tucked his good paw into the pocket of his robe as he looked at the roaring waters. Why were they wasting time talking to a half-mad hermit like Grobian? What had he done but mutter to them about demons?

"What do you think?" Ambrose asked, as they watched the sea crash against the rocks.

"He's a—a unique fellow," Esther said.

"Grobian has suffered," Ambrose said. "But he still cares for the Blessed Beasts and their holy teachings. And he still sees and listens. In his own way. What do you make of his talk about demons?"

"He said they're in the caves." Nathan tugged up his hood for the cold. "But there's no such thing as demons."

"But he must be hearing something down there." Esther looked at Ambrose. "Are there caves under the island?"

"Many sea caves," Ambrose said. "Tunnels too. You see, the Abbey di Ecco used to be a prime target for Lupine Corsairs. Those sea wolves would raid without warning and so the monks excavated numerous tunnels and chambers below the rock, some leading to the sea caves and safety."

"The demons." Esther bounced up and down, squeaking excitedly. "Maybe those are beasts using the tunnels. Making noises that Grobian could hear?" Her tail flicked back and forth and her crimson eyes gleamed. "Brother Ambrose, is there a map of the tunnels? We could see if one leads under this area—if it connects to a cave?"

Beasts in the tunnels. Demons. Was it Tarr's work? And what did it have to do with Abbot Odo's death?

Ambrose smiled. "You've got a very clever friend, Nathan."

"I know," Nathan agreed. "Is there a map like that?"

"If there is, I know one place it would be." Ambrose blinked his dark eyes and tugged up his hood as he turned into the wind. "Follow me."

+++

They returned to the abbey, this time taking one of the winding hallways that passed the great church, the smaller chapels, the scriptorium where some monks still worked their art in copying holy manuscripts by paw, and finally reached the library—one of the grandest chambers that Nathan had ever entered.

It seemed to stretch in all directions, endless shelves containing so many volumes that you could spend your whole life reading and never see the last word. They walked past shelf after shelf, the spines of books done in gold and silver glittering like stars. Ladders allowed beasts to reach books on the top shelves, though some were so high that it would take scholarly mountaineering to get the right volume and make it back to the ground.

"Amazing." Nathan let his paws drift across the spines of a few different books. Most of them were probably rather boring —dealing with matters of worship of the Blessed Beasts—but there had to be a few good adventure stories, chivalric romances, somewhere in the library. More than a few.

"You like books, young Nathan?" Ambrose asked. "It makes sense. You're a character in one."

"Yes, I suppose I am." Nathan let his good arm hang limply. "The Rat on the Road. Bold Sir Squeaky. The Orphan Prince of Tock." He looked at Esther, who had gone ahead in search of Sister Cecilia, the librarian. He struggled to find the right words. "I find it hard to live up to him, sometimes."

"What do you mean? The Rat on the Road, Bold Sir Squeaky, is you, isn't he?"

"He is, I suppose." This sounded absurd. Of course, it was him! "But that Nathan, the Rat on the Road, is never scared. He never gets hurt." He looked at Esther, who waved them toward a table where Sister Cecilia was carefully stacking small books. "His heart—his heart never hurts."

"Ah." Ambrose smiled. He figured it out—of course he did. "But this Nathan does, doesn't he?"

"Yes, sir."

"Well, my boy, there is fiction and real life, and one is always more complicated than the other. We love our stories of heroes and villains. They thrill us and give us hope and move us—but sometimes, there's nothing as important as being a simple, decent creature." He pointed to Esther. "Including accepting the friendship of one who clearly cares so much about you."

And Esther did. She stood by him in Nestovich. She had been his friend from the beginning. Maybe she didn't want to play the role that he'd written out for her in his head—and that was all right.

"Brother Ambrose!" Esther had been talking to the aged, blind ferret. "Sister Cecilia—she knows exactly what we were talking about. A map of the Isola Di Ecco—she's got just the book."

"That I do." Cecilia faced Ambrose and Nathan, a smile making her whiskers dance. "This way." She led them around the table and toward a shelf, walking along with utter confidence. Blind or not, she navigated the library better than Nathan, who nearly tripped over a stack of books waiting to be reshelved. "Tell me, Brother Ambrose, would this particular tome have something to do with the terrible death of our poor abbot?"

"That it might, Sister Cecilia," Ambrose agreed. "But we need to know for sure. What is the book in question?"

"*Historia di Ecco, Volume Two.*" She went to a set of thick books on a waiting shelf, the spines all done in matching stripes of red and blue. "The old abbot conducted an exhaustive mapping of the tunnels and caves beneath our feet. Now, if I'm not mistaken..." Her claw tapped each spine. "Volume Two should be right...here..."

It tapped only empty space.

"Gone," Esther said.

"Yes." Sister Cecilia clapped her paws. "Sister Agatha—bring the records!" A young hedgehog came dashing out, bearing a vast scroll of parchment. Cecilia took it and rapidly spun through the paper, which spilled and pooled on the ground in a papery mass. "There—who last checked out *Historia de Ecco, Volume Two*?"

Agatha squinted. "Why, Abbot Odo did. Just early this morning."

He had checked it out—and then faced his killer a few moments later. "But the book wasn't in his chamber," Nathan said.

"He couldn't have misplaced it." Cecilia's paws rested at her side. She seemed old now and tired—her face full of lines and faded fur. "Not Abbot Odo. And he was so excited to start reading again."

"Start reading again?" Esther asked.

Sister Agatha bobbed her head. "Oh yes. He always loved books, the abbot—but then his eyesight was fading—"

"And he sent away to the mainland for a pair of spectacles

that would help him read." Cecilia sighed. "But he never got a chance to use them, the poor fellow."

"He is with the Blessed Beasts now," Ambrose said. "Free of all the trials and suffering that mark the days of the living. And perhaps, if we are clever enough, we can bring his killer to justice. Thank you for your help, Sister Cecilia." He nodded to Sister Agatha as the old librarian returned to her organizing. "Would you be so kind as to bring me a bowl of water? I'm feeling a little parched, as I often do when thinking. Thank you so much." The hedgehog nodded and scurried off. Ambrose pulled a chair at the nearest table and motioned for Esther and Nathan to sit down. "Now, I believe we know everything we need to know to find Abbot Odo's killer."

"We do?" Nathan asked. "We have a lot of questions. What's making the noise in the tunnels? Why did Abbot Odo check out the book showing all the underground passages in the island? What happened to that book? What poisoned him?"

"And what about the spectacles?" Ambrose asked.

"But there *weren't* any spectacles on his desk."

"Exactly." Ambrose smiled, his dark eyes shining. "Esther?"

"Someone took the book—and the spectacles." She was shaking with excitement, her paws clicking against the scuffed wood of the reading table. "Only the killer could have done it. I don't know why—why would the killer want to steal some reading spectacles?—but that's what happened. Perhaps there was something in the book that they didn't want Abbot Odo to see." She let out a sudden squeak and covered her mouth. "I know who the killer is."

"Who?" Nathan demanded.

"The first person to enter the room, to find Abbot Odo dead and Zipporah and Zoya Schall standing next to them."

Abbot Odo's murderer? Nathan breathed out the name. "Brother Flavian."

"He knew he would find Odo dead when he went to fetch him for morning prayers. He went into the room and saw him—and Zipporah and Zoya. So he blamed them, let them run—and as they escaped—scooped up the spectacles and the book." She pointed to Nathan's clothing. "You can hide a great deal in the folds of a monk's robes."

Sister Agatha had returned with a bowl of water. Brother Ambrose accepted it, soaked both his hands, and bathed his face. Water ran down over his speckled skin like tears, even as he smiled. "Esther, you possess a keen and insightful mind. But can you prove any of it?"

"If we find the *Historia* and the spectacles in Flavian's room," Nathan said. "That'll prove it." A surge of pride warmed his heart. He had helped.

"Then come along, while there is yet time." Ambrose stood. "We must pay Brother Flavian a visit."

+++

Flavian was important enough to have his own rooms, the window of his chamber looking out over the courtyard garden where Nathan began his day. They passed it, turned the corner into the stony hallway, and stopped outside the closed door. Nathan's heart pounded. Was a murderer lurking inside? He shouldn't be afraid—he'd dealt with a true maniac like Smiling Spike and clever killers such as Semyon. But they were open about their evil. Brother Flavian had done his murders in the shadows.

If he was the murderer after all, and they weren't about to accuse an innocent beast.

Esther seemed just as wary. "What exactly do we do?" she asked. "We're not the bailiff, though he should be arriving soon." They'd spent much of the day investigating this mystery and the sun was now cresting gold across the isle's rocky hills.

"I'm aware," Brother Ambrose said. "But we don't need to

catch the culprit. Just ask him questions. If he's the murderer, he'll lie—and then we'll know." He knocked on the door, his soggy hand leaving a wet mark against the wood.

No answer.

"Brother Flavian?" Ambrose knocked again.

No response at all.

"Could he be somewhere else?" Esther asked.

"If so, we're in luck." Ambrose grinned at Nathan. "A chance to snoop. That's what you and young Esther do, isn't it? When we're at prayers or our meals or when you think no one notices?" Supreme Rodent! He knew everything. "Well, perhaps we can peek inside. If we find the *Historia di Ecco, Volume Two*, and a pair of mole's spectacles, then we'll know that Brother Flavian does indeed have something to hide."

"You want us to sneak into his room? That's not exactly pious behavior."

Ambrose shrugged. "I'll make a confession afterwards. Now, how are we going to gain entry?"

This was something Nathan could manage. "I can do that."

He gave them a wave and scampered off, clutching his wounded arm as he rounded the corner. Back into the garden, the colorful flowers growing dim as the sun crept down in the distance. He slipped into the shadows, pressed himself close to the wall, and reached the window. It was open, letting a spring breeze drift inside. Flavian certainly wasn't worried about leaving it open—it was too small, he must think, to let anyone slip through.

He must not know many rats.

Nathan pulled himself over the casement and into the window. He poked his nose first, slipping into shadow, and then wedged in his shoulders. His wounded arm banged painfully against the sill, the solidity behind the cloth jabbing into his belly. But he winced, held his breath, and gave another wiggle. Rats could squeeze through just about anything. Nathan's father told him that often enough: 'the doorway may be narrow, but a rat can get through.' He proved that now, slipping his waist through the window and squeaking a little in triumph as momentum brought him inside.

Then he tumbled down and plopped on the cold stone floor.

He yelped as the flagstones banged against his belly—then went silent. He wasn't alone.

Brother Flavian lay in a simple cot in the corner, his back to Nathan. Sleeping. Oh no—had Nathan's clumsy fall woken him up?

Nathan went to his feet, as quietly as he could. The breath iced over in his throat and cold trickled to the end of each whisker. Still no motion from Brother Flavian. Nathan held his breath. All Flavian had to do was roll over and he'd see Nathan.

Quick—a place to hide. But there was nothing, apart from a simple desk and the bookshelf by the wall.

Wait—what was that on the desk?

Nathan tiptoed closer. His heart thudded in his chest and his stomach had gone hollow—but he had to know. His eyes flicked from the desk to Flavian. Still nothing.

He reached the desk. A book sat there, with a spine of striped red and blue. Nathan knew the title without even looking at it.

Historia di Ecco, Volume Two.

The missing volume, taken from Abbot Odo's desk. Resting on top were a pair of reading spectacles, shining glass within two dark circles. Nathan leaned closer. He picked up the edge of the spectacles and hoisted them up to the fading light streaming through the window.

There, on the bridge that had settled over the mole's nose, was a tiny needle. You had to strain your eyes to see it and if you had poor vision—like poor Abbot Odo—you wouldn't notice it all. Until it gently poked through fur and skin and deposited lethal poison into your veins.

Just like the poison that had sickened Rinaldo in Katzenberg, but a lethal dose.

The work of Contessa Vivaldi. On the orders of Titus Tarr.

Nathan glanced at Flavian again. No motion from the badger. Not even the rising and falling of a sleeping chest.

Oh, Supreme Rodent.

He walked closer and extended his paw. His fingers shook. They settled on the shoulder of Brother Flavian—and there was nothing but cold below his fur. At the touch, Brother Flavian rolled over, eyes staring sightlessly at the ceiling. A dagger had been buried to the hilt in his belly. Little silver bells danced on the pommel, and they made a gentle, merry ringing as Flavian's body settled.

A jester's weapon.

"B-Brother Ambrose?" Nathan raised his voice. "E-Esther?"

Something creaked behind him. He spun around.

The bookshelf swung open on hidden hinges, revealing the mouth of a tunnel. There was a secret passage in the Abbey di Ecco after all. But this wasn't a good way to discover it.

Not when Smiling Spike, his jester costume bloodied and his spiked mace with its ringing bells dancing in his paws, emerged from behind the bookshelf and stood before him.

A grinning, spiky nightmare.

"Hello, Nathan." Spike snapped his teeth. "When I heard the noise, I was confused. The dead don't walk, after all, and I killed Flavian as well as I've killed any beast." He drew closer, his quills clicking against the desk. "Now I find you here, next to the unfortunate monk."

Don't be afraid. Don't back down. "He killed Odo for you?" Nathan posed the question carefully, putting a foot closer to the door. Ambrose and Esther—he had to warn them.

"No, no. Flavian just cleaned up the mess. Vivaldi was able to find the spectacles that Odo ordered and made some minor alterations before they were delivered. The annoying little froggy finally earned her keep." Spike made an exaggerated sigh, rolling his eyes and shaking his quills. "She was supposed to kill your Rinaldo on the stage of the show. Wouldn't that be something? His eyes bulging and spittle crusting his swollen tongue as he dropped dead before the audience. Now, that's a show. That's entertainment!" He passed the mace from paw to paw, making the bells ring. "But no—she thought there'd be no chance of her escaping if she up and killed an actor. So your play went on and you beat Tarr's performance, and he became so very upset. I find him quite tiresome sometimes."

"Why'd you kill Odo?" This was good. Keep Smiling Spike talking—something he clearly loved to do. Nathan reached the door now, pressing his back against it. Just a little more time—a little more and he'd make his escape.

"Odo was about to discover our little secret. Flavian—our pet monk—told us that Odo was researching the tunnels, and he'd catch on soon enough, so he had to go. Now, I had another idea." He hoisted up the mace. "Dance my way in, smash open the skulls of Odo and as many monks and nuns as I could find, tie the others up in their library and burn the place down. Make them sing their holy hymns as they roast." He reached for Nathan. "I didn't get to do that, I'm afraid. But with you—" He rested the mace on his shoulder—ready to swing. "We're going to laugh long and hard, you and I. Tarr promised."

Nathan slammed open the door and darted in the hall—and stopped.

Brother Ambrose and Esther were frozen—held at the point of blades. Reynardine kept his rapier leveled at Esther's face, the blade a deadly, thin line, while Jacopo Draco had a thick arm around Ambrose's belly, his falchion at the monk's throat.

"Don't worry, Nathan!" Spike chuckled as he walked into the hall. "Your friends are invited too!"

"Nathan—" Esther started.

"Not a word from you." Reynardine's rapier sliced her cheek. "You took my eye. I will make you pay before I see you die." Blood shone bright on her fur. Esther gasped and pressed her paw over the cut. Nathan tried to run to her, but Smiling Spike grabbed the back of his monk's robe and tugged him back.

It was Nestovich, burning again. His friends, in danger—and he couldn't help them.

"Not here." Spike pointed back into Flavian's chamber—and the secret passage. "We'll go down. Away from witnesses—and Tarr wants to see it done."

"The monk too?" Draco asked.

"Oh yes, indeed." Spike made an exaggerated gesture, ushering them on. "There are enough laughs to go around."

No chance of escape. No chance of calling for help.

They had solved the murder of Abbot Odo—but it seemed that death was not finished with them yet.

+++

Their captors led them back through Brother Flavian's chambers, Smiling Spike pausing to wrench his dagger from the badger's belly, and then into the secret chamber and down steps hewn into the sand-colored stones. The tunnel dipped low and wound back and forth, cutting into the heart of the Isola di Ecco. Silence mostly, apart from the click of their shoes on the ancient stones—and Smiling Spike, who sang a little ditty and waved his mace to ring the bells in time with his song. He capered along, pausing every so often to look over his shoulder, shake his spiky tail, and smile at Nathan and his friends.

"I truly dislike that porcupine," Esther muttered.

"Not a word, I said." Reynardine yipped.

She gave him a sweet smile. "How's the eye, dear Reynardine?"

He let out a rageful yip and pulled back his rapier, but Draco raised a claw. "Wait. We're here."

The tunnel ended in a cave—a grotto. A stony shore faced the sea, the waves crashing against it. The water rushed out through the mouth of a rocky cave, the open ocean beyond a silvery seascape in the moonlight.

The grotto had been transformed into Tarr's workshop. Docks stretched out into the water, ships waiting an anchor. Torches had been set into the walls, casting shimmering light over the stones. Shadows danced from the fire, playing against the cave walls and ceiling. Laughing Company guards lounged around assorted crates and packing materials.

In the middle of it all, a giant printing press worked tirelessly. A platform slammed down, stamping letters in a dozen languages and blocky pictures on waiting parchment. Further on, bladed machinery snipped the papers into pamphlets, and Laughing Company soldiers folded them and tucked them into the waiting crates, where they would be shipped all over the world. One large stack waited at the edge of the jagged bank, lantern light revealing the Carrion King's grim features.

This was his birthplace.

All thanks to the printing press. Nathan's mother had invented that. She had put all her creativity, her spirit, her love of Nathan and his love of stories, into that machine—and Tarr was using it to spread messages of hate.

For a moment, Nathan wasn't afraid anymore. Only angry.

Titus Tarr stood on the dock with his back to them, his paws set atop a walking stick of white ash. He turned slowly. "The

Blessed Beasts reward the patient hunter." He walked closer, cane tucked under his arm. "Give the quarry enough time and it will come to you."

"We're not alone, you know." Esther glared at Tarr. "We've got allies all over."

"Then I will find them and dispatch them." Tarr looked at Ambrose. "I'm afraid you'll be the first. I apologize, my good monk. I doubt you wanted to get wrapped up in the business of rats—but I can't have you telling the world, now can I?" He smoothed the fur at his chin, sighing—a child given an unpleasant chore. "I'll make sure Smiling Spike doesn't have too much fun."

Grobian had been right. This cave was home to demons.

Brother Ambrose's dark eyes went wide—taking in everything. Then his slick tail slapped out. It upset the stack of pamphlets which toppled down in an avalanche of paper. They caught the sea winds, dancing and shifting—a swarm of snowflakes—before settling into the water. The tide drew them out, streaming white and pale like dead fish, flickering as they drifted through the cave and toward the sea.

"Apologies." Ambrose raised his slim shoulders in a mocking shrug. "I'm a clumsy salamander."

Was that it? No—Ambrose never did anything without a reason. But why upset a bunch of pamphlets? Some last bit of defiance before death? There had to be something more.

Smiling Spike closed in, giving the mace a spin. "Shall I make him pay, sir?"

"We'll put the body in the water," Tarr agreed. "But the Essen girl—I have use for her. Her parents will be here soon and I—"

"What?" Esther asked. "My mother and father—here?"

They had been in Erminium, in the palace dungeons. But Tarr must have brought them here. He had all the Essens now—but why?

"Don't interrupt." Tarr's eyes flicked to her. "Yes—I thought your parents' lives might be useful. Bargaining chips. But now, I have you and you'll be the bargaining chip. Your father, Mistress Essen, will do everything in his power to keep you alive." So that was it. "He still has holdings. He still has power. I'll take them all, as I move to my new castle in the Copperbright Kingdom, where they know how to treat beasts of worth. He'll do it for your sake —and it will destroy him."

"I'm going to destroy you." Nathan spoke quietly. They hadn't mentioned needing him alive—and if all he could do was insult Tarr, then that was fine by him.

But he did have one more card to play.

Tarr gave his tail a shake. "I long ago learned to quell my temper. To think only in terms of logic and cunning. But you, Nathan the Rat, are truly testing me."

"Sir?" Jacopo Draco pointed.

"What?" Tarr glared at him—exasperated at being interrupted.

"There's a ship coming in."

Every looked at the mouth of the cave. A sleek, dark shape slid inside, cutting easily through the water. A little triangular sail caught nighttime winds, oars helping to guide the vessel over the fallen pamphlets, which formed a white trail in the tide. Sweeney stood tall in the prow, gripping his poleaxe. Artemisa De Leon waited next to him, drawing free her rapier as Sir Thomas Mulberry hefted his mace and let out a low, threatening croak which echoed like thunder in the cave. Flammarion worked the tiller, then scampered down to where a curious cannon—an eight-barreled monster known as an organ gun— waited, ready to fire.

"Your little moth, Nathan," Ambrose explained. "I set it free this morning to summon your friends. Thought you could use the help."

And when you truly needed help, it was a grand thing to have friends who would come bearing a lot of guns and swords.

CHAPTER 7. WHEN RATS TAKE WING

Tarr overcame the confusion first. "Kill them!" he cried. "Essen, Nathan, the monk—kill them all!"

Now it was time for Nathan to act.

He drew the dagger out of the sling holding up his wounded arm, then wrenched his paw free and flexed his fingers. In truth, the arm was still sore and ached like boars had been stampeding over the bones. The barber-surgeon from the Orphans would doubtlessly wriggle his whiskers in anger if he knew that Nathan was freeing it—and that he had used his splint and sling to hide his Winterborn dagger this whole time.

But the ruse might help Nathan and his friends stay alive. Any doctor would respect that.

He lunged out for Smiling Spike, hoisting up the dagger with both paws, and drove it down as the porcupine tried to bring up his bell-draped mace. Not quite aiming, his tail lashing out as he sucked in breath and the blade hummed through the air.

It bit into something. Stabbed deep and kept going—before stopping completely. Spike shrieked. Nathan let go of the dagger and stumbled back.

He'd nailed the mad jester's arm to the middle of the printing press.

The whole thing had taken less than a second. Spike stared up, the rasping screech dying on his lips, and gripped the dagger with one hand. Was that a pained grimace fused to his face that kept his teeth in a clenched, awful smile? Or was it mirth? Was he starting to laugh and giggle as he gripped the dagger and worked it free? Tarr was shouting, Reynard and Draco had drawn their blades, and the Beasts-at-Arms of the Laughing Company moved in.

"Nathan!" Esther grabbed his arm and pulled him back toward Brother Ambrose. "We've got to get to the boat!"

He went with her. She was right. They could escape.

But Nestovich was still burning. Death had come again. He didn't know if he could be brave or strong enough to save his friends.

Esther rammed her shoulder into a tower of boxes containing Carrion King pamphlets. They tumbled over and crashed to the floor—children's blocks falling to a swift kick. Wood splintered. The pamphlets rushed out in a blizzard of hateful paper, the Carrion King's snarling skull visage dancing and fluttering through the sea winds of the cavern and forming a temporary paper barrier between Nathan, Ambrose, Esther and Tarr's hired killers.

Saving their lives.

Thunder boomed, loud and long. The sea cave echoed it, the pounding making Nathan wince. The organ gun on the ship, Flammarion working the cannons. Fire blasted into the stony roof of the cave. Chunks of rock rained down, crashing onto the printing press, the paper, and Tarr's soldiers. Nathan peered through the smoke to see the possum working fast, his lean, pink fingers swinging the organ gun around and reloading.

A fancy weapon, a fine toy—but the battle would come down to blades in the end. It always did.

One such blade cut through the falling papers. A thin rapier. "Mistress Essen!" Reynardine rushed through the torrent of pages, followed by Jacopo Draco. The fox had his sword raised, firelight catching the hateful gleam in his remaining eye. "We have much to discuss." Draco hoisted his falchion, forked tongue flicking out—just as ready to kill.

Essen turned, her ears flicking up. Nathan grabbed her paw, and they ran, Ambrose helping them along.

No blade of his own now. Nothing to defend her with.

"You'll not have her!" Sweeney roared louder than the cannon fire. He had jumped from the deck of Fortunate Few's ship, yowling as he descended. The poleaxe hummed down above him, a silver comet. Draco turned to face him, had time to raise his falchion and suck his tongue in a final time before the poleaxe struck down and buried itself in the scales of his head. He dropped and Sweeney wrenched the axe free as more Laughing Company beasts charged to meet him.

A chittering squeak followed as Artemesia De Leon leapt in, landing before Reynardine. She seemed happy enough to join the fray.

Her rapier rushed up, as fast as the fox's blade, and they clashed together with the same terrible speed. Two fire-furred swordsbeasts, battling back and forth across the stones as the sea crashed below and pamphlets danced through the air. Their swords moved with the precision of masters, De Leon parrying, shifting, striking, dancing and matching Reynardine's movements—but this was no fencer's bout, and blood flowed from wounds delivered too swiftly for Nathan to see.

De Leon stumbled back, a scarlet gash marring her sleeve. No hesitation. A flick of her rapier and she was back in the fight.

"Nathan!" Ambrose waved to him as he stood at the edge of the cliff. "Grab a torch, my boy. Whatever they're printing has no place below my abbey." He'd pulled one torch free from its stanchion and motioned to another.

"Right." Nathan hastened to join him, wrenched the torch from its post, and hurled it.

Not his best throw, but it landed next to the spilled pamphlets. Ambrose's torch thudded amongst a large stack of crates.

Dry paper and flickering fire. It caught quickly.

Firelight danced and cast mad shadows over the stone wall. Burning crates gave way and flaming chunks of paper drifted everywhere, painting the air in choking smoke and burning scraps of paper. Nathan tried to breathe, tried to see.

They were doing battle in a dragon's belly.

"Young Master Nestovich!" A croaking voice from somewhere in the chaos. Mulberry. He stood in the prow of their ship, webbed hand extended. Flammarion had sailed closer, and the deck bobbed and danced in the subterranean tide. Close enough to jump—if they could make it. "Come aboard, young sir—and Esther and your salamander friend too! There's room enough for all!"

He didn't need to be told twice.

Nathan dashed for the edge, Esther next to him. He stumbled on a chunk of burning pamphlet, and she caught him, squeaking encouragingly. They scrambled through the fire and the smoke until they reached the edge, Ambrose stumbling along behind them—and then the jump.

Hot wind around them, chaos behind.

Mulberry caught Nathan and Esther by their shoulders. He had real strength in his amphibian arms. "Up you go!" He plopped them down and then helped Brother Ambrose aboard. "And you too, my monkish friend!" Then his wide cheeks spread like a full moon, and he was bellowing over the chaos. "Sweeney! De Leon! Come aboard—we are leaving!" He hopped down to the tiller. "Master Flammarion, give them a parting gift."

The organ gun thundered again.

Nathan didn't look to see if the cannon hit anything. He

crouched on the desk, breathing heavily.

The ship creaked and twisted around on the dark water, making its escape. Tarr was uttering commands back in the grotto—their escape wouldn't come easy.

Nathan made it to his feet, Ambrose and Esther helping him up, and managed to look back. Darkness, burning paper, a smashed, fiery printing press. They'd done some damage.

They'd struck like the paw of the Supreme Rodent—and now they just had to escape.

Sweeney and De Leon jumped through the smoke together. They clattered to the deck—De Leon landing nimbly, despite the numerous cuts staining her orange fur red—but Sweeney dropped hard on his belly. Esther squeaked so loud that Nathan's ears hurt and ran to him. He planted the haft of his poleaxe in the deck and pushed himself up, a paw on his belly. Blood seeped between his claws.

"Sweeney." Esther hugged him. "Oh—oh no."

"Easy there, lass." He coughed. "A cat doesn't always land on his feet."

The tide was rushing out, carrying them to the mouth of the sea cave. The ocean waited before them, the gold of sunset giving way to the silver of night. A little more and they'd be out on the open sea, away from the Isola di Ecco and out of reach of Titus Tarr.

But they were forgetting something.

"Wait!" Nathan sprang up. "The Schalls. Zipporah and Zoya."

Ambrose patted his arm. "No need to fear, young Nathan. Your friends managed to find their freedom without our help."

Sure enough, a rope had descended from the mouth of the cave. Zipporah Schall shimmied down, her small, round furry form outline against the mantle of the night's first stars. She descended with swift, quick and sure movements, her tail dangling below her to match the rope, and Zoya was right above her. The mouse and the rat, working their way down with the sureness of spiders.

Mulberry squinted at them as he worked the tiller. "Friends of yours?"

"Dear friends," Nathan agreed. "Let them aboard."

They sailed through the cave mouth. The Schalls dropped down, Zipporah first—and she caught her daughter—just about her size—in her arms and set her safely on the deck.

Nathan ran over. Zoya was safe. She'd done all she could to protect him, to help him—and he'd paid her back. He had protected her, and her mother too.

Or perhaps they'd protected themselves.

Zoya clasped Nathan's paw. "Sorry, Nathan—we didn't wait for you and your friends to prove us innocent."

"We did, though." Esther looked up from where she clung to Sweeney. "Brother Ambrose can vouch for that."

"That I can," Ambrose agreed. "But I think you were wise to leave when you did."

Zipporah flexed her paws. "I've escaped dungeons—a wine cellar wasn't so hard. Then we heard the noise and came to visit." She waved toward the vessel. "It seems you've got all sorts of friends, Bold Sir Squeaky."

Nathan looked at Zoya's dark eyes, which caught the shimmer of the stars. "I do."

Something crashed into the water, louder than the thunder of waves against the coastal stones. "Except that we're far from safe!" De Leon shielded her eyes from the glare and peered back, her tail a thrashing, worried eel. "Hellfire. They're giving chase."

A great pale shape emerged from further in the grotto. A white ship, far bigger than the little one-masted vessel that the Fortunate Few had brought for the rescue. This one had three masts, the sails extended, and a deck bristling with Laughing Company mercenaries. Cannons protruded as well, jutting out like the tusks of a boar from the front of the ship and ringing the sides.

A warship, powerful and terrible and coming right for them.

Nathan caught the name of the vessel, etched on the hull. The *Sovereign*.

Mulberry sputtered. "What a name. That wretch Tarr thinks himself a king."

"More powerful than a king." Nathan looked to Flammarion, who tugged down a line to extend another sail. "We can outrun them, right? We're smaller. Faster."

"Doesn't work that way, Nathan!" Flammarion rasped. "Bigger sails—more wind—and they've got more guns."

Those cannons fired now. The first two, thundering together and burning through the air. Nathan's ears ached again as one walloped the water and sent up a fountain of salty spray. The other sheared into their side, making a torrent of splinters cascade away. They'd be nibbled up by those guns, or just blasted into driftwood, and Tarr could take his time picking up the survivors.

To kill them. Or to join Esther's parents as prisoners.

"Sweeney!" Esther cried as Sweeney let out a yowl and came to his feet.

"My darling girl." Sweeney leaned on his poleaxe. He took one halting step and then another until he reached the stern of their vessel. Esther's fingers linked with his paw, and he pulled it free. "I've done nothing but fail you." He gripped the haft of the poleaxe, his ears flicking back as his whiskers shook. "I've failed your father. Your mother too. I had a job to protect them—and I didn't." Supreme Rodent—what was he going to do?

"Sweeney, that's not true—you couldn't have—" Esther was

crying now. She reached for his arm and caught only air.

"I'll not fail you again."

He ran to the railing and leapt up, grabbing a rope dangling from the rigging, and kicked off. Wind stirred his fur, and his tail flashed behind him as he hurtled through the air, momentum and the rope carrying him along. The poleaxe shone in the moonlight. Esther was crying, running to the stern like she was going to jump after him. Nathan and Zoya reached her and held her back. Her red eyes misted with tears as she squeaked again and again.

They all knew that Sweeney wouldn't be coming back.

He landed on the foredeck of the *Sovereign.* The Laughing Company soldiers stared at him in surprise for just a moment— and he used that time to swing his axe into the ropes fastening the first sail. The canvas came free, ocean wind twisting it and bunching it up. The *Sovereign* listed to the side, smashing into the edge of the sea cave. Rocks crashed down from the ceiling and spars shattered and broke. The poleaxe struck again and again, chopping apart ropes and other bits of important nautical wood and then spinning around to meet the soldiers who now swarmed him at Tarr's shrieked commands.

Sweeney vanished behind a tide of mercenaries. Nathan tried to peer through the press. A glimpse of Sweeney carving a weasel nearly in half, then braining a stout mole, then slamming his shoulder into a hedgehog.

Reynardine's rapier flashed out and caught Sweeney in the back—the blade driving straight through and bursting out the other side.

And then Sweeney was down, the Laughing Company surrounding him. Their weapons rose and fell.

Esther had stopped crying. Nathan and Zoya sat next to her.

No one spoke for a long time.

"We've got a good current," Flammarion said. "We'll make it to Kostamare. Tarr won't dare an attack on us so close to the city."

So they had made it out. They had escaped.

All because Sweeney had given his life.

They hadn't escaped anything. They hadn't won any war. Esther had started to sob again and slipped into Zoya's arms as Nathan walked to the railing and looked out at the crashing sea and the fading outline of Isola di Ecco. It was Nestovich all over again.

The ones he loved gave their lives and all he could do was run.

+++

Three nights and two days and Esther stayed in her chambers at the Drunken Gull, the seaside tavern they'd transformed into the headquarters for their motley company. Nathan and Zoya brought her meals from the kitchen—good fish stew with fiery Westlands spices—and she took them in silence. A few times, Nathan tried to go in and join her, but Zoya kept him outside.

"She wants some peace. She wants to mourn," Zoya said. "That's something you and I never had. She deserves it."

Down below, the common room of the Drunken Gull now hosted their friends. It seemed the most comfortable place on the Kostamare waterfront, and since it was mostly patronized by pirates, the owners knew to keep their beaks shut.

It certainly looked the part. A ship's wheel dangled from the ceiling, mounted with flickering candles, and old nautical charts hung on the walls. Like everything in the Drunken Gull, they seemed a little soggy.

Mulberry was mourning by getting drunk. He sat at the scuffed bar, the counter and seats made from shipwreck salvage and driftwood, and guzzled tankard after tankard of grog. Nathan gave him a wide berth as he swayed on the seat, his drink waterfalling into his vast open mouth.

He slammed it down. "Here's to you, Sweeney! You were a fine warrior, a better friend, and a truly excellent cat!" He croaked loud enough to wake the dead at the threadbare parrot bartender. "Another, sir—and quickly!"

"You haven't paid for the first six," the parrot muttered.

"I'm drowning my sorrows. I'll pay when they're drowned—now fetch another!"

Nathan and Zoya went to the table in the corner, where De Leon waited with Zipporah. Fresh bandaging, courtesy of Brother Ambrose, formed numerous white stripes on the monkey's fur. She looked as miserable as Nathan felt, her formerly carefully combed mane bedraggled and stained with salt. De Leon pushed a bowl of bread their way and flared her nostrils as Mulberry began a tuneless song.

"Is Flammarion back yet?" Nathan asked.

"Still seeing to business on the docks." De Leon chirped. "Blessed Beasts—if I had just killed that wretched fox, or wounded him, or—or done something—" She clenched a fist. "No. I'm too old for that sort of thing. All the friends I've lost, you think I would know better."

"You fought as well as you could," Zipporah said gently. "You're a legend, Mistress De Leon."

"Aye," De Leon agreed. "And so was Sweeney." She swiveled to the side. "What do you think of that, snowball?"

She had asked Sir Volkbert, who huddled in a booth near the back. They didn't bother tying him up—with no armor and no sword, he had no means of defending himself or escaping. Even a wolverine's teeth were nothing against Mulberry's mace and De Leon's rapier. Besides, Volkbert looked as threatening as a newborn kit still in his swaddling cloth.

Perhaps he was beginning to realize how much pain his

master had caused.

Volkbert just stared at his table and shivered in his tunic.

It wasn't right. "He didn't do anything." Nathan said the words quietly. "Maybe we should let him go?"

"You have a good heart, my boy. It will get you nowhere." De Leon slid from the booth, her paw drifting to the basket hilt of her saber. "Zoya, perhaps you should take Nathan for a walk about the docks. See the ocean. Volkbert may very well have more to tell us about his employer—about his plans, and he just requires the proper persuasion to make him squeal."

Volkbert looked at her, his eyes huge and pink. Frightened—but not surprised.

"No." Nathan was on his feet next. "Mistress De Leon—you're upset. You're angry—but he's not so bad—we don't have to—" Words jumbled together. His tongue had turned into sun-warped driftwood. "It's not what Esther would want."

That stopped De Leon in her tracks.

The door opened and Brother Ambrose stepped in. "Hello there—" He stopped and looked around the room, staring from De Leon to Mulberry, who was muttering some drunken battle song, and then to Nathan, Zipporah, and Zoya. "Am I interrupting anything?"

"Not at all." Zoya smiled weakly. "Come to say farewell?"

"And to give a parting gift." Ambrose joined them, still a little hesitant. He knew their heartache and was calm and pleasant as always. A welcome relief. "I've found passage back to the Abbey di Ecco. I'm lucky enough to have a home and I need to return. But I'd like to give you something—a little memento of our time together." His dark eyes flicked to the stairs. "Is Esther ready to receive visitors?"

"Um." She had still been crying when he'd left her. "I'll pass along your good wishes, sir."

"Please do." Ambrose drew a little book from his coat and pressed it into Nathan's paws. "I think you'll both enjoy this. A volume of herblore. I've been keeping records of herbs and their effects since I started gardening, and this little volume includes some of my favorite bits of research and discoveries."

The pages revealed countless expertly done sketches of plants, berries, fronds, flowers, and grasses, the vegetation captured in elegant swirls and surrounded by close-packed writing. A book about plants? That didn't sound too exciting, but any gift from Brother Ambrose meant a lot.

Nathan set it carefully into the pocket of his cloak.

"Herbs can do almost anything. That's why I've been so taken with my work in the gardens. You don't need to be a mighty adventurer or a wandering hero to get good results from the earth. Patience, gentleness, care, gratitude—and faith. You give that, and you'll find there's no end to the rewards that can come your way." Ambrose looked at the stairs. "I trust you'll remember that, Nathan."

What exactly was he talking about? But Nathan nodded. "I'll try, sir. And thank you. For taking me in and helping me and Esther solve the mystery—and for keeping secrets."

"It was no trouble at all." He patted Nathan's shoulder, the slickness on his webbed hand leaving a watery stain. "For the famous Nathan of Nestovich."

Then he walked away, his robe swaying behind him. Bright sunlight blazed through the door as he joined the throng outside —and held the door for someone else to come in.

Septimius von Stahl.

The ferret had undergone a transformation greater than Nathan could ever imagine since he'd been in his courtly finery in the Ermine Palace. He'd gone from mud-stained, cage-trapped prisoner in the chaos of a Dark Forest battlefield to something else: a smuggler kingpin, and he looked the part.

Von Stahl now wore a ragged cloak and a rough homespun shirt open to reveal the pale fur on his belly, which he'd now draped with a necklace bearing an oversized shark's tooth. A broad-brimmed cavalier hat alive with peacock feathers completed the look.

Von Stahl's clothing choices weren't all that had changed. Since Tarr had ruined him in the Ermine Court, he'd used his connections to forge a smuggling empire, and he'd been more than happy to help Nathan and Esther. It was his careful planning that put them on a boat to the Isola di Ecco, and he'd arranged to keep them here after they'd returned.

"Greetings, my friends—greetings!" He swaggered to the table, pausing to snatch up a chunk of bread. "I've got news."

"What sort?" Zipporah asked.

"Concerning a certain Titus Tarr."

Everyone listened with a new intensity. Mulberry slammed his tankard down and ended his mournful song and De Leon sprang up from her seat. Von Stahl had put out the call since their return, sending out flocks of messenger moths to his allies across the coast, asking for any sign of Titus Tarr and the *Sovereign*. Von Stahl settled down and snacked on the bread, not caring about the crumbs staining his fur. He took his time chewing and swallowing—probably enjoying the audience.

"Well?" Zipporah asked. "Speak, speak, you furry sausage, and don't keep us waiting."

A cough, a rough swallow, and Von Stahl started. "His ship's been sighted at Renzi Cove, the easternmost port of the easternmost island in the Archipelago. Taking on supplies for a decent voyage. My sources say he's bound north."

Volkbert released a sort of half-growling bark. They stared at him. "The Misty Isles."

"What?" De Leon snapped her teeth. "What did you say?"

"The Misty Isles—and the Copperbright Kingdom that rules them." Volkbert stepped from his seat. His head stayed wedged between his shoulders, his eyes fixed on the dusty floorboards. "The Copperbright nobles and merchant princes love Tarr. He's brought them a lot of business—so why shouldn't they? It's given him numerous holdings around the country."

More holdings. More printing presses. If he could reach the shores of the Copperbright Kingdom, he'd find a sanctuary to tighten his stranglehold of the continent. The trade routes would flow from the west to the east, from the Copperbright Kingdom to the Grand Sable Empire and on to the Winterborn Dominion. Cutting right through the now pacified Dark Forest. His wealth would only grow, and rats and mice would pay the price.

"Something else." Von Stahl looked at around. Searching for Esther. "I'm reliably informed that he has two prisoners aboard. Two rat prisoners."

Eleazar and Yelena Essen. He'd brought them along.

Nathan spoke up, the words spilling out of him. "We'll sail after him. We'll stop him."

"So we shall!" Mulberry let out a war cry croak, waving a tankard in the air like a battle standard. "The Fortunate Few will ride to battle once again—and Tarr and all his hirelings will dye the ocean red. Let the winds billow our sails, let courage hoist our blades, and then we'll...we'll..." He trailed off. "We'll sail as soon as the Lady Essen is ready."

"Can I speak with her?" Von Stahl asked. "Is she—is she receiving visitors?" He snorted. "By the Blessed Beasts, that makes her sound like some empress, and not a squeakling child —"

"Hold your tongue." De Leon leaned across the table. "We wait for the Lady Essen's command." Lady Essen? That's what they had taken to calling her and it fit well—even if Esther wasn't there to hear it. "Besides, Flammarion's still seeing about our ship. When we go after Tarr, it won't do to be outgunned." She pointed to the ancient clock in the corner. "I wonder what progress they've made?"

"Perhaps I should go and have a look?" Nathan asked.

It would be better than waiting around here—waiting to give comfort to Esther when she wasn't ready, to try and act like Zipporah and De Leon and be some cunning general waging war against Titus Tarr, when all he felt was anger and sadness and fear.

And he really wanted to see what Flammarion had built.

"A fine idea," Zipporah agreed. "Zoya, go with him. Make sure he doesn't fall into the ocean."

Zoya put up her hood. "I think he'll manage." What? No snide insult? Not even a cutting remark? Truly, she must have become fond of him. "Come along, Sir Squeaky. We'll leave them to discuss their strategy. And Esther—the Lady Essen—could use the time."

They headed for the door as De Leon, Zipporah, and Von Stahl commenced their plotting and Mulberry launched into another song. Volkbert slid closer, standing awkwardly by the door. "Nathan." He swallowed. "I wanted to thank you—and—and to give my condolences. About Sweeney."

Though it was his master who caused Sweeney's death. But the wolverine sounded sincere. "Thank you."

"He was a mighty warrior."

"He was—he was a good beast." Nathan choked back the sob and Zoya patted his shoulder. He couldn't cry. Couldn't let grief claim him. Tarr was still out there, with Esther's parents. Still a danger to every rat and mouse in the world.

Zoya had been right. Beasts like them never had the luxury of mourning.

+ + +

A short walk from the Drunken Gull brought them to the grand harbor of Kostamare. It was a wild place, a sprawling world of dockside alehouses and gambling dens facing a forest of masts and sails. Nautical trade and piracy fueled Kostamare and sailing beasts streamed into the taverns and dice rooms where they drank and brawled with the same irrepressible energy. Nathan and Zoya skirted one such melee, a sea otter and a river otter wrestling together in the shadow of a sailor's inn while a surrounding crowd cheered and took bets.

Zoya pulled Nathan to the side as the river otter kicked his seaborn counterpart and sent him rolling across the wharf, right past them, and into the water with a splash. "Careful there, Nathan." She waved aside a squawking seagull merchant pushing along a wheelbarrow of suspicious-looking half-submerged oysters. "Kostamare's a tough town."

"I've known a few of those." You couldn't find much worse than Stenchtrench, the slum of Katzenberg. "I'm betting you have too."

"It's all I've known."

What sort of life had she led? He hadn't really thought about it before. Zoya Schall was an orphan, just like him, and while he had found shelter and safety in the home of the richest rat in the Grand Sable Empire, she had been adopted by a queen of thieves. Thanks to a twist of fate, his adventures—mangled though they might be—were famed worldwide. Maybe Zoya deserved that kind of fame? No wonder she'd been a little rude with him when they first met.

But he was glad she was his friend now.

"This way." Zoya led Nathan down a rickety pier. "My mother took me to have a look at your possum friend's work when we first arrived. Prepare yourself, Nathan—he's outdone himself."

They reached the vessel, and it was certainly the strangest

ship he had ever seen. It seemed like a slightly shrunken version of the surrounding ships, with two masts supporting proud sails—but that's where the similarities ended. This ship had a stooped foredeck, which seemed like it was so low it would dip under the water during sailing. The stern jutted up like a scorpion's tail, an assortment of carpenter beavers working hard to hammer wood into place while hired otters prepared the rigging. But the strangest part was the back. A great wooden wheel rested in the water, dripping with sea spray, like some huge, coiled tail. To make it even stranger, the whole of the ship had been painted in shimmering white and red stripes, apart from its gilded name.

The *Fortune.*

Flammarion scampered across the gangplank, popping in a new pair of spectacles. "Nathan and—Zoya, was it? Well, what do you think?" His pale ears flicked back as his mouth opened, sharp yellow teeth catching the sun. "The paddlewheel's my own invention. Ups the speed considerably. And in terms of armaments—"

"You don't have any cannons," Zoya said. Nathan hadn't even noticed.

"Cannons? Pah!" Flammarion spread his pink paws. "Loud, clumsy, stupid things. Who needs them?" They had used an organ gun last time, but Nathan didn't bring that up. "We don't want to sink the *Sovereign.* We want to board it, to rescue Lady Essen's parents, and leave them crippled and floating in the water. For that, I've got just the thing."

They followed him to the gangplank, heading for the deck of the bizarre ship.

"Call me St. Nicodemus. I've brought gifts for the good little kits and cubs, even though it's far from Winter Night." He pointed to a set of giant sticks, each tipped with lean paper packages ending in conical points. "You know what those are? Rockets. My own design." He beamed, a proud father. "These are more than fireworks to be set off on festival days. They pack a punch, and that's only—" An annoyed rasp. "Put that down!"

Zoya had hoisted up a crossbow, with a strangely bulbous bolt mounted on the string. It seemed about the size of an apple, composed of dark metal wrapped round with cloth. She did as she was told, placing it gently next to a bundle of similar bolts, and held up her paws with overstated caution.

"Explosive bolts," Flammarion explained, a mad twinkle in his eye. "That'll help in the boarding. One shot to the mast and they're dead in the water."

"Supreme Rodent," Nathan whispered.

"And that's not all." Flammarion walked around the barrels, revealing another set of devices set evenly on the deck.

Bizarre harnesses of leather and wood, topped with sections of canvas held aloft by struts. Were they weaponry of some kind? Armor that couldn't stop a simple club? They seemed too small for an adult to even wear.

Flammarion knelt, fiddled with one device, and the canvas toppings snapped out and extended.

A pair of wings.

"Fledermaus Flyers, I call them." He stood. "Flying machines."

This was beyond amazing. A flying machine? It would be like taking to the sky on the back of a dragon. A sorcerer would conjure up something like that. But Flammarion was a sorcerer, who worked with alchemy and clockwork to cast his spells.

"I can't manage to offset the weight of heavier creatures, but a rat kit might use them." Flammarion jabbed a finger at Nathan. "Don't get any ideas. They're not ready. After this little misadventure is over, we'll go somewhere safe, and you'll take on the role of my apprentice again. Then, once I'm certain you won't go sailing to your death, we'll see if I can make you properly fly."

He hesitated, strangely nervous. "Would you like that?"

All Nathan could do was nod silently.

Zoya went to her belly and sniffed at the Fledermaus Flyers. "This is wonderful. This is what we need—but we need more. We've got a ship, but we need a crew. We need soldiers."

Flammarion grinned. "Have a look. You've got your wish."

Goat hooves and pounding feet clattered on the wharf. The beavers and otters stopped their work. Everyone looked up as an army emerged. Ragged, weary, battle-hardened, with their wagons splintered, their uniforms tattered, and their harquebuses and weaponry on their shoulders, the Orphans had arrived. Captain Uttz led them, riding a gray goat.

Niko Nikaros marched along at her side.

A raised fist from Uttz stopped the Orphans. "We hear you're going after Tarr," Uttz said. "Got room for a few Dark Foresters?"

Nathan hurried to the gangplank and ran to Niko. They clasped paws and embraced.

"I came as soon as Sweeney's moth found me." Niko grinned. "Where is the old cat?"

He had to tell him. His mouth opened—but the words didn't come.

But that was enough. "Oh." Niko's grin vanished. "Well. That's the price we pay, you know." He looked back at Uttz. "Esther, the Pale Maiden, needs us."

"The Lady Essen," Flammarion corrected.

"Aye—and we'll fight for her." Captain Uttz's ears extended. "Where is she?"

Esther hadn't even been talking to Nathan. Was she ready to discuss strategy? But what choice did they have? The *Sovereign* was sailing closer and closer to the Misty Isles with every passing moment. Tarr was getting away. They had marshaled their forces, and their ship was nearly armed and ready.

It was time to finish the fight.

"We'll go back to the Drunken Gull," Nathan explained. "That's where she's staying. I'll fetch her and—"

"Nathan." Zoya tapped his shoulder. "She's beaten you to it."

As always, Esther was one step ahead of him.

She rode on the Empress's mouflon, sitting tall in the saddle. She wore fine traveling clothes, purchased in one of Kostamare's most exclusive tailoring shops, and every hint of mourning, fear, and sadness was gone. Esther looked like a statue of a hero, standing tall and proud before an unconquered castle. Her white fur shone in the sunlight and her ruby eyes glowed.

She was the Pale Maiden—regal and commanding.

Artemisia De Leon, Zipporah Schall, Sir Thomas Mulberry, and Septimius von Stahl, walked behind her, weaponry at the ready. Sir Volkbert trudged along too, with his paws bound. Even Emperor was there, trotting along with his tusks raised proudly.

The Orphans watched her silently, as did the beavers on the *Fortune*.

No one spoke.

Esther faced them. "Tarr has wronged all of us. For no reason but greed, he has hurt us—and he will pay." Her ears flicked back and her voice, high and calm, carried over the crash of waves and the sounds of the port. "We're going after him. For my family. For revenge." Nathan's heart pounded. She wasn't at all like the kit who had asked him to skip his schoolwork and play in the forest just a few weeks ago. "For a better world. We sail at dawn."

Every beast cheered. Nathan did too.

+++

Good weather and calm seas sped them on their chase after the *Sovereign*. The *Fortune's* bizarre paddlewheel played its part too, churning away—a creaking, groaning organ that cast up wild bursts of water but propelled them along at a decent rate. The coast was never far, but soon they had left the Sunstone Archipelago and reached the shores of the Argent Empire. Cold winds scoured the deck, bringing sheets of spray, and Nathan thanked the Supreme Rodent for his good cloak and the scarves and knit cap that Esther had bought for him. If only the seasickness didn't send him sprinting to the railing to hurl his lunch into the churning surf every few hours, it wouldn't be so terrible.

Up in the crow's nest, it was even sort of cozy.

Nathan sat there as the sun set in the distance, reading the book of herblore by lanternlight. A blanket, courtesy of Zipporah Schall, kept away the night's chill. Brother Ambrose's book was fascinating. Herbs could cure a toothache, instill instant sleep, burn for hours to create fairy lights, and make many more miracles.

If only he had some on the ship that could help with seasickness.

Zoya poked her head up through the trapdoor. "Had a feeling I'd find you up here." She hauled herself up and joined Nathan, far above the deck and the water. "Your friend Lady Essen's keeping busy." She pointed down to the quarterdeck, where Esther stood next to Mulberry and Captain Uttz.

"I know." He hadn't talked to her much since they sailed. He hadn't had the chance.

"Everyone calls her the Pale Maiden now. Or Lady Essen. She's not a noble—far less pompous—but I guess the name's stuck." Zoya accepted some of the blanket from Nathan and tucked it over her shoulders. "She's living up to the role of a legend."

"Better than me." Nathan marked his place and carefully closed his book.

"I don't know if she wants to." Zoya's oversized ears flicked upward. "Do you want to?"

"I don't know." He folded his paws, cold from the ocean seeping through his fur and clinging to his bones. "Maybe I'm tired of being the Rat on the Road. Maybe I want to be myself —but maybe it doesn't matter what I want. The character of Nathan, Bold Sir Squeaky, the Orphan Prince of Tock—he's strong. But me? I'm not. I couldn't save Esther's parents, or Sweeney, or Nestovich, or—" He stopped suddenly. "I'm not strong enough to save Esther."

Zoya looked at him for a few moments as the waves sloshed against the hull. "You think too much, Nathan. I'll tell you what Esther Essen needs: a friend. And you can do that just about as well as anyone."

"What about you? Do you need a friend?"

A dismissive squeak. "I have my mother and the road. That's more than most rats get."

"That's sad."

She smiled at him, the flash of her teeth white and sudden. "I can see why you have so many friends, Nathan of Nestovich."

They sat together for a little while, watching the ocean, and then Nathan worked his way down the mast and left her to play lookout. Not an easy journey, but he put paw after paw and managed it. Climbing up that cage on a pole on the Dark Forest battlefield had been far harder. Soon enough, he had the solid, rolling deck under his feet. He passed Mulberry and Niko, who were examining assorted bladed weaponry, and went to join Esther on the quarterdeck.

He stood next to her. Neither said much.

"How's your seasickness?" Esther's eyes stayed fixed on the dark horizon.

"Better, I suppose. Zipporah cooked me up some soup, and that's helped, I think." He smiled. "It still feels like there's a storm in my stomach, though." He wrapped his cloak tighter around him as the wind coursed over the sea. "I don't think that will make it into the next volume of *The Adventures of Nathan the Rat.*"

"Probably not." Esther matched his grin. The same Esther as before, for just a moment—not the Pale Maiden. Then she hesitated. "You held a special place in your heart for me, didn't you?"

Oh Supreme Rodent—not that!

The storm in Nathan's belly transformed into a hurricane. He had the urge to make a run for the railing and abandon her. Instead, he managed a little nod.

Esther's red eyes gleamed. "And I—I do not feel the same way about you."

"How did you know how I felt?"

"It was, well, rather obvious." She sighed. "I'm sorry. Did what I said—did it hurt?"

"Just a little," he admitted. "But I still get to be your friend, don't I?"

"You do." She offered her paw. "And I'm grateful for it."

She wasn't the Lady Essen now. She was Esther. Nathan clasped her paw.

Loud chattering came from the crow's nest, followed by the ringing of a bell. It was the Artemesia De Leon, dangling from a line as Zoya worked the bell endlessly. The ringing echoed over the ship and all conversation ended, paws slid toward weapons, and feet pounded across the deck as the sailors ran to positions.

Every knew what it meant.

"The white ship!" Flammarion cried. "The *Sovereign!*"

Mulberry had reached the tiller. "What do we do, Lady Essen?"

She hurried to the quarterdeck, Nathan joining her. "Raise the sails. Work that paddlewheel. We chase them and finish them."

It was time. Battle would rage on the sea.

Either the Essens would be reunited, or the ocean would claim them all.

+++

On land or sea, battle had the same slow and tedious pace. The *Fortune* roared through the choppy water and first drops of rain. Nothing to do but check weapons and wait. Nathan wore a good short sword and a matching scabbard from the Orphans' armory. It had a hilt and pommel shaped like a goose, so that Jan Hoppensen would never be far from an Orphan's arm. A gift from Niko since he lost his Winterborn dagger—he hadn't had time to pull it free from Smiling Spike's paw. He clutched it tight and waited while he stood with Esther, Captain Uttz, Mulberry, and the Schalls by the tiller.

That was all he could do.

Finally, they were close enough. The *Sovereign* was sailing ahead of them, all sails billowing in the rushing wind and falling lines of rain. A white wake followed the white hull. They weren't stopping, weren't coming about to use their cannons, though Nathan could make out beasts darting into place on top of the deck. No, Tarr had nothing to gain with a battle in the water, where the results were uncertain. Better to flee to the Copperbright Kingdom and put his allies to use.

Except they wouldn't let him.

The rockets roared to life. They had been arrayed in a sort of giant candelabra before the quarterdeck and they rushed out in a fiery torrent. Smoke seared the air, dark charcoal lines flowing over the crashing waters—and then the explosions. Some rockets struck the sea and cast up torrents of water, but others blasted into the sails and rigging and deck of the *Sovereign*.

Wounding her. Slowing her.

"Now we close in," Captain Uttz said. "And let our blades and paw-guns do the work."

Esther didn't say anything. Instead, she pulled open the crate near the tiller. Inside, the Fledermaus Flyers waited. What was she doing? Nathan hurried to her side as she plopped one Fledermaus Flyer over her shoulders and snapped open the wings. It looked absurd, a mad beast's costume that wouldn't be out of place in a carnival parade.

Then she grabbed the crossbow with explosive bolts and hooked it to her belt.

"Esther!" Nathan scrambled over to her. "What are you doing? Flammarion—he said those aren't ready—they haven't been tested—"

"Keep harquebus fire on their decks, Captain Uttz." Esther's commands came crisp and calm—a confident general. She pulled herself onto the railing, the wings clumsy on her back. "Mulberry—bring us in as close as you can. I'll land, sunder their masts, and find my parents. Cover us as we make our way back to the deck and then to our ship."

Right into danger—Supreme Rodent, she couldn't!

But Captain Uttz nodded. "Leading from the front. Just like Bunzika would." She saluted. "Blessed Beasts guide you, Pale Maiden."

"Esther—" Nathan squeaked.

"I wanted to be a legend—like you." She tensed her legs. "Not sure if that's true anymore, but I don't have a choice. Stay safe, Nathan of Nestovich."

Then she leapt off the ship.

For a terrible moment, she dropped down, plummeting toward the ocean, and then she was up, the wings catching the air and sending her skyward in a mad glide through the silver rain. Another volley of rockets streamed through the sky above her and she wove through lines of smoke before arcing upwards and dropping right onto the deck of the *Sovereign*.

Where she vanished.

"Fighters to the side!" Mulberry didn't hesitate. "We'll do her honor today!"

The sailors heeded his command and *Fortune* creaked as it swung to the side. Now, the *Sovereign* had given up trying to run. It was fight or die. Everyone knew it. Her cannons extended and opened fire, sending up gouts of smoke that blanketed the rainy sea in gray gauze. Hard to see anything on their ship—or much of anything at all in the gathering storm.

Some luck. But not much of it.

A cannon ball rushed in, screaming, and then a sudden explosion somewhere in the prow of the *Fortune*. Shattered wood and screaming beasts. The clatter of harquebus fire followed as the Orphans worked their guns, adding to the mad music of seaborne war.

Nathan looked at the ship and then at the Fledermaus Flyers. Two left in the crate.

Zoya caught his eye. "Oh, Supreme Rodent!" She reached for him. "You're as big a fool as she is!"

And it was foolish—but Esther was his friend, and he needed to help her. Nestovich couldn't burn again.

He grabbed the Fledermaus Flyer and squeezed his arms through the harness. Snapped the buckles into place. Zoya was shouting something at him, her words stolen by another peal of thunder from the *Sovereign's* cannons. The leather straps bit against his shoulders. A punch of a button and the wings snapped to life. Flammarion was a grand engineer. He wouldn't make a flying machine that came apart and dropped him right in the ocean. Or splattered him across the hull of the enemy ship— would he? Besides Esther had made it across.

So at least one of the Flyers worked.

No time to think. He ran to the railing, banging a wing against the tiller. Mulberry croaked and reached a paw to stop him, but he kept going. Then he hopped up, pulling himself onto the railing as a storm started churning in his gut. He risked a look back. Zoya was reaching into the barrel. Was she getting a set of wings for herself?

Then he slipped on the rain-slicked wood and dropped.

The world screamed past him. The ocean waves rushed up, cold and dark and hungry. Sea spray stung his eyes and clung to his fur. He squeaked louder than the cannon fire.

The wings caught. A pair of talons grabbed his shoulders and hauled him skyward—a giant bird of prey, dragging him toward doom. His heart pounded to match the match the churning sea. Wind tore at his face, salt stung his eyes, and when he opened his mouth to scream, rainwater surged down his throat, chilled his tongue like ice, and punched him in the gut.

It wasn't nearly as fun as he thought it would be.

The hull of the *Sovereign* was coming up. A white wooden wall, split with cannons. One boomed away and the cannonball rushed past him, the whine putting an ache in his ear.

The wind made him spin to the side.

Nathan tugged at the little lever, flailed with his tail, trying to right himself. He couldn't fail—couldn't go into the sea or smash into the hull. He had to be the hero rat.

Bold Sir Squeaky—the Rat on the Road.

A final twist, so hard that his bad arm felt like it would break again, and he leveled out.

Just as he reached the deck of the *Sovereign*.

His feet slid down. Struck a bit of rigging and tangled up, and then he dropped down, the world going upside down like he was a particularly clumsy bat—before he plummeted onto the deck.

The thin wooden struts snapped. The wings lay limp and soggy below him.

Nathan sucked in air. No time to rest. Find Esther—find her parents—get back to his ship. He had to be like the Nathan of the stories now.

He pulled his arms free from the harness and rolled away. Made it to his feet.

There was chaos all around. A fire had started near the stern, burning bright despite the rain. The Laughing Company ran to the railing to meet the Orphans and the Fortunate Few as the *Sovereign* and the *Fortune* careened closer and closer. No sign of Tarr or Smiling Spike, though.

But there was Esther.

She'd cast aside her wings as well and was hurrying up the deck, running toward a set of double doors built below the quarterdeck—the way to the interior of the ship. Nathan drew his short sword and ran after her. "Esther!" he called her name as she slid to a stop. "We're going in, right? To get your parents?" He clutched the Orphan blade tight. "I'm going with you."

A smile on her face. She hoisted up her crossbow, one of Flammarion's special bolts on the string. "And I'm glad to have you at my side. Now, do me a favor and duck."

He did. The crossbow twanged. The bolt whined over his head, and he spun around to watch it speed upward, vanishing in the darkness and rain. Had she missed?

No—Esther had practiced well in the forest outside her home.

The explosion in the middle mast proved that. A great gout of fire coated the rigging, sail, and mast. Burning splinters and strips of sailcloth joined the tumbling rain, cascading down and covering half of the *Sovereign*. The fire everywhere was matching the ship now, steaming and burning like they'd sailed into an oven.

"Now, we get my parents." Esther reached for the door—but it opened first.

Reynardine stood there, his rapier drawn. Esther reached for another bolt as Nathan hastened in with his sword, but the fox's fancy boot lashed out first. He kicked Esther in the gut and sent her sprawling back on the deck. She slid back, landing next to Nathan. Fear flashed in her red eyes. She was a kit once again.

"You have come to me, yes?" Reynardine drew his rapier. Behind him, bells jingled. "Look at this, Spike. The little rats—we do not even have to seek them out. They have found us."

Smiling Spike emerged next, hoisting up his mace. The bells rang. He smiled. "What a wonderous bit of luck."

Nathan swung the sword. Spike's ringing mace crashed against it as the *Sovereign* and the *Fortune* did the same. A good blow, one that Sir Konrad would be proud of. The metal rang out, clear and true, and Smiling Spike even shook his quills in distress —but then he brought his mace down again and again. Rapid chopping motions, striking like thunder, and Nathan couldn't match the speed or the strength. He parried, stepped back, slipped on the deck—and caught a blow from Spike's fist that dropped him hard to the deck.

The mace came down again. He rolled, got out of the way, scrambled to a crouch. Spike was laughing. Playing with his food.

Next to him, Esther had blocked Reynardine's rapier with the crossbow—but she was losing that fight too. Beyond her, battle raged all along the edge of the deck as the Orphans, the Fortunate Few, and the Laughing Company fought above the sea. No cannons, rockets, or harquebuses now. It came down to blades, to clubs, to claws, and teeth. Lightning carved through the sky, bold and terrible, and painted everything in grim white for just a second before giving way to rain, darkness, smoke, and fire.

He slashed blindly at Spike, making him step back, and started for Esther—but he slipped. He wouldn't make it. Smiling Spike stomped on his leg, pinning him in place.

"Leave him be!" The shout came from the sky. A shadow cut through the fire and two boots rammed into Smiling Spike's face and sent him stumbling away.

Zoya landed in her Fledermaus Flyer, next to Nathan. He looked at her through the firelight.

"You came to rescue me?"

"Somehow had to." Zoya snapped the wings shut. She at least had managed to land without breaking anything. "Now, let's get Esther—"

She squeaked. Reynardine had grabbed Esther's throat and hauled her up, his rapier poised as she struggled.

A lean shape emerged from the battle. "Fox!" Niko's voice. "You cut down Sweeney, didn't you? Or you helped?" He slid through the battle, running toward them.

Reynardine looked up. "I've beaten him and many more." He tossed Esther down and spun to face Sweeney, expertly hoisting up the rapier. "I'll add you to the list."

"I would take you up on that challenge, friend." Niko hoisted up his harquebus. "But I'm tired."

The gun thundered. Reynardine's body twisted back, his fancy sword tumbling away as he crashed back. He seemed to gain a bit of flight himself, tumbling away and slamming into a set of barrels lashed to the sundered mast. His body crashed against them, wood splintered, and a barrel tilted to the side. Black powder spilled out, more joining the deck as the barrel rolled.

"Run!" Zoya was grabbing Nathan's arm—and reached for Esther. "That's gunpowder—"

It struck one of the fires dancing on the deck and then the

whole world vanished in smoke and flame.

+++

Everything was cold. Nathan's eyes flickered open. Nothing but black smoke, black water and pouring rain. Saltwater was so thick on his tongue it seemed like he was drinking the ocean. There wasn't a bit of him that wasn't soaked through and aching. He'd landed on a chunk of wood, which bobbed and floated in the water. Chunks of wood, some still burning, floated, and danced around him.

No ships. Nothing but the sea.

Zoya. Esther. Niko. He needed to call them—but he couldn't speak. He didn't have the strength.

Then something grunted from the shadows. A friendly oink. He looked around.

Emperor. The piglet paddled toward him, managing the water with the same grace that he showed on land.

Well, maybe a little clumsier.

He reached Nathan. A push from his snout plopped Nathan onto his back.

Nathan's eyes had managed to adjust—just a little. A scrap of mottled brown fur, ahead of him, swimming in the water. "Emperor." He whispered and gave Emperor a gentle push. Emperor swam along and they drew closer, pushing aside the flotsam as waves and rain drenched them.

Zoya—floating on her back. Still breathing.

Nathan pulled her onto Emperor's back, and they continued, as the sunrise revealed a craggy beach in the distance.

CHAPTER 8. THE LAST WORD ON MICE AND RATS

Somewhere in that black ocean, with the rain coming down like daggers, the surf crashing against poor Emperor's flanks, and the darkness broken only by burning chunks of broken ships, Nathan slipped away into the relief of unconsciousness.

Only for the nightmares to come again.

Somewhere, Zoya's grip on his paw and Emperor's determined squeals faded away, replaced by burning and screams. Nestovich, again. His parents, his friends—he hadn't been strong enough to save them then, and he wasn't now. Esther was gone, the Fortunate Few had vanished somewhere in the wreckage, and all the beasts who had shown him kindness were wiped away.

All because they had stuck with him.

When true darkness stole even that away, it was a relief.

Something warm played on his fur. His eyes flickered open. A sky, clear and blue—the kind of spring sky that you only see after a terrible storm. A rainbow stretched in the distance, half-lost in the clouds. Nathan blinked a few times, rolled over, and coughed an ocean's worth of saltwater and gunk into the sand. He stumbled to a crouch.

Emperor sat on his flanks next to him, munching placidly on gathered shore grass. He rubbed his snout against Nathan, squealing in delight and jabbing his hooves happily into the sand. That brave boar had carried Nathan and Zoya through the ocean, saving their lives. They must not have been too far from the shore—of where exactly, Nathan didn't know—but it was still a phenomenal feat.

Sir Konrad's warboar could do no better.

+++

Nathan hugged Emperor. "Good piglet. Very good piglet." His words came out as a raspy whisper.

Feet crunched in the sand. Nathan looked up.

Zoya walked across the beach, a waterskin slung across her shoulder. She looked how Nathan felt—waterlogged, exhausted, broken, with seawater transforming her fur into a bristly disaster and a beleaguered sway with each step.

Still, she brightened when she saw him, and hurried over. "Nathan! You're awake. Thank the Supreme Rodent." Zoya pressed the waterskin into his paws. "Take this. It washed up, along with a few other things." She waved to a mass of flotsam—or was it jetsam?—cast up by the waves lapping at the shore.

He accepted the water and drank greedily. Good, clear water, without a trace of salt in it. He emptied the waterskin without thinking and let it drop to the sand, then collapsed on his back and breathed the clear air.

"Are you feeling all right?" Zoya asked.

"I—I think." He sat up and walked to the detritus that Zoya had gathered. "Where are we?"

"Your guess, Sir Squeaky, is as good as mine." She gestured with a tired paw at the beach. The gravely dunes ended in a curtain of shore grass, which gave way to dense forest. Morning mist curtained the trees, which stretched into the distance. "Could be the Argent coast. Or maybe we reached the Misty Isles after all. I suppose there's one way to find out."

"Are you feeling up to traveling?"

"Are you?"

He patted Emperor's side and stood. "We'll take turns riding. We'll make it."

"There's one thing you'll want to bring." Zoya passed him his short sword—the Orphan blade. "If we're in the Misty Isles, in the Copperbright Kingdom, we'll need to be careful. Not many rats or mice around here, after all. So be ready."

"Just in case," Nathan said.

"Just in case."

He'd lost the scabbard but tucked the blade into a loop in Emperor's saddle.

Then they set off, leaving the beach, and crossing under the trees, taking turns in Emperor's saddle while they rested. Soon enough, both walked along on foot. It was at least sort of nice to stretch his legs, to feel grass under his sodden and tattered boots as the sun dried them, and to wander under mossy boughs in a sunlit wood filled with the music of buzzing insects.

Soon enough, they reached a road. Not much of a one, more a stretch of gravel, but it was the best they could find. Nathan went onto Emperor's back and stretched out. Was that smoke creeping up in orderly little puffs over the tops of the trees? Maybe it was a town. No—too small for a town. A village.

A place to go.

They took the road. Zoya sang a little as they walked, an old rat lullaby that mingled with the insect hum and the rush of water. Nathan settled back in the saddle and Emperor carried him along. He was tired after all.

Zoya tapped his leg. "Nathan—someone's up ahead."

They turned a corner and found a rickety wooden bridge crossing a deep canyon split with a torrential, waterfall-fed stream. The water surged and crashed below them, white and wild as it flowed out toward the sea. The poor bridge had seen better years, with splintery edges, gaps in the planks, and one railing completely missing. How much more weight could it take before it cracked completely and sent its occupants tumbling down to their doom in the rocks below?

Right now, that occupant was a hedgehog in a broad-brimmed hat, tugging fruitlessly at the reins of a sick mud-brown goat pulling a wagon of potatoes. He looked back at them, his quills shaking. "Can you offer me some help? Blessed Beasts, I beg of you!" A Misty Island accent, but a more rural twang than the studied upper crust tones of Sir Thomas Mulberry. "My poor Lucky's sick, he is, and trapped us over Foulberry Falls!"

A bad situation. Nathan swung down from the saddle. "What's wrong with him?"

"Nathan." Zoya lowered her voice. "Is it really our business? Tarr's still about, for all we know. We ought to play it sneaky."

That was smart, but the hedgehog's voice was quivering, and the poor goat was hacking and coughing, shaking his horns as his wild eyes flashed back and forth. He knew what Esther would want, and Sweeney, and his parents.

"It will just be a moment." He hurried to the edge of the bridge. "Sorry—is he sick?"

"Aye. Swallowed something that disagreed with him." The hedgehog smoothed down the goat's scraggly white fur. "I shouldn't be asking for assistance from some kit on the road. It's all right, lad. Maybe we can try and pull Lucky through—but watch yourself. Foulberry Bridge has been weak for years, and too much weight will—"

"Hold on." Nathan dug into his coat. There—the book of herblore. He drew it out and flipped through the pages. They were waterlogged and some of the ink had turned into dripping, illegible swirls. It was like trying to read the waters in a storm. But the covers had been made of some waterproof material, and there was enough left to find what he needed.

He peeled wet page after wet page and then he found it.

"Zoya—do you see any of this sort of flower?" He held it up. "Demon's Kiss it's called? It's native to the Misty Isles and—"

She scanned the side of the road and pointed. "Is that some?"

Green stalks with yellow flowers flicked with orange—little miniature suns. Nathan dashed over. It might be Demon's Kiss. It might be something else.

He tugged a bundle free, his paws clumsy. Three flowers, ripped out at the roots. That would do. Then Nathan dashed back to the bridge, slipped over a half-broken plank, and went to the goat. A splinter came free below him and tumbled down into the water.

"Be careful, young sir." The hedgehog farmer clutched his hat. "The bridge, you know—what have you got there?"

"I think this might work." He held the flowers out toward the goat. "Come on. Eat up. Please?" He jabbed them closer. The goat looked at him with pained eyes. He might be sick—but he was also hungry. His muzzle curled back and his teeth tore into the Demon's Kiss flowers. Petals rained down on Nathan's feet as the goat munched away. He gobbled up the flowers and the stalks too.

Then his ears flicked back, and he bleated miserably.

The farmer stepped closer to Nathan. "What's that supposed to do then?"

"Um." Nathan flipped back the pages of his book. "I'm not sure. It's supposed to remove poisons—it's an emetic, but I, ah, don't really know what that means and—"

Lucky's mouth opened wide. His bleating became a hacking repeated cough, split with deep belching—transforming into a bizarre instrument. Then a blast of pea green vomit burst out of the goat's mouth, a fountain that washed over Nathan and the hedgehog farmer. The puke sent Nathan tumbling back. The goat twisted his head back and unleashed more and more chunky vomit. The strangest dragon imaginable. The smell of it, sour and stinking, made Nathan's own stomach clench. Was he going to vomit too?

Another cough, a blast, and then a great hacking noise—and something solid burst free. It clattered onto the bridge next to Nathan's head.

The farmer picked it up. A toy knight, carved of wood—now painted in goat puke.

"Ah." He wiped vomit from his face. "My little one was wondering where this went."

Another belch from the goat and then a happy bleat.

Nathan sat up. Drenched in seawater and now goat vomit—what a day. "He's all right?"

"Right as rain." The farmer helped Nathan up and took the goat's reins. "Come along, Lucky. Quickly now." Hooves clattered and wheels churned. The bridge creaked and shuddered—but held. They made it across.

Zoya followed on Emperor. She grinned at Nathan. "The conquering hero."

All he could do was smile back.

"Well, young sir, you have my undying gratitude. I'm Bobbin Brumley." The hedgehog shook Zoya's paw and reached for Nathan's—then stopped himself. "You'll be wanting some shelter and a place to take a bath, I expect. Well, you're in luck. Woolery's up ahead and it's the day of their Wool Fair. The inn will be open and doing good business."

"Woolery?" Nathan had never heard of it. "Is that, ah, in the Copperbright Kingdom?"

"Where else would it be?"

So they had landed in the Copperbright Kingdom after all. A

distant land, where Titus Tarr had numerous allies. But had his vessel even survived the battle in the water? What about Esther and the others? Had they made it? Bobbin Brumley, concerned only with bringing his potatoes to market for this Wool Fair, certainly wouldn't know.

"What's your name, then, young sir?" Brumley asked.

"Nathan of Nestovich." He stopped—he should have lied—but he was tired.

Zoya glared at him. "I'm Zoya Schall." No point in keeping up the ruse now. "Yes, yes. He's the one from the books."

"Books? I'm sorry, young miss, but I'm not much for reading. I've never heard of him."

He was unknown. That was a mercy.

+ + +

Woolery wasn't a grand city like Katzenberg, a riotous port town like Kostamare, or a gilded fantasy like Erminium. Instead, it was a small village consisting of two intersecting circles of cottages and business: a bakery, a cobbler's shop, an inn, and a little church, with a stretch of green in the middle for festivals and games of pawball. Only the inn had tiles on the roof and glass in the windows. The beasts wore simple homespun tunics and jerkins, and good wool cloaks to keep off the spring chill. It was a quiet place, with its own local dramas and troubles, far from the intrigue of kings, merchants, and soldiers that decreed the way of the world.

Another Nestovich.

Right now, the Wool Fair took over the town. Great bales of fleece formed fuzzy mountains in the village green, and local buyers and shepherds haggled over the price as wagons waited to carry the cargo away.

But the fair wasn't only about wool. The locals offered frothy beer, fresh-baked bread and creamy butter, and spicy sausage to all, a band fiddled and piped on a little stage at the edge of the green, and village kits, pups, hoglets, and hatchlings played with the excitement you only got on holidays.

Nathan's eyes went to the food, as they neared the inn. A hook-topped staff below a sign named it as the Shepherd's Respite.

Zoya followed his gaze. "First, a bath," she said. "Then you can eat."

Fair enough. Being coated in goat puke didn't exactly help his appetite.

They went to the inn and Bobbin Brumley waved to a mole in an apron. "Nathan, Zoya, this is Moll Mullen, the owner of this fine establishment." Mullen gave them a quick curtsy. "They saved Lucky's life on the road, they did. I'd like to buy them a night here, and a meal, and—" He pointed to Nathan. "A bath."

Mullen pointed inside. "A bath you'll have. First floor, second door. The water's already hot. I'll have my daughter take care of your piglet there." She offered her paw to Zoya. "And you, my dear, look like you could use something to eat."

He went inside, Zoya giving him a quick nod before the door closed. She'd be all right—she could take care of herself. But he slid the Orphan Blade from Emperor's saddle and brought that in with him. Just in case.

The bath was wonderful. He dunked himself in the warm water again and again. Got rid of the puke and the salt—or most of it. But he couldn't rest—couldn't let the warmth wash over him and uncoil the turmoil in his belly. What about Esther? And her parents—and Niko? They had to get on the road and find them. The capital of the Copperbright Kingdom was Brightstone —maybe Esther would go there?

Maybe Tarr was waiting for her.

After he was close to clean, he went outside. Zoya sat at a little table overlooking the square, working at a vast collection of food. Some cheese, matching the bright whiteness of the moon, a few links of sausage, and a berry tart. She matched his bad manners. Nathan settled across from her and both shoveled food into their faces. Crumbs rained down on their clothes and stained their paws.

Halfway through, they looked up at each other. Zoya laughed and Nathan joined in.

When the grub was mostly gone, Zoya settled back. "We'll spend the night here. Get properly provisioned—I want some more weapons—and then we'll set out tomorrow."

"Tomorrow? But Esther—"

"Can take care of herself." Zoya held up a paw. "When we left her, she was close to the Fortunate Few—close to rescuing her parents. You can trust her to protect herself. The same with all of them." She hesitated, her whiskers shaking. "Is it always like this? Are you always afraid?"

He didn't say anything.

"Since Nestovich?"

"Yes."

"Oh." Zoya reached over and rested her paw on his. "It was easier for me, I suppose. I never saw my home destroyed. Never knew my parents. Zipporah was always there to look after me, and when she was away—thieving—she'd leave me with someone she trusted, and I knew that she'd always return. That's how I feel now. I was afraid, of course—I still am. But I don't live in fear." She gripped his paw, and there was iron in her fingers and the shine of polished steel in her eyes. "You don't have to either. I know your fear will never fade, and that's all right—but the trust you have in your friends won't fade either. You've got plenty of that. I know it."

She was comforting him. Helping him—another friend. One he could trust—without fearing for her safety. The same with Niko, and Esther, and the others. He nodded silently as his ears flattened.

Moll Mullen came back. "No bread? I'm sorry, Master Nathan, Mistress Zoya. I thought I told Maggie to bring you a loaf." She raised her voice. "Maggie? Where's the bread?"

A mole pup, her apron bearing a maze of embroidered flowers, hastened to their table. She was a little older than Nathan and had a wrinkle to her muzzle that Nathan recognized: the guilt of a kit who had failed. "I'm so sorry, mother." She hoisted up a tray, empty apart from crumbs. "We're out."

"All that dough I sent to Wheatley's to be baked and we're already out?"

Maggie Mullen stared at her shoes. "I'm sorry, mother. I delivered the dough and brought back what he made—but it wasn't much."

"Hmmm." Zoya slurped her water.

"What?" Nathan asked.

"Nothing. It's not our business." Her tail swirled in the dust. "But you want to get involved."

His whiskers shook. She knew him well. "Maybe they could use the help?"

Moll Mullen smoothed down her apron with a large paw. "Oh, Master Nathan, you needn't worry about it. Wheatley's a turtle with a short temper, and I'd hate to see one of my guests get into trouble on our account."

"What a minute." Maggie leaned closer and sparks of recognition flickered in her dark eyes. "A rat—a rat kit named Nathan? With brown fur?" Heart sizzled in his cheeks as his ears flicked up. "This is Nathan the Rat—the Rat on the Road!" She patted the table, excitement putting a dose of speed in her words. "He's a hero, mother, a wandering trickster hero who always acts nobly, shows true courage, and never loses a fight."

He didn't have the heart to correct her.

"So much for anonymity," Zoya muttered.

Maggie clasped his paw. "Nathan—can you help? I know it's a far cry from slaying dragon skunks and making a deal with the Swamp Baron to save the world from his toad army, but we do need our bread—and you're the great Nathan of Nestovich. I read about the time you saved an entire village from a rampaging bear by besting it in a game of riddles, and—"

"I'm not—that's not me." But Nathan couldn't turn her down. "But we'll help. It's the right thing to do." That was what Brother Ambrose had said.

Sometimes, you just had to be decent.

He wiped his whiskers on his sleeve, picked up his sword, and followed Maggie. Zoya let out an annoyed sigh and joined them. They crossed the village green, passing the booths and their heaps of wool, as the band switched songs into a fast-paced reel. A collection of villagers danced along, their shoes slapping in the dirt as they switched partners.

Nathan's heart pounded in time. Solving village problems— was this the right thing to do? Was he acting like the Rat on the Road? Becoming a storybook character who had escaped the page?

No. A village baker was hardly a skunk dragon. He was being himself.

They reached the door of the bakery, a squat, square structure. Rich baking smells clung to the air. A wooden pretzel dangled on a post above the door, looking good enough to eat.

Maggie knocked on the door. "Master Wheatley? Sir? It's Maggie Mullen?"

The door creaked open. "Distract him." Zoya whispered to them both. "Keep him talking."

"What?" But when Nathan turned around, she had gone. Her tail slithered around the side of the house. Then the door was open and a turtle, his green speckled scales well-powdered with flour, jabbed his head out of his shell at them. "Um—excuse me." He smiled. "I'm Nathan of Nestovich."

Maggie seemed as nervous as Nathan. "We'd like to talk to you, Master Wheatley. About your bread."

"What?" Wheatley waved a paw at them. "What's wrong with it? Crust too hard for your liking?" His eyes fixed on Nathan and narrowed. "Why'd you bring a rat to my door?"

So even here, some beasts hated rats. Maggie looked at Nathan, her eyes sad. "He's a guest in our village—and he's Nathan of Nestovich, the great hero. My mother says that all beasts are welcome at the Shepherd's Rest, and—"

"Your mother's an innkeeper. She gets paid for every beast who stays at her inn. But I'd be careful if you let a rat under your roof—"

"How about you stop talking?" Nathan patted the pommel of his sword. "Before you make me angry?"

Wheatley's dewy eyes widened. Rats weren't supposed to act like that. Rat kits certainly weren't. But Nathan was tired, and worried about his friends, and completely out of patience. "Maybe I should fetch the bailiff and tell him—"

"You'll have quite a tale for him, baker!" Zoya called from inside the bakery. Wheatley spun around, the door swinging open. A clean kitchen with a huge clay oven lurking in the corner like a pet dragon in a wizard's chambers. Zoya popped out behind it, shaking some flour from her fur. "You can tell him all about the little hole in the bottom of your oven."

Wheatley stumbled into the room, moving toward the table where rolling pins and pans waited in a heap. "What—how did you—"

Zoya sprang up. "It's an old trick. I stayed with some crooked bakers in Minkleberg and they showed me how. A hole in the oven. You pop out some of the dough, bake it yourself, and sell the extra bread. Steal from your neighbors and enrich yourself."

"How dare you?" Wheatley's scaly fingers curled around a rolling pin. "I should—"

Nathan drew the Orphan Blade. He let the point rest on Wheatley's throat. "Drop it." Wheatley's fingers opened and the rolling blade tumbled away. "From now on, you bake everything from the Mullens for free. You plug in that hole. And if there's any extra loaves, you give them away."

"Otherwise, we'll come back." Zoya grabbed a slice of rye waiting on the table. "And we'll be after more than bread." She popped it in her mouth.

Wheatley hid his head in his shell.

They left him shuddering in the bakery and went outside. Maggie pumped their paws, one after the other. "You wait until I tell mother that Nathan of Nestovich and Zoya Schall defeated that wicked baker. You'll stay in the Shepherd's Respite for as long as you like and eat to your heart's content. I promise you that. Come along, I'll get our best quarters ready."

Zoya grinned at Nathan as they trailed Maggie back through the fair. "That was rather fun. How long do you think we can stay here?"

"A night to rest and half a day to prepare," Nathan explained. "No longer."

"A pity." Zoya shrugged. "My mother would tell me to milk this for all its worth."

"It wasn't so hard," Nathan said. "Compared to a lot of what we've done.

"Besting an evil baker—what a feat." She skipped ahead. "What's next?"

Tomorrow would tell.

+++

And what day it was. Nathan was pulled from a dreamless slumber by Maggie Mullen's gentle paw. She'd brought him breakfast, with strong tea—and a visitor. The village bailiff, an ancient falcon named Fielding, had need of him.

He explained the situation as Nathan munched on some of Wheatley's fresh bread topped with cheese in the inn's messy common room. "It's the Gang O'Green. They're a bunch of drunks, rascals, and misfits who like playing outlaw in the woods out past Foulberry Falls. Led by a fox named Harry O'Green. Now, usually Harry will just kidnap visitors, make them listen to him play a lute and sing a ballad about himself, and then let them go without some of their valuables, but now he's stolen something far worse."

"What?" Nathan asked. Treasure? Gold? A rare gem, maybe?

"Some of our prized wool."

Zoya emerged from her quarters then, and Nathan told her that he was going to have a word with Harry O'Green and get the wool back. She rolled her eyes. "We're really staying here and helping these beasts with all their little problems?"

"They need their wool."

"And I need a break." Zoya sighed as Maggie put a teacup on her table. "Mistress Mullen asked me to fix the tiles on her roof. The spring rains are due soon and if there's leakage, this whole place will be underwater. I'm a surefooted sneakthief, so I can do some climbing and replace the broken tiles without much trouble. I suppose I can manage that." She drained her tea. "Or maybe I'm becoming just as stupid as you are, Nathan."

"Could be," Nathan agreed. "Be careful, all right?"

"You too. I'll see about getting us provisioned and find a map that can point us to Brighstone after I deal with the roof. You watch out that this outlaw fox minstrel doesn't play his lute too loud."

Then it was off into the forest to find the Gang O'Green,

which turned out to be rather simple. They weren't at all like the bloodthirsty outlaw bands, fueled with out-of-work mercenaries and renegade soldiers who made travel in the Dark Forest so dangerous. Instead, they were more like a collection of overgrown kits who liked sleeping under the stars and playing their instruments aggressively to passersby. Fielding tolerated them and it was easy to see why. Their leader, a fox elaborately dressed in green doublet and matching cape, was lounging on a tree stump when they entered his camp.

"Oh, you wretched falcon—have you come to deliver me further into the grave?" He hoisted up his feet, his shoes removed to reveal red welts marking his fur. "This injury has finished me, finally ending the fabled career of the greatest outlaw prince of the age! No longer can I traipse whimsically through the underbrush, sneak with stealthy tread to some guarded caravan, and—"

Nathan knelt and examined the welts. "I think I can help, sir. If you'll let me search for some herbs." A squawk from Fielding followed. "Oh—and if you'd return the wool you've stolen. I know Woolery would be very grateful. And you are a heroic outlaw, aren't you? You wouldn't steal from the commonfolk."

Harry O'Green bobbed his head. "Please, my dear little rat, end my agony and you shall have your wool."

Once again, Brother Ambrose's book came in handy. Nathan scoured the woods, slipping under trees and poking under bushes for the proper herbs—dark black flowers called St. Caspar's Wort. He chewed them up himself, spat them in a bowl, and rubbed them on Harry's feet.

"Does that feel all right? You'll need to rest the feet and apply pulped flowers twice a day. How do they feel?"

"How do they feel?" Harry bound from the tree stump and drummed his feet against the dirt. "They feel good enough— for a jolly jig!" He held out his paws and a plump vole dutifully tossed him a lute. Harry O'Green began playing merrily while skipping around the clearing, the rest of the beasts following as they sang together.

Mostly offkey.

Nathan looked back at Fielding, who shrugged. At least they had the wool back.

When they returned to Woolery, in the midafternoon, Nathan found Zoya seated at a table outside the Sheperd's Respite. A large trout dangled from wooden tripod, the fish big enough to have gobbled down Nathan and Zoya and probably still have room for more. Moll and Maggie Mullen were hard at work, scraping off the scales to reveal the juicy white flesh within.

Zoya waved. "Have fun with the outlaws?"

"I did," Nathan admitted. "And you went fishing?"

"Bobbin Brumley's idea." Zoya pointed to the fish. "He wanted to pay us back for saving his goat, so he offered to take us fishing. I figured I'd do it for the both of us while they're getting our provisions together. When we got to the shore, some ancient river otter wouldn't stop yapping about the legendary King Trout, so we landed him. Or one of his princes. I used some dagger throwing to weaken him, and then we dragged him out." She grinned, proud of herself. "Enough to feed the whole village, which is precisely what we're going to do."

"That's wonderful." Landing legendary fish, dealing with musical outlaws—they were keeping busy. "But what about the provisions?"

"I've seen to that, Master Nathan." Moll waved to them from the fish. "Arranged everything at the store, including a map and directions to Brightstone. It's all being loaded on your boar, along with a new saddle and blanket and all the other tack such a fine riding creature might need. It'll take them just another hour to collect everything and get it ready."

Another hour—could they wait that long? "Thank you. I

think I've got some coin left…"

"No, no." She waved her paw. "It's our treat. For all the good you've done here." She hesitated. "But well, there is one more thing…"

Nathan and Zoya exchanged a look. "What?"

Maggie grinned at them. "Sister Alice, she comes down from the abbey over in Greenmouth and teaches the little ones their letters and numbers and such. That's how I learned to read. She's over in the church now, probably finishing up class for the village children and—" She gulped. Supreme Rodent—this was how Nathan had been around Sir Konrad the Courageous. "—and she and I think it would be a wonderful thing if you two were to come by and talk of your adventures."

Talking to a bunch of younger beasts about his adventures. Would he be like some performing beetle, doing tricks? Would they laugh at him? And there was still Esther and the others— they needed to find them.

"I don't know," Nathan said.

"Nathan." Zoya left her seat and stood next to him. "You owe it to them. You owe it yourself." She patted his paw. "Go on. We have the time. Tell your story."

He bobbed his head. "All right. Just while we're waiting."

Maggie beamed.

They left the village square and crossed to the church, Maggie going with them—doubtlessly wanting to hear the Rat on the Road's adventures. Sister Alice, a cheerful stoat in a rumpled wimple, greeted them at the door. Inside, seated on the pews, a collection of Woolery's youngsters seemed more intent on playing than learning. Chicks, cubs, kits, hoglets, and more talked excitedly. Two young squirrels played a rapid clapping game, waving their bushy tails in time. A beaver kit had transformed a stick into a catapult and was sending pebbles and dirt clods humming through the air. They were carefree, the day's lessons almost done, and the warm spring air beckoning. Sister Alice had to shout to get their attention.

Was this what Nathan had been like before destruction had sent him into the world? Esther too, perhaps. But those days were gone.

Still, it was nice to remember them.

Nathan and Zoya went to the front of the class. The children fell silent. How many of them had ever seen a rat before? And now there were two—including one who had stepped out of a legend.

Alice chirped and the children quieted. "My dear children, we have two special guests today." She waved to Nathan, who stood before the pew. Carved statues of the Blessed Beasts looked down. They seemed to be watching, along with the children. "These are two rats, strangers in our land, and one of them is Nathan of Nestovich."

Excited whispers rustled through the class like wind in a brewing storm.

"Now, does anyone have any—"

The young beasts began shouting their questions immediately.

"Is it true you fought a skunk dragon? What'd it smell like?"

"When you filled up the Castle of the Crows with gunpowder and blew it up, was it loud?"

"How many beasts have you slain in single combat? A hundred? Or more? How many heads did you chop off?"

He stepped back, ears flicking up and looked to Zoya. She gave him a gentle nod. His friend was with him. It was all right.

"Well, I've never fought a skunk dragon—but I did battle an evil porcupine jester. And, while I never put gunpowder in a castle, I stuffed a bed with it—and I blew that up. I don't think I've slain any beasts in single combat. As far as I know—but I've fought more than a few." They were all listening now, fixed on every word.

A tiny owlet raised a mottled wing. "What was it like?"

There was nothing for it. He told them.

+ + +

When the class ended, the younger beasts dashed out, hurrying into the golden spring air for a chance to play before they had to be home for afternoon chores. Sister Alice walked Nathan, Zoya, and Maggie out. "You made their day, Nathan. Your stories—so amazing. But it's not just that—it's the way you've helped us in Woolery. Not many beasts would spend their time sharing tales with a classroom of children, after all."

"He's a child himself, Sister," Zoya said.

"That he is," Alice agreed. "Come along. I'll buy you lunch before you leave."

"Thank you," Nathan said. But leaving, going out into the dangerous world once again—would that be such a good thing?

They were kind in Woolery—even if he had earned that kindness.

But Esther was still out there.

They'd tarried long enough. He had to go.

They went back to the Shepherd's Respite. The air had cooled a little, so Maggie brought them to the common room. A good roaring fire in the hearth kept the chill away, and the great trout had been sliced up and plated. It seemed that all the village had stopped by for a bite. Nathan even spotted Harry O'Green, who was playing a fiddle in the corner along with some of his merry-making outlaws. The fish smelled fine, and all his work had given him an appetite.

Moll Mullen greeted them at the door. "Nathan! There you are —and Zoya too. I was looking all over for you." She pointed to a table in the corner. "Look. Another rat's arrived."

Another rat? Nathan forgot to thank Mullen as he pushed his way through the crowd, slipping under Bailiff Fielding's wings, and reached the booth.

Firelight danced on white fur.

Supreme Rodent! It was her.

Esther Essen sat at the booth, a dainty pile of fish bones on her plate. Niko Nikaros sat across from her, gnawing on a roasted potato.

He ran to join them. "Esther!"

"Nathan." She sprang from the table and embraced him. They were kits again, longtime friends grateful to see each other. "You're safe. You made it."

"I was about to say the same for you!" Esther slid to the side and had him sit. "After the chaos on the sea, with the *Sovereign* running aground and sinking, we searched the wreck for nearly a day—and couldn't find you, or—" She beamed at Zoya, who hurried over as well. The two embraced. "Emperor charged out of the ship and leapt into the water soon after you went over. We couldn't find him either. That convinced me you made it."

Niko crunched on a chunk of potato, butter running through his teeth. "Looks like you've done all right for yourself."

"We have," Zoya agreed. "Woolery's a—a nice place. And the beasts here seem nice enough." That was probably the best compliment they were going to get from her. "But what about Zipporah? And the others? And your parents? And Tarr?"

She asked the questions before Nathan could.

Niko guzzled a mouthful of beer and explained. "Your mother's fine, Miss Zoya. Already ingratiated herself with the local thieves in Brightstone—it was her who talked to some smuggler otters and learned that this town was the closest to the beach near our tussle on the waves, and the most likely place to find you." Zoya's whiskers quivered like reeds in a storm with relief. "We don't know what happened to Tarr. He might have drowned when his ship crashed—but several lifeboats left the *Sovereign* and paddled away. The storm hid them. We caught the Contessa Vivaldi, at least. Turns out she's wanted in the Copperbright Kingdom. Poisoning numerous victims."

"And your parents?" Nathan asked.

Esther smiled. "Safe. I got them out."

Kind Yelena. Wise Eleazar. They were safe. Something unclenched in Nathan's belly.

"We're in Brightstone. My parents, Zipporah, the Fortunate Few—resting before we search for Tarr." Esther smoothed back her pale fur, looking like some regal princess in the cluttered, countryside inn. "I met with the Copperbright Queen, Gloriana. Convinced her to help."

"It's not all good news." Niko hoisted up a walking stick next to him and patted his leg with a wince. "Did some damage to myself in that fight. Our barber-surgeon stitched me up, but I don't know if it will heal." Oh Supreme Rodent—Niko! "Don't look like that. I can still get about just fine. My adventuring days are far from over." He clicked his teeth. "And Sir Volkbert escaped. Snuck away during the battle, stole a jolly boat, and paddled his way to freedom."

The white wolverine knight—their prisoner, now free. Somehow, that didn't bother Nathan. Sir Volkbert had never seemed like much of a threat.

But Smiling Spike and Titus Tarr—they were another story. They were like scorpions in the dark. You wouldn't notice them until the pincers clenched and the stingers struck.

"But you don't know where Tarr and Spike went?"

Both shook their heads—with the same worry that he had.

"Well, we can stay here for a while." Nathan looked back at the crowded bar. Harry O'Green had finished his fiddling and bowed to a smattering of applause. "Woolery seems safe."

A knife slammed into the wood of the counter. A loud noise —cutting through the remnants of clapping and the absence of music.

Nathan spun around.

His dagger, the Winterborn dagger that he had left embedded in Smiling Spike's paw, rested in the bar.

Smiling Spike, seated at the bar, was the one who had put it there.

Conversation hushed and several townsfolk slid out of the way, as if sensing that something terrible had entered the inn. Smiling Spike looked more nightmarish than ever. His jester face paint had been turned into a smeary mess, his quills hung limp around a cruel crooked smile, and his checkered motley had gone ragged and torn. Bloodstained bandages marked his body, but he still had his bells, wrapped around his wrists and the haft of his spiked mace, which he hoisted up and shook in a mocking, ringing salute.

Titus Tarr was next to him. Tarr's pale finery was similarly tattered, kept under a dark traveling cloak.

Sir Volkbert, in half-plate and armed with a broadsword, flanked the merchant prince.

Everyone stayed still and quiet for a moment that seemed to trickle on for an eternity. Spike waved his mace back and forth, letting the ringing fill the Shepherd's Respite. Then he hoisted up his paw and gave Nathan and his friends a little wave.

"Hello, Nathan. Good to see you again."

Niko was on his feet, swinging up his walking stick as he limped closer. "Nathan, Esther, Zoya—get out through the back. I'll hold them off and—"

Spike bashed him with the mace, sending him sprawling to the ground. Nathan sprang up next, drawing the short sword from his belt.

Only for Tarr to throw back his traveling cloak and reveal a crossbow, which he aimed straight at Zoya. "Drop it." No grand pronouncements. No threats. He sounded too tired.

Nathan looked at Zoya. She shook her head.

But Nathan let the sword clatter to the ground. He couldn't risk it. Sir Volkbert, his eyes downcast, crept out, grabbed the sword, and carried it back. He looked miserable, uncomfortable, like his armor was some tiny cage that had trapped him.

"Outside." Tarr pointed. "To the village green. All of you—and if you speak at all, I'll have Spike rip out your tongues."

Nathan walked to Niko and helped him up—Spike kicked the walking stick aside to force him to limp. Esther slid from the bench. She took hold of Nathan's paw. Zoya took the other. They huddled together and went outside, into the bright spring sun, with Tarr and his allies behind.

Tarr raised his voice. "Everyone who wishes, come and see!" His raspy voice echoed through the Shepherd's Respite and out into Woolery. "Come and see, I ask of you! Come and watch as a trio of rats finally receive their justice!"

+++

The village green sparkled emerald in the sunshine. Speckles of flowers grew and danced in the gentle breeze. Tarr pointed to the middle with his crossbow, forcing Nathan and his friends to gather there. Behind Tarr, it seemed that everyone in Woolery had come out to watch. Sister Alice and the youngsters from the church, all terrified. Harry O'Green and his outlaws, still clutching their now silent instruments, and old Bailiff Fielding. Moll Mullen, holding close to Maggie. Even Bobbin Brumley, his eyes wide and gleaming below the brim of his hat.

Tarr faced them, the crossbow still aimed at Nathan. "You've heard of the Carrion King? No doubt you have—and if not, you'll learn. A monstrous rat tyrant, who moves in secret to despoil and corrupt our world." He pulled a pamphlet from his cloak and tossed them in the air. The skull-faced Carrion King fluttered his way to the grass. "And these three rats and their marten servant are his agents. Do not trust them—do not trust any rat!" There was no trace of the silver tongue now—just exasperation. "After they're gone, I'll cut a deal with Good Queen Gloriana. No rat shall tread upon this kingdom's shores. It will be safe, and you'll watch the first blow struck today."

"Don't you say that about young Nathan!" Moll Mullen stepped closer, hoisting up a heavy paw. "He's a good young beast —saved our inn, helped our town."

"He saved my goat!" Brumley agreed.

"And Zoya—she caught the biggest fish in the river." Mullen's voice grew in strength. "And helped my daughter fix our roof. This Carrion King business sounds like nonsense—you let those two young ones go or you'll pay."

They were on his side. Not because of grand heroism or some fancy legend—but because he had been nice to them.

"Volkbert." Tarr glared at his knight. "Draw that sword. Get rid of them."

Sir Volkbert pulled his broadsword free. A heavy, hulking blade, which caught the sunlight. But he merely held it up and made no move to use it.

"White-furred lummocks!" Spike hissed.

Tarr clicked his teeth, eyes darting from Nathan and his friends to the crowd. Esther glared at him. "Looks like your pamphlets didn't work, Tarr."

An orange blur hummed out through the air—a roof tile, thrown from Maggie Mullen's paw. It bashed into Tarr's face, the tile shattering with a crack. His crossbow hummed a moment later. The bolt thudded into the sign for the Shepherd's Respite, striking the wood and making it swing back together as its hinges screamed. Cries from the crowd—but they didn't run.

Spike and Sir Volkbert slid in front of Nathan—blocking their escape. "The Hell with it!" Tarr drew another bolt and slid it into place. He twisted the crank. "Volkbert, Spike—kill a few and scatter them. Then we can leave."

Smiling Spike hoisted up his mace. Nathan's heart pounded —there had to be a way out—some hidden weapon, or careful stratagem—some warning—but there was nothing. Only Smiling Spike, looking at Sir Volkbert, daring him to put the broadsword to use.

"Go on, snowball." He rattled his quills. "Be a good knight. Follow your master's command."

Sir Volkbert closed his eyes—then spun the broadsword around and drove it straight through Smiling Spike's belly.

The broadsword punched through motley, flesh, and made the quills rattle as it burst out the other side. Spike gasped, his spines shaking as life left him. Volkbert pulled him close, teeth barred, some stains settling on his pale fur. He tore the blade free, and Smiling Spike dropped to the village green in a heap.

His bells jangled a final time.

"You know nothing of knighthood," Volkbert muttered.

Tarr stared at him and the sword—and moved. He grabbed Nathan's arm, smacked him with the butt of the crossbow, and dragged him across the green. The world spun and pain flashed in Nathan's eyes. Fear too—a fire burning yet again. An iron grip, and the crossbow jabbed out, poking into his belly. Nathan squeaked and kicked, delivering a good blow to Tarr's side, but then they had reached the edge of the green and a wagon, pulled by a mud-brown goat. Lucky—Bobbin Brumley's goat, and this was his wagon.

Tarr hurled Nathan into the back, pulled himself into the seat, and cracked the reins.

Esther and Zoya were running after him, calling his name, the townsfolk too, but Lucky's hooves went to a gallop, and he was running down the village road, bleating all the while, and they couldn't catch up. The wagon rattled away from the village of Woolery and into the forest.

Tarr kept the reins moving, the crossbow on his knees.

Nathan wiped blood from his nose. The world was sliding back into place.

"I'll get them on my side." Was Tarr talking to Nathan—or himself? "The common beasts. After I dispose of you and your friends, I'll win them over."

"You won't." Nathan glared at him. "You don't need Carrion Kings or great legends to get beasts on your side. You just need some decency—and that's something you'll never have."

Tarr's mouth opened, his tail jutting up.

That was the best opening Nathan would get. He lunged out and grabbed for the reins.

Tarr's grip held, but Nathan pulled back, and poor Lucky bleated in terror as he galloped along. The wagon wheels churned up mud and grass. Dirt sprayed behind them—but the wagon kept going, right up to the nearly broken bridge over Foulberry Falls.

Nathan had a decent grip on the reins, and he pulled them back as hard as he could, forcing Lucky to twist to the side—and the wagon to swing around, a stone from a sling, and break free of reins and ropes.

The wagon left the goat completely and crashed over and rolled, bearing Nathan and Tarr with it.

Trees, earth, mud, sky—and the bridge. Nathan hugged onto his seat as the wagon plopped onto rickety Foulberry Bridge.

Which shattered.

He leapt for the stony cliff as bridge, wagon, and Tarr went down below him, Tarr screeching as the waterfall churned and an avalanche of splintery planks, broken wheels, and shattered wood cascaded around them.

Wood crunched on the stones along with a wet, meaty plop—the end of Titus Tarr.

Nathan's paws reached out, sunlight burning his eyes and spray from the waterfall drenched his fur, and his fingers settled on something solid and slick.

He started to slip.

Until a firm grip settled on one of his paws. Other fingers took hold of his right arm. He looked up.

Zoya and Esther were pulling him up, Maggie Mullen behind them. Bobbin Brumley was there too, and old Fielding, and Sister Alice and the village kids. All working together, grasping the shoulders of each other, and pulling him up and to safety.

He didn't need to be afraid. He didn't need to think of the fears of his past.

He could trust his friends to save him.

They settled on the grass. He lay next to Esther—weak, bruised, bleeding. Alive. "You saved my life. Again."

She laughed. "It's a habit I'll keep."

Niko reached them, limping up, and put a good warm cloak around Nathan's back. They led him back to the village.

Woolery, safe again.

It was a grand thing that so many cared about him.

+++

A day later, and it was time to say goodbye.

Esther and her parents, along with the Fortunate Few, bid their farewell to Nathan at the royal docks in Brightstone, within sight of Good Queen Gloriana's magnificent palace. The queen's own barge, painted a deep red and escorted by a honor guard of swans, waited in the peaceful waters. The Orphans, led by Captain Uttz, stood ready to sail. Esther, Yelena, and

Eleazar Essen walked across the cream-colored wharf to join them. The Fortunate Few trailed after them, Niko still limping, Flammarion fiddling with his tools, and Sir Thomas Mulberry and Artemesia De Leon arguing excitedly about some details of swordplay. Zoya and Zipporah brought up the rear, garbed in thief's finery and ready to return to the continent.

Nathan accompanied them.

Yelena stopped suddenly, knelt by Nathan, and embraced him. "Are you certain you won't come with us? I feel wretched, leaving a kit to fend for himself."

"I'm hardly a kit, Mistress Essen. I'll be in Woolery, surrounded by friends." Nathan took her paws in his. "But I'll visit. I promise. And I'll write, to you, and Master Eleazar—and Esther."

"I'll be in Erminium, often enough." Esther joined Nathan, her ruby eyes shining. "Helping my father." But she'd be doing more than that—Esther was a leader now, Lady Essen—the Pale Maiden—and she'd work to make things better for rats and all beasts with her wit and determination. Nathan knew it.

"The Lady Essen," De Leon said. "Living up to her name."

She had become a legend herself. "But you will visit me, Nathan? Won't you?"

"I promise," he agreed. "And if you need help—"

"If she needs help, she can call on us." Mulberry slapped Niko's back, nearly knocking him over. "The Fortunate Few, together again."

"You're really going to remain a mercenary?" Nathan asked.

Niko shrugged. "A mercenary who soldiers away from the action. Maybe that's what my life needs. It has certainly had enough excitement. Perhaps I'll settle down. Is that what you're planning to do, Nathan of Woolery?"

"Nathan of Nestovich," he corrected. "And yes. Partially.

There's something I must do."

Zoya bound over to join him. "I hope it doesn't take too long." She took his paws. "Mother and I are going to have a little crime spree on the continent, and then we'll come back and join you. Woolery's a fine place to lay low." She looked back at her mother, who was already tapping her foot. "She's a little tired of charitable work."

Zipporah squeaked indignantly. "And tired of long goodbyes, my Zoya. Tell him farewell and let us be gone."

"You heard her." Zoya gave Nathan a quick hug. "But I'll come back."

"That would be amazing." He looked over all the beasts who had fought for him and helped him over the years. "All of you— please—I owe you everything."

"That's quite enough," Niko said, with a laugh. "But tell me, Nathan—what are you going to do while you rest in little Woolery?"

He smiled. "One more adventure. A difficult one—but I'll manage."

A final round of clasped paws and then they were piling onto the barge that would take them out to the *Fortune*. Mulberry was singing another song, his booming voice echoing over the clear water. Nathan stayed on the shore and waved to them until the oars carried them out of sight. He shivered a little—he was alone.

But at the edge of the pier, another figure waited. A hulk in iron that somehow looked small.

Sir Volkbert.

"Hello…" Nathan had his dagger and sword now, both on his belt—but it was clear enough that Volkbert was no threat. "Are you—are you all right?"

"I turned against my master. That's not something knights should do." Sir Volkbert lowered his head. "But the chivalry you showed, to me, to the beasts of Woolery—that was honorable. I'd like to follow you, Master Nathan. To aid you on your quest."

"My quest?" Then again, what was the job he had given himself to do, if not a quest? And maybe he could use some help. "Well, that sounds fine."

"Wait—I can? I can join you?"

"Yes. I'll appreciate the company." Nathan pointed to edge of the pier, where Emperor munched grass. "Come on. We'll have to get you something to ride and then we're going back to Woolery. There's much to be done."

+++

That evening, Nathan settled into the desk in his room in the Shepherd's Respite. Sir Volkbert snoozed in the adjacent chamber. It had taken a great deal of persuasion to get him to set his sword down and rest, but he'd finally been convinced that Nathan was safe enough in this quiet inn in a quiet village. That gave Nathan time to prepare.

Maggie stepped into the room, a bundle under her arms. "Here you are, Nathan." She set down a stack of parchment, followed by an inkwell and a set of quills. "A quail was nice enough to part with them—for a reasonable price."

"I'll pay you back." He needed to pay Sir Volkbert too, and the rent for their rooms and for his meals. This new adventure was already becoming expensive.

"Ah, I wouldn't worry." She winked. "The famous Nathan of Nestovich, in our inn. It'll make us a true destination. Especially if you have much luck with your work."

Luck—he'd need a great deal. More than ever.

"Thank you." Be polite—his parents had taught him that. Maggie gave him a nod and slipped out, closing the door behind him.

He settled in the chair. The candle danced and flickered, an expectant kit ready to dash free from its parents' side and run free in a field. He carefully arranged the papers, dipped a quill in the ink, and settled back. How to start? It was tricky, that was for sure. Should he follow the example of his favorite Sir Konrad tales? Or some of the humorous trickster stories of clever foxes and the mischief they caused?

No—he needed to do what he did on the Katzenberg stage and for the young beasts in the Woolery Church.

He needed to be himself.

The title came easily: *The True Tale of Nathan of Nestovich— And of All Those Who Called Him Friend.*

Then he switched to the next page and began to write.

-The End-

ABOUT THE AUTHOR

Michael Panush

Michael Panush is a lifelong writer and Sacramento native.
His books with Curiosity Quills include The Stein and Candle Detective Agency, featuring a pair of occult detectives in the 1950s, Dinosaur Jazz, a story about a Lost World battling against the forces of modernization; The El Mosaico series, an occult Western about a Frankenstein bounty hunter. With Pro Se Press, he created Ape's Honor, an alternate history adventure of a noble gentleman gorilla in a world of talking animals. With Airship 27, he created The Dagger Men, a Novel of the Clay Shamus—a story of a golem detective, and The Dead Sheriff, Volume 5: A Cold and Lonesome Grave, a novel about the undead Western avenger created by Mark Justice. His short fiction has been published in Towers of Metropolis, George Chance: The Green Ghost, Pulp Mythology, Volume Two, and Bass Reeves, Frontier Marshal, Volume 5. The Stone-Law: Blood-Spiller's Quarry is his prehistoric crime novel starring a neanderthal detective. Nathan the Rat, A Tale of the Dark Forest, is a medieval woodland fantasy about an orphan rat in a world at war.
With Charles Santino, he's created his newest novel, Metropolis: Resurrection—a prequel to the famous German Expressionist Sci-Fi Classic.
He lives and teaches in Sacramento.
Follow him on the web at https://michaelpanush.com/ and on twitter at https://twitter.com/Michael_Panush

www.ingramcontent.com/pod-product-compliance
Lightning Source LLC
Chambersburg PA
CBHW060315260626

47160CB00007B/2616